"I told you I n...
you again!"

Ty's heart slammed against his rib cage like a punch being delivered by a boxer. The woman glaring at him like an Amazon warrior was Catt. *His* Catt.

It couldn't be! Ty tried to take a deep breath, but it was impossible. Ten years ago, when he was just a shavetail lieutenant fresh out of the naval academy, he'd fallen hopelessly in love with a red-haired beauty. Was *this* the same woman?

Then Ty saw the desperation in her narrowed blue eyes, the anguish in the way her full mouth compressed. She didn't need to say a thing. He knew this was his woman.

His heart reeled. His emotions exploded violently within him when he realized the woman he'd loved and lost so long ago was now standing in front of him.

And she was furious....

***

Don't miss HUNTER'S PRIDE (SE#1274),
the next exciting adventure in
MORGAN'S MERCENARIES: THE HUNTERS
series, coming in Special Edition in October 1999.

Dear Reader,

Summer is a time for backyard barbecues and fun family gatherings. But with all the running around you'll be doing, don't forget to make time for yourself. And there's no better way to escape than with a Special Edition novel. Each month we offer six brand-new romances about people just like you—trying to find the perfect balance between life, career, family, romance....

To start, pick up *Hunter's Woman* by bestselling author Lindsay McKenna. Continuing her riveting MORGAN'S MERCENARIES: THE HUNTERS series, she pairs a strong-willed THAT SPECIAL WOMAN! with the ruggedly handsome soldier who loved her once—and is determined to win her back!

Every woman longs to be noticed for her true beauty—and the heroine of Joan Elliott Pickart's latest book, *The Irresistible Mr. Sinclair,* is no different; this novel features another wonderful hero in the author's exciting cross-line miniseries with Silhouette Desire, THE BACHELOR BET. And for those hankering to return to the beloved Western land that Myrna Temte takes us to in her HEARTS OF WYOMING series, don't miss *The Gal Who Took the West.*

And it's family that brings the next three couples together—a baby on the way in *Penny Parker's Pregnant!* by Stella Bagwell, the next installment in her TWINS ON THE DOORSTEP series that began in Silhouette Romance and will return there in January 2000; adorable twins in Robin Lee Hatcher's *Taking Care of the Twins;* and a millionaire's heir-to-be in talented new author Teresa Carpenter's *The Baby Due Date.*

I hope you enjoy these six emotional must-reads written *by* women like you, *for* women like you!

Sincerely,

Karen Taylor Richman
Senior Editor

Please address questions and book requests to:
Silhouette Reader Service
U.S.: 3010 Walden Ave., P.O. Box 1325, Buffalo, NY 14269
Canadian: P.O. Box 609, Fort Erie, Ont. L2A 5X3

LINDSAY McKENNA

HUNTER'S WOMAN

Published by Silhouette Books
America's Publisher of Contemporary Romance

SILHOUETTE BOOKS

ISBN 0-373-24255-7

HUNTER'S WOMAN

Copyright © 1999 by Lindsay McKenna

Visit us at www.romance.net

Printed in U.S.A.

LINDSAY McKENNA

is a practicing homeopath and emergency medical technician on the Navajo Reservation in Arizona. She comes from an Eastern Cherokee medicine family and is a member of the Wolf Clan. Dividing her energies between alternative medicine and writing, she feels books on and about love are the greatest positive healing force in the world. She lives with her husband, David, at La Casa de Madre Tierra, near Sedona.

A letter from That Special Woman, Dr. Catt Alborak:

Dear Readers,

I like to think I'm a woman with a mission in life to make this world a safer place. When I decided to be a crusader for this purpose, I knew I was going to take it on the nose—and I have. But I'm one of those tough Texas women, and you just can't keep us down! I've worked hard for every scrap of anything I've ever done in this life. And in my line of work—virology—I'm up against viruses that would just as soon kill me as they would the patients I'm trying to save. I like to think my hardscrabble life growing up on a Texas ranch prepared me for the challenges I face every day as a doctor.

Life is always hectic, because I could be called at any moment to hop on a plane and head anywhere in the world to combat a deadly microbe. But I love it! I love the danger. I like the challenge of pitting my intuition, my heart and gut, against killer diseases.

On my latest mission, all hell has broken loose. The last person I expected to see when I got down to Brazil was Ty Hunter. Suddenly my past has crashed into my present! I don't know if I can walk on that saber blade between my work and my personal life now that Ty is watching my every move. Life has suddenly gotten dangerous, not only physically, but emotionally. I just hope I can hold myself together long enough to save the people of this village—and keep myself from succumbing to Ty as I foolishly did once before.

Yours,

Dr. Catt Alborak

Dr. Catt Alborak

Chapter One

"Sit down, Ty, I've got some very bad news for you." Morgan Trayhern scowled and placed his hand on the back of his chair, his fingers tightening perceptibly on the dark brown leather. He had asked Ty to join him here in the war room, hidden deep below an innocuous-looking turn-of-the-century Victorian on the outskirts of Philipsburg, Montana. Morgan saw the wary look the tall, tightly muscled ex-marine officer gave him as he quickly closed the door to the inner office where all planning took place for Perseus missions.

"That bad?" One corner of Ty's mouth lifted derisively, in more of a pained expression than a smile. He noted that Morgan looked very tired; there were shadows beneath the older man's eyes, and his mouth was tightly set against the emotions he was clearly holding back. Although Morgan was dressed casually in a pair of jeans, cowboy boots and a long-sleeved white shirt, nothing could hide his military background. Ty was glad he'd been in the Marine Corps, too. It was something they shared, something good and solid, something that could be counted on. Ty knew that if anyone could be trusted, it was Morgan.

Morgan pursed his lips as Ty took the rustic pine chair in front of his desk. The leather seat cushion creaked as he sat down.

"Two words I hoped I'd never have to utter," Morgan admitted with a sigh as he walked around his own chair and sat. Resting his arms on top of the highly polished red cedar desk, he ran his fingers through his short black hair, now peppered with white strands.

Ty frowned. "Which two words? I can think of a lot of bad things that start with two words." When Ty saw the various top-secret faxes, e-mails and courier service information scattered atop the desk, he realized why Morgan looked so tired. He obviously hadn't been doing much sleeping. As haggard as Morgan appeared, Ty saw a glint in his eyes. He recognized that look. It was the look of a predator on the trail of his quarry. At heart, Morgan was the ultimate hunter-warrior, and a planner and catalyst to boot. It was one of many reasons Ty was glad he'd left the Marine Corps and come to work for Perseus, the covert government agency Morgan ran. Maybe, as Ty's younger brother, Reid, once said, all the men at Perseus were throwbacks to the era of cavemen, true hunter-warriors who knew instinctively how to track, hunt and kill their quarry.

In the case of Perseus, the quarry was always a dangerous criminal element somewhere in the world.

Heaven knew, there were plenty of evil men who wanted to bring harm to people, communities, or even countries. It didn't bother Ty that he was a hunter-warrior. He lived for it, thrived on the danger, just like his three brothers, who also worked for Perseus, did.

"Black Dawn?" Ty wondered aloud as he watched Morgan sort haphazardly through the missives on his desk.

"You're damned close. How about biological attack?"

Ty's straight, dark brown brows dipped instantly and his hands came to rest on the arms of the pine chair, his fingers automatically curling around the warm wood. "What?" The word came out as a harsh whisper tinged with disbelief.

"You heard right," Morgan muttered, pulling out a couple of papers and thrusting them across the desk in Ty's direction. "We think that Black Dawn has chosen what they consider a 'safe' target to test out their goods before they assault a much larger city. Take a look at this. It's from the Brazilian government."

Ty rapidly scanned the report Morgan handed him. It was in Portuguese, the official language of Brazil. Luckily, he was proficient in it. "This is a handwritten report from a backwoodsman by the name of Rafe Antonio, who works for that government," he said as he slowly tried to make sense of the scrawl. "He's saying that people in one of the villages he has responsibility for, of the Juma tribe, have suddenly come down with a mysterious illness. It's killing them off within forty-eight to seventy-two hours of infection. He's asking for…" Ty looked up at

Morgan "...*your* help? Not the Brazilian government's? What's this all about?"

Morgan grunted and sat back in his chair, which creaked in protest. "We've got moles all over the world, wherever we suspect things can go very badly wrong in a very short time. Brazil is one of them. Their government is trying its best, but they've got their problems, too," he continued wearily. "Unbeknownst to the Brazilians, Rafe is our operative and mole. He also works for the CIA. From time to time, if he ferrets out anything interesting, he passes it on to Perseus. His report came in yesterday." Rubbing his face tiredly, Morgan rasped, "I suspect Black Dawn used an airplane, flew over that village, dropped a load of some deadly biological material and is monitoring to see if it worked and how well."

"Rafe suspects Black Dawn?" Ty asked, rapidly perusing the rest of the report.

"No, I do. All Rafe knows is that the natives of one of the villages he's taken care of for years are suddenly dropping dead like flies. He's been in the Manaus region for ten years. He knows the area and its inhabitants better than anyone. Actually, he's been keeping tabs for the CIA on the cocaine plantations that are springing up all over the Amazon basin. The CIA then informs the Brazilian government, which does nothing about them because they just don't have the logistical support and trained manpower to go after them."

"So, Antonio functions as your eyes and ears out there on the rapidly growing drug trade?"

"Among other things, yes. Because Rafe works for the city of Manaus in that state of Brazil, he's in a very valuable position. He's alarmed that the Juma are dying like this. That second report came in hours ago from him. Right now he's heading down the Amazon River from Manaus with a load of antibiotics he got from a local hospital, to try and save some lives. You can see where he mentions that the chief of the village told him a plane flew very low and slowly over the village and 'spit upon them.' That was the old chief's word, *spit*. I think it was an aerosol spray that was released.''

Ty's brow wrinkled as he sat there and read through the second, even more hastily written report. Rafe Antonio's writing left a lot to be desired, but Ty could pick out the salient points of the document. Looking up when he finished, he asked, ''What else have you put into motion on this?''

Smiling a little, Morgan said, ''I called OID—the Office of Infectious Diseases—immediately because of what we suspect. I know you know Dr. Casey Morron, the medical doctor who is number two in charge of the Hot Zone and other outbreaks around the world. She has sent her best field epidemic specialist down to Manaus.'' Morgan looked at his watch. ''Chances are they are getting ready to land there by now. A tug is to take them downriver to the Juma village. The OID team is being headed up by Dr. Catt Alborak. She's got three other people working with her. They know how to handle a field assignment like this during an outbreak.''

''But do they know it could be a biological attack?'' Ty asked in concern.

''I haven't told them yet,'' Morgan said, ''I want to keep this under wraps until we're sure our target is Black Dawn.''

"And the Brazilian government? Are they in on this?"

"Not yet. We need to get the OID team in place, make a diagnosis, send blood and tissue samples back to OID headquarters in Atlanta, so that we know what the hell is happening first."

"Is there some chance this is really an epidemic outbreak and not the work of Black Dawn?"

Morgan shrugged and gazed at the map of Brazil behind him on the wall. "It's possible, but after that strategic feint they employed against us earlier, which made us think they were going after the Ebola virus in the Congo, I think this is real."

"Gut hunch?" Ty knew how much Morgan operated off that primal survival sense deep within him. Hell, Ty did, too. It had saved his worthless life many times over.

"Yes."

"Where do you want me to play in this sandbox?" Ty grinned a little as Morgan rallied from his teasing.

"I want you to join the OID team just as soon as humanly possible. I've got the Perseus jet waiting at the Philipsburg airport right now for you. They're fueling her as we speak. You've got the kind of background necessary for this. Your primary mission is to protect Dr. Alborak. She's our point person in the field. We are going to be relying heavily on her diagnosis, what she sees and observes. We need to keep her alive and out of danger while she does the necessary testing in order to get this info back to OID headquarters for verification one way or another."

"In other words, I'm her glorified bird dog?"

"Yes. She's not to suspect who you work for. For legitimate cover, OID, through Casey, is sending you down as her special assistant. Your background includes field work and you know how to draw blood, take samples and so on. No one is to know what you're really looking for. I don't want to alarm anyone in the village, nor do I want anything getting out that we've got a Perseus operative down there. *That* would tip off the Black Dawn. It could spring them into action before they're ready—or we're ready—and I don't want to risk that.''

''You really do think Black Dawn is working up to an aerosol attack on a major city, don't you?''

Morgan closed his eyes and kneaded the bridge of his nose gently with his thumb and index finger. ''Yes,'' he whispered finally.

The heaviness in the room permeated Ty's being. Some of the initial excitement he'd felt dissolved. The anguish in Morgan's voice told him of the terror the man was feeling over the possibility. ''We all know that a terrorist attack with a biological weapon is going to happen eventually, Morgan,'' Ty said finally. ''Anyone in the military or CIA knows that. This isn't anything new.''

''No,'' Morgan admitted as he allowed his hand to drop from his face. He opened his eyes and studied Ty. ''But my gut tells me Black Dawn is going to attack the U.S.A. We're going to be their prime target sooner or later.''

''It makes sense.''

''Exactly.'' He sighed. ''It's just a matter of time and what city. That's what we've got to find out. Somehow, we've got to get ahead of them on this curve. They sucker punched us once with their Congo bluff, and we fell for it.''

Ty sat quietly. He could see the tumultuous feelings reflected in Morgan's face, the pain in his eyes. "Depending upon what they use, hundreds or maybe thousands of people could die," he said at last.

"Yes," Morgan replied, "and that's why it's so important to get down to Brazil and find out what was used. Knowing at least that much will be a help." He tapped his fingers on the cedar desk. "Not much, but a help...."

Ty rose. "You got the mission brief prepared for me? I'll get out to the airport pronto."

Morgan nodded. "What there is of it. My secretary had a helluva time collecting stuff last minute. She managed to scare up photos of two of the four OID team members. Unfortunately, Dr. Alborak's isn't in there, but you'll know her. She's the only one with red hair on the outbreak team."

Ty brightened momentarily as he took the file from Morgan. "Redhead, eh?"

"Yeah. You like redheads?"

"My favorite," Ty said with a chuckle.

"Well, don't be too happy about this particular redhead," Morgan warned him, one eyebrow moving upward as he looked in his direction. "Around OID, Dr. Alborak is known as a Texas hellion. She doesn't put up with fools, from what I understand from Casey. This woman is a one-woman army. She shoots from the hip. She's got no diplomacy. She's all action and demands results. You get in her way and don't operate at the speed of light like she does, she'll chew you up and spit you out before you can say boo."

"Sounds like a military-officer type."

Morgan said, "She's not, but she could be. Casey thinks highly of her. She said if things get bad, Dr.

Alborak is the person you want at your back to protect you.''

Grinning slightly, Ty said, ''Sounds like a woman right down my alley. I like Type A go-getters.''

Snorting, Morgan rubbed his watering eyes. ''Today OID had a major computer crash involving their personnel department. I have nothing to give you on Dr. Alborak presently, just what Casey told me. By the time they get the software problem fixed, you'll be down in Manaus and on her trail.''

''That's okay,'' Ty said, ''I'm sure with this kind of description, I won't have a problem knowing who she is or how she operates.''

''Casey said to warn you that Dr. Alborak is intense, focused, stubborn and bullheaded. She's also got one hell of a temper if you cross her.''

''Must be that Texas breeding?'' Ty chuckled.

Morgan lightened momentarily. ''Maybe. But in this arena, we *need* someone with Dr. Alborak's gutsiness. Casey said she can shoot and spit with the best of 'em. I guess that's a Texas euphemism?''

Ty headed toward the door. ''I don't know. I'm from Colorado, remember? But Texans do have a helluva reputation.''

Morgan raised his brows. ''Just don't tangle with this hellion, all right? Work with her, not against her. I just hope she can take well-meaning direction from you.''

''My taste in women has always run to the independent types,'' Ty assured him smoothly. ''I'll find a bridgehead with Dr. Alborak and make it work. Too much is at stake not to.''

Morgan raised his hand. ''Rafe is expecting you. He's the only one who knows who you really are.

He'll do all he can to assist you. Just ask. Trust him and rely on what he knows. After ten years, he knows that area like the back of his hand. Literally.''

''Yes, sir.'' Ty opened the door. ''I'll see you when I get back.''

''Come home in one piece,'' Morgan growled in warning. ''Or else...''

Nodding, Ty quietly closed the door behind him. As he moved through the darkened passage to concrete stairs that led up to the first floor of the house, his heartbeat quickened. He reveled in the opportunity to be on a mission where so much was at stake. He had no idea what he was going to step into. If Black Dawn had delivered a deadly biological disease via aerosol spraying, that meant he and everyone on the OID team were also in jeopardy until they could verify what it was.

As he reached the top of the stairs, opened the door and stepped into a carpeted room at the rear of the house, Ty wondered what Texas hellion Catt Alborak was like. A brief smile lingered at the corners of his mouth. She might be the best part of this mission. Was she married? He resisted the temptation to open her file. Once he was on board the Perseus jet, he'd sift through all the information, commit it to memory and then try to get some sleep during the long journey south to Brazil.

Stepping out on the ornately carved front porch and automatically eyeing the thick cape of snow on the shoulders of the Rocky Mountains rising above the tiny hamlet of Philipsburg, Ty smiled. He was between relationships. Dr. Alborak sounded alluring. He liked a woman who knew her own mind, who had a definite sense of herself, who she was and where she was going in life. And if she was a little spicy and hotheaded, well, all the better. Ty liked women who challenged him. And he never ran from a fight. He stepped off the porch into the glare of bright sunlight. Putting on a pair of sunglasses, he hurried to a dark blue car parked out front.

As he settled in the back seat, the driver took off for the airport. Frowning, Ty amended his earlier musings. He *had* run from one relationship, he remembered now. A twinge in his heart made him unconsciously rub his chest. But that was a long time ago. He was thirty-one now and that relationship had happened ten years before. Long gone, but somehow, never forgotten. With a sigh, Ty opened up the file, his curiosity getting the better of him. The facts collected there were meager, but one of them piqued his interest. Dr. Alborak had attended Stanford University. So had the woman he'd loved so many years ago. Ty considered that a sign of good luck, if nothing else. He smiled to himself. Soon he'd be on Brazilian soil again. And he'd be facing this infamous Texas hellion in the flesh....

"Where the *hell* is that tugboat!?" Catt Alborak paced up and down the old, weathered wooden dock that jutted fifty feet out into the muddy headwaters of the Amazon. To her right was the distant skyline of Manaus. To her left was jungle. She saw her assistant, Maria Sanchez, pick up the cellular phone. Standing for a moment, her fists jammed on her hips, Catt glared up and down the river. There were a number of docks scattered along the bank, and plenty of tugs and tugboat captains. But where was *their* tug? Arrangements had been made before they arrived. A tug was to meet them at dock six and take them downriver for five hours, to the affected Juma village, where people were dying from some unknown bacterial or viral epidemic. Damn! People were suffering, and she and her team were standing here like they didn't have a better thing in the world to do. Frustration ate viciously at Catt. She was never in good humor when things went wrong. She didn't get paid to sit back, smile and be passive. No, responsibility for the lives of her team and those they were racing to help rested squarely on her shoulders.

Nostrils flaring, Catt started pacing again. Taking off her sunglasses, she stared out across the massive, slow-moving expanse of the Amazon. Two major rivers combined at Manaus, the largest city in northern Brazil. Once, there had been a very rich rubber trade here, which had made this city experience an economic boom for the first half the century. As the need for natural rubber died, so had the industry. Since then, Manaus had remade itself into a very profitable white-collar city, and with its high-tech computer companies, it was a leader in communications in South America.

"I could scream," Catt muttered as she moved back to her team waiting on the bank. All around them were portable trunks filled with dry ice and antibiotics, boxes of lab equipment and laptop computers. The software contained information on every possible epidemic. The database would help them as they collected information about symptoms that would, she hoped, help them identify the killer of the Juma people. All would be needed to fight this epidemic. *If* they got to the Juma village at all!

"We've got to get a tug," she said firmly to Maria, who had just gotten off the cell phone.

"You aren't going to like this, Catt. The man who was hired to take us said he won't do it. He doesn't care how much money is involved. Word's gotten out that half the people in the Juma village have died in the last two days. He's scared," Maria said unhappily, "and he said he loves his wife and kids too much to take us out there."

"He's afraid he'll get infected and die," Andy Foltz said. "Understandable, but that puts us in a hell of a fix."

Catt's patience was rapidly thinning. She ran her fingers through her short red hair in an aggravated motion. Her eyes burned with anger. "Maria, you call the city of Manaus. Get the mayor on the line. I'll talk to him. I'm not going to beat around the bush. We'll go to the top and take 'em apart one at a time if that's what we have to do in order to get down there to help those people."

Maria nodded sympathetically and rapidly punched in some numbers. She was of Hispanic blood and knew Spanish, which was a close cousin of Portuguese. Catt knew some Spanish because her father's spread near Del Rio, Texas, was right across the border from Mexico. Still, Maria's command of the language was stronger, and whether Catt liked it or not, Maria was her intercessor at the moment. Unfortunately, Maria wasn't pushy like her, and Catt knew in order to get Manaus officials to help them, push was going to come to shove.

None of the team spoke Brazil's first language, and they were at a decided disadvantage because of it. Now, Catt wished fervently that OID had either sent along an interpreter or brought in someone with field experience who spoke the language. It was too late now.

Catt saw a cab moving rapidly toward them, much like the one that had dropped off them and their medical supplies. This dock was out in the middle of nowhere. They'd been waiting for this tug for over an hour. A precious hour during which they could have been heading down the Amazon toward those suffering people.

Andy Foltz and Steve Tucker sat on large olive-green metal lockers, looking glum. They were just as frustrated as she was at not being able to get to those dying people. Aggravated to the point of blowing her infamous temper, Catt moved quickly back onto the dock. Immune to the beauty surrounding her, she jammed her hands into the pockets of her beige slacks as she walked quickly, her head down and filled with the turmoil of how to get out of this jam. Hearing the squealing of brakes, she stopped, turned and looked to where the asphalt ended, about a tenth of a mile from where she stood. The cab was delivering a passenger to their dock. Who? The tugboat captain? An official envoy from Manaus to help them? The man who emerged from the cab was tall and well muscled. He wore a short-sleeved white shirt, jeans and work boots, from what she could tell at this distance.

He looked vaguely familiar, Catt thought, then shrugged off the notion. Worried for the dying people downriver, she turned her attention back to them and their ongoing plight. She shouldn't just be standing here! She and her team should be on their way downstream right now. She snarled unhappily under her breath, spun around and headed back toward her team again. Maybe this man really was an official come to help them, someone who could get them out of this miserable mess. Catt wasn't sure, but he looked like he knew what he was doing just by his proud carriage and the confident way he walked toward them. Her heart skipped a beat. Who was he? She frowned and halted near her team, waiting impatiently for him.

The way he walked reminded Catt of a lithe animal—a jaguar, perhaps. The man had dark brown hair, cut short and close to his skull. He wore sunglasses, so she couldn't see his eyes, which to her were the most important feature in a person's face. Catt knew from experience that looking into someone's eyes told her everything she needed to know. What was this man hiding? Suddenly the sun was masked behind veils of misty clouds that moved sluggishly above them. The heat was oppressive and she was perspiring profusely beneath her white cotton shirt. Still, she couldn't help but notice the way his own shirt clung to his upper body, shouting of his athletic shape. His chest was well sprung, his arms lean and tightly muscled, the dark hair thick upon them.

It was his face, though, that drew her gaze—an oval face with a hard, uncompromising jaw. His mouth was pleasant to look at—full, with the corners tipped slightly upward, so she knew he smiled a lot. Maybe he was a joker, someone who liked to laugh. His brows were thick and straight. There wasn't a handsome bone in this man's face, Catt decided. Instead, it was a face carved by crisis; she could see the heavy, indented lines between his brows and the

slashes at either side of his pursed lips. He hadn't
shaved for a while and the darkness of his beard gave
him a dangerous look, warning her that he was someone to be wary of. Who *was* he? She didn't like the
way he strode confidently toward them, as if he knew
them. But unless he was a tugboat captain or someone who could get them one, Catt didn't have time
for him—at all.

He carried a large canvas bag slung over his broad
shoulder. Olive-green in color, it reminded Catt of
the military. In fact, she realized now, he walked like
he was in the military. Her mind spun with questions.
Had he been sent down by OID? Or some other gov-
ernmental agency? Observing the deep tan of his
skin, Catt wondered if he was an official from Manaus come to help them. Warning bells went off
within her. She was no stranger to CIA or military
types, because she frequently rubbed elbows with
them out in the field, especially during outbreaks in
foreign countries. They were instrumental and necessary—even if they were often arrogant about the
crucial role they played in helping Catt get medical
attention to those who suffered.

This man most definitely had an air of danger
around him. She could sense it. And why, oh why,
did he look so *familiar* to her? Catt found her attention torn between getting them downstream to the
people who needed her and searching her memory in
regard to this stranger.

The rest of her group stood up in anticipation as
the stranger approached. Catt lifted her chin at an
imperious angle and allowed all her internal radar
systems, which she relied on so heavily, to focus
directly on him. Her heart sped up. The shape of his

face, that arrogant, confident walk...she couldn't shake the feeling that she knew him. But from where? *Where?* She was almost ready to hurl the question at him, demand to know his name when he slowed down and took off his sunglasses. His icy-cold, cinnamon-colored eyes locking onto hers made Catt gasp.

Everyone in the team heard her strangled cry. They all turned in unison, bewilderment and surprise on their features.

Catt's eyes widened. Her hands fell nervelessly from her hips. Her lips parted. And then her anger surged through her like a volcanic explosion, her voice cutting through the lazy, humid afternoon air.

"You bastard. I told you I *never* wanted to see you again!"

Chapter Two

Ty's heart slammed against his rib cage with the force of a punch being delivered by a boxer. He halted, his mouth dropping open before he quickly snapped it shut. The woman glaring at him like an Amazon warrior was Cathy Simpson. Not Dr. Catt Alborak. Or was it? His mind spun. Fingers tightening around the dark glasses in his left hand, he met and held her sizzling glare.

"Cathy Simpson?" he growled, on guard. It couldn't be! It just couldn't. Ty tried to take in a deep breath, but it was impossible. Ten years ago, when he was just a shavetail lieutenant, fresh out of the naval academy, he'd fallen hopelessly in love with a red-haired woman who was going to medical school at Stanford University. Was *this* Cathy? She'd changed. Her once-long, gloriously thick hair had been cut short and her athletic frame had filled out. She was more beautiful, if that was possible.

She'd winced visibly when he'd called out her name, and now Ty saw the pain, anger and desperation in her narrowed blue eyes, the anguish in the way her full mouth compressed. More than anything, he saw in her expression the devastating effect of his sudden appearance. She didn't need to say a thing. He *knew* this was Cathy Simpson.

As he stood there, every set of eyes on him, Ty felt horribly vulnerable in front of this group of strangers. His heart reeled. His emotions exploded violently within him when he realized the woman he'd loved and lost so long ago was standing here, now, in front of him—and that she was furious. What kind of torturous trick was being played on him— and her? Ty saw all too clearly that Catt, as she called herself now, wanted nothing to do with him. Her face had flushed a dull red, and now that it was whitening, he recalled all too well her hair-trigger temper. Whenever she turned pale again, that meant all hell was going to break loose. This time at him.

Trying to prepare himself, Ty felt an avalanche of old pain surge violently through him. The hurt from the past was alive in Catt's eyes. And he'd been the bastard to hurt her but good. Helplessly, he stood there. This was the kind of emotional assault he had absolutely no defense against—nor did he try to shield himself from what was justly his to take. The ugly past, the sordid details, all started to rise with vivid clarity into his conscious mind. Lord knew, he'd buried them deeply, but with the beautiful, furious Catt standing before him, they were all coming back with the speed of a laser-fired rocket.

"I *used* to be Cathy Simpson," Catt snarled in a low, throttled tone. She found herself trying to hate Ty, but how could she when she saw the absolute surprise and unsettled pain in his expression, the agony in his cinnamon-colored eyes? She wanted so hard to hate him, but her heart was pounding and crying out for him! Choking, she rasped, "I don't know what the hell you're doing here, but whatever the reason, just do an about-face and march back from wherever you came. I don't *ever* want to see you again, Hunter. I thought I made that clear a long time ago."

The sudden prick of tears made Catt blink strongly. Tears! Not now. Not ever! Oh, Ty Hunter had such a vulnerable-looking face! Wasn't that what had snagged her, entrapped her before—that helpless expression that he was now wearing for her benefit? Well, it was a damned game that he was very good at playing. She'd been a greenhorn of a sophomore in medical school when she'd fallen for him heart, body and soul. And Lord knew, he'd taken her soul, used her and then thrown her away when it came time to take responsibility for their choices. No, Hunter was a user, a manipulator of the worst kind. In her hour of greatest need, Ty Hunter had abandoned her. He'd left her. He'd said to hell with her and had walked away, pleading more important duties to take care of than the predicament she'd suddenly and inexplicably found herself in.

Ty opened his hand in a gesture of conciliation. He tried to speak, but his voice failed him. He could almost feel Catt's fury pummeling him as she stood tensely, as if prepared for combat. So much of the past, the bittersweetness of their torrid love affair, came smashing back to him. How much he'd tried to forget! And now he realized he'd forgotten nothing about her. Not the thick, silky quality of one strand of her auburn hair. Not the way her soft, firm skin smelled and tasted as he grazed it with his fingertips or tongue. Worse, he remembered her hungry lovemaking and how they'd met, matched and soared to the heights together like two eagles in mating season, high in the sky, hooking claws and tumbling thousands of exhilarating feet in the lovemaking process.

A serrating pain gutted him. What kind of awful trick was being played out here? "Look," he managed to say in a low, soothing tone. "I don't know anything about this, Catt—"

"It's Dr. Alborak to you."

He winced at the coldness of her words. She meant business—he could tell by the iciness in her eyes.

"Yes...Dr. Alborak." Ty dragged in a ragged breath. He was reeling so badly from this terrible surprise that, for once in his life, he didn't have the glib words, the quick comebacks he normally employed to defuse such situations. Lifting his hand in a pleading gesture, he rasped, "I've been sent here by OID. I'm your assistant."

"That's impossible! What the hell do you know about epidemic lab facilities? Last I heard, you were still in love with your precious Marine Corps. There's no way you're part of OID, so don't try and get me to swallow that lie." Catt tried to steady her shattered emotions, but it was impossible. Her heart was pounding wildly in her breast. Her breathing was shallow. Her employees were glancing back and forth between her and Ty Hunter with more than mild curiosity. Steve and Andy, who had been with her on just about every mission she'd been assigned to handle in the last five years, really looked baffled. Fortunately, they were smart enough to let her handle the situation. Catt was sure they would have questions later—questions she wouldn't want to answer. Ty Hunter showing up was the worst possible thing that could have happened in her life—other than the painful tragedy she'd suffered through alone, so long ago.

Now all Catt could feel was bitterness, and she wanted to hate Ty for leaving her when she'd needed him most. "There's no way you're going anywhere with me and my team," she sputtered. "These people I trust. I don't trust you. I need staff I can rely on, not someone who'll run out on me when the situation gets tough or dangerous." She shook her head. "No, you get out of here, Hunter. I don't care what you say. You are *not* a part of my team."

Grimly, Ty pulled a paper from his shirt pocket, opened it and stepped forward, bringing himself almost eye-to-eye with Catt, who was tall at five foot nine or ten inches. As he held her edgy look, the fury of her gaze burning him, a picture from the past flashed before his mind. He vividly remembered the first time he'd seen her. He'd gone into Mountain View, a small town outside the gates of Moffett Field, the naval air station where he'd just been assigned after graduation from Annapolis, for a breather from his duties. The immense responsibilities on his young shoulders had driven him off to find a place to relax. Colorado had always afforded him unlimited open spaces to walk when he was upset as a child. Nature was healing to Ty and helped him when he felt lost or needed to release stress. By chance he'd wandered into a park, and relieved to find a piece of land that didn't have steel, glass and concrete buildings on it, he began walking aimlessly through, until he spied a group of women playing soccer.

What had drawn him so dramatically to them was one woman—Catt. She was the tallest player on the team, and as she ran down the length of the field after the soccer ball, she'd reminded him of a fine-limbed Thoroughbred in top form. She'd been much thinner, but then she was still growing up, a twenty-year-old full of life, her red hair a banner streaming across her proud shoulders....

Ty remembered sitting on the sidelines, in uniform, not caring if they knew he was watching them. Just seeing Catt play, her intensity, her focus, her drive and competitive spirit, completely captured him. He'd never met a woman like her in his life. She'd overwhelmed him with her athletic ability, her beauty and her incredible presence, which shone like a million sparkling suns that day. He remembered how his heart had pounded, underscoring how drawn he was to her vitality, her raw, unbridled beauty. She reminded him of the wild mustangs that lived in the deserts of Colorado. It was her untamed spirit, her challenging, deep blue eyes, her determined smile, that had entrapped him. That still made him stare at her in wonder, even now.

"What's this?" Catt demanded as she glared up at Hunter, who held some sort of document in his hands.

"The paper...the orders."

She held his vulnerable brown gaze. Oh, she remembered those eyes, all right. Grabbing the paper, Catt tried to focus her attention on the words that blurred before her. It was impossible. Ty Hunter was too close, too virile, too damned powerful for her. Her wildly beating heart cried out that she could not bear to be embraced by him again. The thought made Catt turn on her heel and walk about ten feet away, just to escape the overwhelming sense of protection she felt radiating from him. Oh, Hunter was good, all right. He always had made her feel cared for, protected and supported. But she knew now it was all a sham. When things got dicey, he jumped ship. He'd abandoned her once, and she would never forget that day, that single defining moment of her life. Nothing had ever been so traumatic since then. Nothing.

Steadying her breathing, she held the paper with both hands. At first glance, she saw that it was on OID stationery and it was signed by her boss, Casey. As she read the terse paragraph, Catt scowled. She read and reread the document, which apparently was her newest set of orders.

Ty Hunter is to act as your immediate subordinate in all activities. He will be your assistant during this epidemic outbreak. I've sent him because he can potentially help you in difficult situations you may encounter. Use his talents. He will be your second-in-command.

Slowly turning around, Catt raked Ty with a glare, from his booted feet to his close-cropped hair. Damn him for being so handsome in his own rough kind of way. If anything, in the intervening decade, Hunter had grown far more handsome than when she'd known him. Back then he'd been a naive twenty-one-year-old. Although the clothes he wore hid his athletic prowess, Catt knew he was hard and well muscled. There was nothing soft about Hunter. There never had been. But that baby face of his was gone. In its place was the face of a man who'd seen and done a lot. Now his features had character and plenty of it, judging from the crow's-feet at the corner of each of his intelligent eyes, the lines across his forehead and the indentations bracketing his mouth. His mouth... Whether Catt wanted them to or not, memories of him kissing her slammed through her.

Stop it! I can't do this to myself! I just can't! Nostrils flaring, Catt walked over and thrust the paper back at him. "Since when did you get epidemic and lab training, Hunter? Last I heard, you were up to your ass in alligators, with the president of the United States flying into your little naval air station." Her voice was taut and choked with feeling, but Catt didn't care what she sounded like. She wanted to hurt him like he'd hurt her. She couldn't stop herself from lashing out at him, even though she knew it was wrong. This was one of the few times in her life that she felt helpless. It was an emotion Catt hated and tried to avoid. Being around Hunter was like being out of control, and she was panicking because of it. She never wanted anyone to make her feel that way again. Yet, as Ty stood motionless, the paper in his hand, his eyes containing that curiously gentle and understanding look, that's exactly how she felt.

Angrily, Catt fought the emotions roiling inside her. After ten years she didn't want to think anything except anger, bitterness, hurt and hate were left between them. "You hear me?" she demanded finally, her voice dropping an octave.

"I hear you," Hunter rasped, purposely keeping his voice low and unruffled. He folded up the paper. "A lot has happened since we last…saw one another."

"Obviously." She sized him up with a withering look. "I don't care who signed that paper. I don't *need* you. You got that? You can crawl back under whatever rock you came out from." She took a ragged breath and gestured toward her stunned teammates, who stood off to one side watching them. Catt felt embarrassed. They'd never seen her fly off the handle at anyone like this. "I've got people I can trust to do the job. I know they won't run out on me when things get a little hot in the kitchen."

Her words were like fiery barbs. Each one hurt like hell. Ty compressed his lips. In Catt's eyes, he'd abandoned her. Well, that wasn't exactly what had happened, but he'd be damned if he was going to air their personal laundry with strangers standing by, hanging on every word fired between them. No, right now he had to be the one to tame her, calm her down and get her focus back on what was important.

Pressing the orders back into the pocket of his shirt, he said, "You look stranded here. I thought a tug was supposed to take you down to the Juma village?"

Rubbing her brow, Catt took a step back. Obviously he wasn't going to leave anytime soon. And she couldn't make him leave. Her heart sagged in her breast and she felt panic mingle simultaneously with rage. This mission was dangerous enough to them physically. Now Catt was feeling like it was her emotions that were going to take the brunt of the beating, with Hunter showing up so unexpectedly. What twisted karma was at work here? She almost mouthed the words, but didn't.

Hunter was right to bring the focus back to the matter at hand. What was important right now was the fact that people were dying. She clung, almost panicked, to the thought of the mission. If she got busy, she could block his presence from her mind— from her crying heart, which longed for him still. Angry with herself for feeling anything for him, Catt whispered, "The tug captain bailed out at the last minute—just like you did, Hunter. He was worried he'd get whatever that bug is out there, die and leave his family without a provider. I guess on that last point, that's where he isn't like you."

The words were a slap in the face. Ty knew better than to try and defend himself. Especially in front of this group of people who didn't know him. Wrestling with the hurt of her unfair accusations, he said, "Okay, let me see what I can do."

She placed her hands on her hips and arrogantly lifted her chin. "Oh, yes, go handle this situation like you handled ours. If that's the case, I don't have to worry about you being around, do I? Out of sight, out of mind. You won't come back now, just like you never came back then."

Ty gave her a grim look. He didn't like her flaunting their private past in front of her team. Maybe they already knew about him—and them. Maybe not. Smarting at her bitter words, he thinned his mouth and turned away. "I'll be back," he growled over his shoulder as he headed up the slight incline toward the awaiting cab.

Catt tried to gather herself together. She suddenly felt embarrassed by her wild reaction to seeing Hunter again. As the cab drove off toward Manaus, she took a shaky breath and tried to calm her shattered nerves.

It was Andy who was the first to approach her. "You okay, Catt?" He laid a hand on her shoulder.

Closing her eyes, Catt nodded. "Yeah, I'm okay, Andy."

"Ghost from the past?" he guessed gently.

She opened her eyes and stared sightlessly toward the muddy Amazon. "You could say that."

Allowing his hand to slip off her shoulder, Andy looked around, running his fingers through his blond hair. "Well, if he can find us a tug and a captain, then we can get back on track." He rubbed his beard thoughtfully.

She heard the hope in his voice. "If I know anything about the bastard, it'll be the last we see of him," Catt breathed savagely. In her heart, she would be relieved if Ty never showed up again. "He's got a past history of only being around when things are hunky-dory. But when things get into a choke hold, he abandons everyone and everything. He's not to be trusted. No—" Catt shook her head adamantly "—if he doesn't return, I'm not going to be sorry about it. We're better off without him than with him, Andy."

"Did OID send him?" Steve asked as he joined them.

Catt looked over at the thin, tall, balding man. Though Steve was in his fifties, he lived to globe trot from one epidemic to the next. Through the silver wire-rim spectacles that sat on his narrow, hawklike nose, his gray eyes were thoughtful as he met and held her gaze.

"Yes," she muttered bitterly. "Casey sent him. I have no idea why. We have our team. We're good at what we do. We always get the damned job done!"

"I wonder, could he be a virology specialist on the new South American bugs?" Maria Sanchez asked as she came over.

Snorting, Catt looked down at her. "Somehow, I doubt it. That bastard was in the Marine Corps, an Annapolis graduate, the last time I saw him. Just because he's not wearing the uniform of the day doesn't mean he isn't in the military now. No, something fishy's going on here. I don't know what it is, but Maria, will you call OID and track Casey down? I want to talk to her."

Maria nodded. "You bet," she replied, digging the cell phone out of the leather knapsack that hung from her shoulder.

"What are we going to do about a tug?" Andy asked her.

"I want Maria and you two to walk down to those other docks and see if you can't bribe one of the captains into taking us to that Juma village. As I understand it, the rate of exchange is about six hundred to one. Flash a twenty in front of them…or whatever it takes. A small amount of U.S. money will make them rich enough that they won't have to work for a year if they'll just get us downstream to Señor Antonio's houseboat, near the Juma village. Get going. And good luck."

The two men nodded and turned as Maria approached Catt and held out the cell phone to her. "Dr. Casey's on the line."

"Thanks," Catt said, and took the phone. Maria, Andy and Steve walked down to the riverboats to find a willing tug captain.

"Casey?"

"Yes. Catt?"

"You got me. You're breaking up a little." Catt turned a bit. "Is this a better connection?"

"Much better. What's going on? Are you in the Juma village?"

Catt grimaced. "Hell, no." She went on to explain what had happened. "Listen, you just sent a guy down here by the name of Ty Hunter. Is that right?" Her hand became sweaty and she held the cell phone a little tighter.

"Yes, I did."

"What for? Don't you have confidence in me and my team to handle this situation?"

Casey laughed. "Confidence? Of course I do, Catt. That has nothing to do with this. Hunter is your assistant. I feel this situation is potentially so big that you need someone who can act like a gopher for you. Go for this, go for that. You know?"

Unhappily, Catt realized Casey did not know of their past with one another. Catt wasn't about to mix personal business with her professional life, either. "I really don't need him, Casey. That was decent of you to send him, but really, you can have him back. My team is all I need. There's no way we can assess the Juma outbreak until we get in there. We've been delayed by an unexpected problem with the tug we originally hired. We're in the process of rectifying it."

"If I know Hunter, he's probably looking for a tugboat for you this very moment. He's a very handy person to have around, Catt. Believe me. He's got a lot of time in grade over in Africa and South America. He's handled a lot of dicey, dangerous outbreak situations. Hell, he almost died of Congo fever a couple of years ago during one of them. No, this guy is a jack-of-all-trades and a master of *all* of them. He's the one person you want at your back if things break the wrong way."

Catt nearly choked. Her lips parted and she almost told Casey she was dead wrong. Hunter was the *last* person to rely on in a tense situation. "So where did he pick up his knowledge of epidemics?"

"He's got a minor in biology. I've used him from time to time on other outbreaks with other teams when the situation was dangerous and the factors were unknown. He's an excellent go-between in many ways, Catt. He speaks Portuguese and no one on your team does. If nothing else, he can serve as your interpreter. Let him work for you. If you need something done, ask him. He'll fill in and get it happening. He's a can-do kind of guy, and my gut intuition on this particular mission is that you need a person with his varied experience to assist you in ways your other team members can't."

"I really don't need him."

"Sorry, Catt, but you'll come to be glad he's with you. Just trust me on this call, okay?"

"But you've *never* done this to me before, Casey. You've always trusted me to run my team in the past and get the job done." Desperate, Catt closed her eyes. She *had* to get rid of Hunter. She just had to!

"Look, Dr. Alborak! Look!"

Half turning at the sound of Maria's high-pitched, excited voice, Catt saw her lab assistant two hundred yards down the bank, pointing out toward the slow-moving, muddy river. Scowling, she muttered to Casey, "Hold on a sec...." Raising her head, she focused her gaze. Her heart dropped. And then it thudded violently. There, less than a quarter mile away, was a tugboat coming directly toward their dock. On the prow was Ty Hunter. Damn! He'd found a tug owner willing to take them downriver before her team could.

Her breath ragged, she turned her back on Maria.

"I can hear shouting in the background," Casey said. "What's going on?"

"It's Hunter," Catt said unhappily. "He's found us a tug."

"See?" Casey said primly. "He's already broken the logjam on your situation down there at the dock. I tell you, Catt, he's a very handy person to have around."

Catt realized that no matter what she said, what fight she put up, her boss was not going to let her get rid of Hunter. Disheartened, all the fire draining out of her voice, she said, "Okay, Casey, he's a part of my team."

"Don't sound so glum. You're the boss, Catt. What you send him to do, he'll do, no questions asked. Okay?"

"Yeah, fine. Look, I'll call in once we get to the Juma village and make an initial assessment, all right?"

"Sure. Just *be careful*, Catt. You and your team are too important in all of this."

Catt pressed the off button and glumly walked to

where Maria was standing. She felt as if her life was draining out of her with each hard beat of her heart. Ty Hunter stood like a proud warrior, his arms crossed against his chest, as the tug slowly paralleled the dock. She saw the triumph in his expression. The bastard was gloating. And then Catt chided herself. What the hell was really important here? People's lives, not her private, sordid affair with Hunter. Somehow she was going to have to put it all behind her and focus on her mission.

She watched as Hunter jumped lithely, like the fabled and rare jaguar that ruled the Amazon jungle, onto the rickety wooden dock. He took the bowline and tied it to the post. Looking up, Catt saw Andy and Steve jogging back toward them, relief written on their sweaty features.

Ty decided that staying busy was the better part of valor with Catt, who stood tensely to one side. At that moment, she looked like a lost waif. He wanted to go to her, to try and smooth things out, but he knew it was impossible. Now was not the time to try and talk about the past, either. He saw the darkness in her glorious, cobalt-blue eyes. He felt her pain. Pain he'd caused her. Guilt ate at him, mixed with his own pain. He had a lot of questions for her, too. But they would have to wait. Walking off the dock, he went over to Maria.

"You need this equipment on board in any particular order?" he asked her.

Maria brightened. "Not really. It just all has to get on the tug." She pointed to three dark green metal chests. "These contain our drugs and antibiotics in dry ice. Let Andy or Steve help you with them."

Ty nodded and picked up a number of smaller

boxes. He'd try and make himself useful—and stay out from under Catt's feet, if possible. However, that tug was only sixty feet long and was going to be crowded at best. There'd be very little room to give Catt relief from his unexpected presence.

His chest ached. Hell, his heart was hurting, too. Every time he walked back for another load of equipment, he saw Catt standing there so alone, so apart from everything going on around them. Her shoulders were slumped. The look on her face was one of utter devastation. It agonized him to know that he was the cause of her turmoil. And more than anything, Ty realized, as he took another box to the awaiting tug, all the old feelings he had for Catt ten years ago were not only alive, but clamoring inside him. He needed to talk to her, to understand all that had happened on that day so many years ago.

Sighing raggedly, Ty handed the tug captain, who'd introduced himself as Hernandez, the box to be placed in the center region of the boat. He knew nothing of Catt's life since their breakup so long ago. And there was so much he *needed* to know. She'd wanted to be a medical doctor and go on to become a pediatrician. She had always loved children.... Wincing internally, Hunter felt pain shoot through him. He turned on his booted heel and walked back for another box.

To his surprise, Catt was standing near the last box. She was waiting for him. He could see it in the challenging blue fire of her gaze, the hard set of her jaw and the way her body tensed as he approached.

Her voice was low and snarling.

"I don't know what strings you pulled or why, Hunter. I don't like it. I don't like the fact that you're here. And there's nothing I can do about it. This smacks too much of our past together.'' She jabbed her finger into his chest. ''I don't trust you at all. From here on out, I'm the boss. You carry out my orders or else. The first time you don't, or you give me lip, I'm making a call on my cell phone to my boss and your butt is out of here. You got that?''

He felt her fear. He saw it in her eyes, even though he knew Catt was very good at making an opponent think she was fearless. Ty couldn't be angry with her. He understood exactly where she was coming from—her last experience with him had hurt her badly. There was no way to explain. Not now… maybe never. That hurt. He didn't like being seen as the villain in another person's eyes. Especially Catt's.

''We need to talk—''

''Like hell we do!'' Her nostrils quivered, and her voice shook. ''Hunter, you screw up just once and you're out of here. Got it?''

He held her gaze, which was riddled with anguish and fear. ''Yeah,'' he growled under his breath, ''I got it.''

Chapter Three

Ty wanted to scream like a wounded jaguar. Struggling against this unexpected surge of emotion, he stuffed his feelings deep down inside, as usual. From his position at the rear of the tug as it left the dock, he could see Catt standing at the bow as the engine *chut-chutted* along. Her profile was silhouetted against the magnificent expanse of the headwaters of the Amazon, and the suffering evident in her face was tremendous. Not only did she have the responsibility of the epidemic and people's lives in her hands, but she had *him*. Maybe that's all he was feeling—remorse for Catt's suffering. Lord knew, he'd made her suffer terribly. His unresolved feelings were like a knife twisting savagely in his gut. But tears and emotions had no playing ground within a mercenary or military person—none at all.

The tug bobbed gently as it putt-putted across the

slightly choppy expanse as the waters of two different rivers met to form the Amazon. Ty tried to focus instead on the beauty of the mighty waterway, where the dark tea-colored water of the Rio Negro, so clear he could see fish swimming in the depths of it, met with the Rio Suhimoes, a milky, muddy river. It looked like someone had poured chocolate milk and iced tea together. The branching of the two rivers was known as *encongtro das aguas,* the "wedding of the waters." And from this marriage, the muddy Amazon was born. There would be a patch of transparent water here, a spot of milky water there as the two currents met and mixed.

It was almost 3:00 p.m. The afternoon haze that always hung over the equatorial country made the sun look like it was shining through opaque white gauze, rather than clouds. The temperature was in the nineties and so was the humidity. Ty was sweating profusely. But then, so was everyone else. So far the rest of Catt's team treated him with respect, not with the withering glares Catt sent him, as if he were some kind of pariah. He sure felt like one. Obliquely, Ty wondered if Morgan or Casey knew of his tragic history with Catt. Probably not. He figured since her name was no longer Simpson, Catt had gotten married, and put their affair solidly behind her. And she could easily have shortened her name from Catherine to Catt. That was a simple enough explanation. But the thought of her with another man made him ache inside. As he sat on the edge of the thick rubber coating that covered the first foot of the tug, Ty had to work to contain all his emotions.

It was absolutely impossible. Morbidly, he swung his gaze back to Catt. She stood on the bow with the cell phone in hand, talking to someone. Probably arranging to get him off the tug and out of her life. Grimly, he realized that wouldn't happen. Casey knew the score. She knew why he was on this mission, though Catt, hopefully, would never find out. She and her team had enough to handle without thinking about the threat of terrorists lurking in the area. That was his job—to be the eyes and ears for the group and protect them, as well as alert the U.S. government of Black Dawn's whereabouts.

Just looking at the way the soft, humid breeze lifted strands of Catt's burnished hair made him ache again. He recalled that fiery red hair streaming freely, like a wild river, across her shoulders as she'd played that soccer game where he'd met her so long ago. Even then she had stood out like the champion she was. Catt was good at whatever she tried. Though she often won, she was a good sport about losing, too, satisfied to simply give her all to the game.

Other feelings, other memories, gently wafted to the surface of his roiling emotions as he sat there on the tugboat, charging down the wide, wide expanse of the Amazon. Closing his eyes, his clasped hands resting between his opened thighs, Ty remembered their wildly torrid lovemaking. Catt had been as hot, assertive, wild and free with him as she was in real life. She was truly an unfettered spirit inside a delicious woman's body. Ty remembered how he'd teased her once after loving her to exhaustion in a motel not far from the gates of the naval air station.

"You know what you are?" he had whispered, placing one small kiss after another on her damp brow as she lay beside him, absolutely spent, a wonderful smile of fulfillment on her soft, glistening lips.

Languidly, Catt moved her fingers across his well-shaped arm and up across his broad shoulder as she gazed into his eyes. "No, what am I?"

"An Amazon warrior." He picked up a strand of her long, damp red hair and held it up, critically examining it in the late afternoon light that peeked around the shade at the front window. "Part child, part woman, part Amazon warrior, part goddess, part sunlight, part warm, rich earth…"

"Mmm, I like that," she sighed, nuzzling his jaw as he cupped her shoulder and pressed her more surely against him. "No one has ever said things like that to me before.…"

"Because?" Ty looked down at her with a grin.

Barely opening her eyes, she smiled up at him. "Because I've never fallen in love before, I guess."

"Hard to imagine. You're so beautiful. A free spirit. You're like the wind in the thunderstorms I used to see every summer over the Rockies, where I grew up," he murmured against her hair. "When I saw you on that soccer field, I thought you must have a hundred men waiting in line for you."

Giggling, she said, "Not many men will take on a female Texas rancher, believe me. Most men feel as if they've met their match. More than met it! And that scares them."

"Texas women are special, not to be feared or run from." Ty smiled a little and pressed a kiss to the tip of her nose. He ran his fingers through her hair, then trailed them across her cheek, marveling at the smoothness of her skin. More than anything, he liked the dusting of freckles across her straight, thin nose and cheeks. Her lashes were thick and long, like dainty fans against her flushed cheeks. Ty savored every moment spent with Catt. They didn't get to meet often because of their demanding schedules. He could never get enough of her, of her husky voice, her touch, her loving, fiery body and that wild, free spirit of hers.

As he lay there and felt her snuggle deeply into his arms Ty had sighed with contentment. He'd never known love was like this. Oh, he'd had girlfriends off and on, but never had he been smitten like this, his emotions bright, his joy higher than the tallest mountain in the world, his senses more alive than he could ever recall. All because of this beautiful red-headed woman in his arms who had crashed into his life two months earlier. He could feel his heart opening powerfully to her as he held her. He'd felt such a sense of fierce protectiveness toward her and he knew he wanted her as his mate for the rest of his life. He was helpless against his longing for her; all he could do was hold her. Simply hold her.

As he sat on the tug now, a ragged sigh of frustration issued from between Ty's lips. He scowled heavily and worked to erase that scene from his memory. Glancing toward the bow again, he saw that Catt was off the phone and talking to Steve, her chief lab man, who would be setting up the work station once they reached the village. Ty knew the responsibilities on Catt's shoulders. He'd worked with outbreak teams before. They had to move fast to chase down the bacteria or virus that was mercilessly killing people.

As he studied the group out of the corner of his eye, Ty considered them modern-day knights, heroes and heroines riding into battle against an unknown opponent—one that could easily kill them, sometimes in as short a time as forty-eight hours after contracting the infection. Most of the world didn't know much about these outbreak teams, the chances they took with the unknown, even when the unknown was a killer of powerful proportions. It took real guts to walk into an area where people were dropping like flies, and hunt down the invisible killer with thorough, detailed, step-by-step analysis and plain hard work. To flush out the culprit meant constantly exposing themselves to it. One wrong move—a prick with an infected needle, or the entrance of the infection into the body through an open cut—would allow the disease to gain a foothold. Just the cough of a sick person could be dangerous if the germ was an aerosol-borne substance and could be breathed in.

There were so many ways to die if one was an outbreak chaser like Catt and the members of her team. Men and women composing such teams were truly courageous in the face of danger, and Ty's respect for them was as high as it was for a military person going into war. The risks an outbreak team took were as lethal as any he'd ever encountered during warfare. Instead of a bullet potentially killing one of them, it would be an invisible bacteria or germ. And the death could be gruesome and painful.

Worried, Ty wondered if Black Dawn had spread a nervine-type gas, such as VX, that would affect the central nervous system and stop a person from breathing, over the village. If they had, the team would see a lot of central-nervous-system symptoms such as paralysis, shaking or trembling limbs or altered states of consciousness in the victims. And a bug like that could easily be inhaled by Catt and her team.

Running his fingers through his short hair, Ty waited until Catt was standing alone at the bow once more. Then he made his move.

Catt's heart thundered as she saw Ty slowly ease to a standing position and head in her direction. She sat down on one of the trunks at the bow. Busying herself with a clipboard, she pretended not to notice his approach. Maybe he'd get the message and leave her alone.

"You got a minute?" he asked, coming to a halt in front of her. Ty saw the rest of her team at the other end of the tug, watching warily. Looking back at Catt, who had her head bowed over the clipboard on her lap in an obvious attempt to ignore him, he waited her out.

"I'm busy," she snapped.

"This will be the most unbusy time you'll have," he began. "When we land at that village, you and your team will work yourselves into exhaustion the first forty-eight hours. You won't even have time to sleep, while you try to find the culprit that's killing off those people. And you won't want to talk to me then, either, so now is as good a time as any."

Putting down the pen, Catt glared up at him. "What do you want?" She tried to hate him again, but it didn't work. He stood there, open and accessible, every emotion he felt revealed in his eyes. Catt knew he wasn't trying to hide anything from her— and she knew how good he was at hiding the truth when he chose to do so. For whatever reason, he was allowing her to see all of him without any walls.

"Mind if I sit down?" he asked, pointing to a green metal trunk behind him. He knew that would put only about three feet between them, and he saw the wariness in Catt's expressive features. It hurt to see how much she distrusted him. Well? Hadn't he earned it? Yes. So now that he'd made his bed, he had to lie in it.

"You'll sit whether I want you to or not."

Grinning mirthlessly, Ty eased back onto the trunk. Opening his thighs, he clasped his hands between them and studied her in the late afternoon light. He could see the stress around her mouth and eyes. Her brow was no longer smooth, but looked permanently wrinkled with the intensity of her concentration on the mission ahead of them.

"Spit out whatever you were going to say and then leave. I've got work to do," Catt warned him. She didn't want to look at Ty. Every time she even glanced into his warm, inviting brown eyes, she felt her heart crying out with need for him. It was a ridiculous reaction on her part. Completely ridiculous!

"I just want to go over some logistics with you," he began in a deep, soothing tone. "Casey wanted me to be a gopher and a guard dog at the same time, for you and your team."

Head snapping up, Catt looked at him. "What do you mean, guard dog? Are the Juma in a territorial dispute with another tribe?"

"No...not that I know of. We'll be meeting Rafe Antonio, a backwoodsman in this area. He works for the state and is the Brazilian equivalent of what we Americans would call a forest ranger."

"He's the one who contacted OID in the first place," Catt agreed, though she felt like fleeing. Just being this close to Ty Hunter was like hell itself. Only it was a hell filled with sweet longing—the kind of longing Catt never would have thought she'd feel if they'd ever met again. Ten years had hardened her heart against him. Or so she'd thought.

"Yes," Ty said tentatively. "He's got a houseboat, which is how he gets around to the various tribes that live in the backwater channels off the Amazon. Casey wanted me to fill you in on the Juma and get you up to speed on the politics of what's going down presently in Brazil regarding them."

"Since when did you become a South American Indian expert?"

Her sarcasm assaulted him. Frowning, Ty refused to let her anger toward him distract him from what he needed to share with her. "I've batted around the world a lot since you knew me," he said slowly and carefully. Noting her surprise, he added, "I left the Marine Corps five years ago. Now I work for the federal government as an expert on outbreak epidemics, with a specialty in South America and Africa." He didn't mention that his real knowledge was in bioterrorism. That would tip Catt off, and he didn't need her knowing the truth—at least, not yet, and maybe never. If Morgan was wrong about this being a Black Dawn experiment, and this was an outbreak situation only, there was no reason to needlessly put more stress on Catt and her team. They'd have enough danger to handle with the epidemic alone, without the possible threat of bioterrorists in the vicinity.

Catt frowned. "I see."

"I was also chosen for this team because I speak Portuguese. I've spent a lot of time in the Brazilian jungle the last three years." He looked around, his voice softening. "It's a beautiful place. Like a Garden of Eden. There're so many plants and animals within the jungle itself. It's like a living, evolving laboratory right before your eyes...."

She tried to remain immune to Ty's unexpected vulnerability, to his obvious love of this humid jungle environment—an environment that only made her feel miserable and hot. "Pretty to you. Dangerous to us," she accused sharply.

Shrugging, Ty studied her. Despite her personal dislike of him, Catt was gradually being less defensive and prickly as they spoke to one another. For that he was grateful. Opening his hands, he said, "No disagreement from me. Rafe will meet us at the head of the channel. He's got a green houseboat with white trim." Looking at his watch, Ty said, "We'll be about an hour late, but that's no big deal. He'll be waiting, and he'll guide us back to the village."

"I just tried to raise him on the cell phone," Catt said. "No answer."

"I'm not surprised," he told her in a low voice. "Cell phones don't work real well out in the jungle. Around Manaus," he continued, looking back upriver, where the skyline of the modern city had disappeared from view, "they work fine. Out here, I'm afraid you're going to find that old-fashioned pony express will be the communication of the day."

Nodding, Catt said, "No different from any other outbreak situation we've been in before—cut off from the outside world except by Jeep, Land Rover, horseback or a good pair of hiking boots."

Ty nodded and grinned a little. Thrilled that Catt was settling down now and speaking to him without such rancor, he breathed an inner sigh of relief. How badly he wanted to reach out and touch her long, elegant fingers. How badly he wanted to tell Catt that the coals of his love for her were still there after all this time. It was a surprise to him, one that made him feel unstable and unsure of himself. He'd thought the love he'd had for Catt had died long ago.

"You should set your lab up near Rafe's houseboat," he suggested. "You don't know what kind of epidemic we're facing yet, and his boat is about as safe as it will get."

"I'd already thought about that. Do you know how far back from the channel the Juma village sits?" Catt found herself falling into companionable conversation with him—once again. Oh, Ty Hunter had always been easy to talk with. How many times had she replayed those wonderful, stolen moments from the past? Far too many. Catt recalled the endless tears she'd cried when he'd abandoned her. In her greatest hour of need, when she'd craved Ty's comfort, his arms, his support, he hadn't been there for her. Tears pricked the backs of her eyes now, and she blinked several times to push them away. Looking at him, she dropped her gaze to his strong, capable mouth. Hotly, she recalled how wonderful his kisses had been. How his mouth had moved with such silken power across her lips, taming her, guiding her, cajoling her and meeting her hunger with his own.

Taking a shaky breath, Catt closed her eyes and rubbed her brow.

"Headache?" Ty asked gently, as she continued to gently massage her wrinkled brow. He ached to reach out and rub the tension out of her shoulders as he had in the past.

"Yes," she muttered uneasily. "It's a migraine coming on."

"Some things don't change, do they?" And he

smiled a little as she opened her dark blue eyes and stared at him. The silence stretched between them. Ty recalled that headaches, the migraine variety, had always plagued Catt. In the past, when they had been going together, he would turn her around and gently knead and massage her tight neck and shoulders, and miraculously, the oncoming migraine would disappear. And when he looked in her eyes now, he saw that she remembered, too, how he had cared for her. And then he saw anger wash the warmth in her gaze away. Realizing he'd overstepped the bounds of their present, tenuous relationship, he said, "Sorry, I just don't like to see you in pain."

Her fingers slipped from her brow and she sat up, fury sizzling through her. "Really?" Sarcasm made her voice brittle, nearly acidic.

Heat raced up his cheeks. Ty realized he was blushing beneath her blistering stare. Well, didn't he have it coming? "I have a friend, a homeopathic doctor," he said, trying to steer their conversation back on track. "She saved my life with this alternative medicine when I contracted Congo fever in an outbreak over in Africa. They had flown me to London to die. The priest had already given me the last rites when Dr. Rachel Donovan-Cunningham came in, gave me one of her little white pills and told the priest to go away, that I wouldn't be needing his services." Ty's mouth stretched a little as he held Catt's furious gaze. Already, as he began his story, he could see her anger fleeing, replaced with curiosity. That was one of the many things he had loved about Catt: her emotions were so open, so easily read on her face. Yes, she had a temper, but it never lasted long. She was like a Texas thunderstorm, erupting suddenly, but quickly returning to calm. In some ways, she hadn't changed at all, and he gloried in that small discovery.

"I've heard of homeopathy. So it saved your sorry neck?"

Hunter chuckled. "For better or worse, yes, it did." He gestured toward her left shoulder. "I remember you got migraines from a tight neck and shoulders. Dr. Donovan-Cunningham taught me a lot about homeopathy as I recovered in that London hospital. As a parting gift, she gave me a repertory and materia medica on the medicine. Over the years, I've gotten more training when I could. I'm not at her level, but I can use it for acute situations like your migraine if you're interested."

Catt didn't like the idea of Ty helping her. All too vividly, she recalled how he'd made her migraines go away before—with his marvelous, kneading fingers that worked a special magic on her tight flesh. Glaring at him, she said, "With you on board, my migraine is coming back. I'll take anything to make it and you go away."

Ty understood. "If I thought jumping overboard and swimming back to shore would cure it, I would."

"Try it."

Stung, but trying not to show his hurt, he took out a pad of paper and pen from his shirt pocket. "If you can answer a few questions about your symptoms, maybe I can find the right remedy to get rid of it. But unfortunately, I won't be able to rid you of myself just yet."

"Fire away," she muttered, as she ruefully rubbed her neck to ease the tension.

He opened the pad and asked, "What does it feel like?"

Grimacing, Catt growled, "Like someone is pulling all the skin on the back of my head and neck so tight that it's going to crack and break."

He wrote some notes down. Pleased that she was going to cooperate despite the fact that she saw him as her archenemy, Ty asked, "The pain? Can you describe it?"

"Dull and aching. Why are you asking me so many questions? Why can't you just give me the pill for migraines?"

"Because in homeopathy, we take all the symptoms of your case first, look them up in the repertory as a unit and then find the one single remedy that fits most of your major symptoms."

"Humph."

"This isn't like the pharmaceutical drugs you're used to," he warned.

"Obviously. What else? This thing is coming on slow but sure."

"When did it start?"

"When I saw you."

He nodded and looked at his watch. "So it's a slow-moving migraine?"

"You know it is."

Unruffled, he said, "What makes it feel worse?"

"Having you sit here. Having you on this tug with me."

The corners of his mouth rose slightly. "I won't find those symptoms in my repertory. Any others?"

She tried to remain immune to his charm, to that little-boy smile lurking around his mouth. Why did Ty have to be so damned ruggedly handsome? He could charm a snake if he wanted to. Nostrils flaring, she lifted her head and rubbed her neck. "I just had a cup of coffee, and that helped ease it a little."

"So, it gets better with stimulants?"

She eyed him. "I guess you could say that. Coffee is a stimulant of sorts."

"That's right," he agreed. "What else?"

It hurt to think at this point. Catt wished Ty would go away, and at the same time, her heart was absorbing his nearness like a desert that hadn't seen rain in years—a decade to be exact—and that made her scared of her own emotions toward him. Fumbling for a response, she muttered, "Bad news."

"Me," he said, scribbling again. "Anything that makes your symptoms worse?"

"With this damned humidity cranking up, I always feel horrible. So I guess you could say heat and sunlight like we're having right now, okay?"

Ty finished writing and got up. "I'll be back in a bit with a remedy."

"Don't worry, I'm not going anywhere." She watched as he nodded and carefully picked his way past the boxes stacked on the deck of the tug. The humid air felt somewhat cooler, but not much. Catt had the desire to leap into the cool waters of the muddy Amazon. She squelched that idea because among the denizens that lived in these fabled waters were schools of flesh-eating piranhas. No, she had no desire to be stripped to her skeleton by those hungry little monsters.

Rubbing her neck once more, Catt sighed heavily. Being around Ty was like holding her hand over an open flame and letting herself be burned. What recourse did she have? None. Her migraine was intensifying. It was because of the shock of seeing him once again, she knew. If only her stupid heart would let him go! Why did she feel hope? Joy when he was nearby?

"I feel like a damned thunderstorm—up one second, down the next," she muttered under her breath. She saw Ty sitting down on the deck, a book in hand and another at his side, deep in concentration. Turning, Catt looked out across the bow of the tug. The Amazon River was nearly half a mile wide at this point, a yellow-gray color against the jungle along the banks. Trees of varying types, including palms, were so thick that light rarely reached the jungle floor, and she could see the darkness within. A flight of red-and-yellow macaws flew overhead in a V pattern. Their color stood out against the clouds that seemed to perpetually hang overhead. Would she ever see direct sunlight again?

"I think I got your remedy."

Catt jumped. She didn't mean to, but Ty's voice was so close, she couldn't help it. Jerking to look upward, she saw he was standing in front of her, a couple of white pellets in the hand extended in her direction. Eyeing them and then him, she growled, "What is it?"

Ty saw that strain was deepening around Catt's eyes—pain from the oncoming migraine encroaching. "It's a remedy called Gelsemium. In layperson's language, it's yellow jasmine." He crouched down in front of her and kept his hand extended. Catt was eyeing the pellets jadedly. "In its natural state, the herb is poisonous and could kill you. But—" he pointed to the pellets "—these are made so that there's no longer any of the crude substance left in it to hurt you.''

''Then what's left?'' Catt demanded. ''Air?''

He grinned. ''Energy. I know we don't have time to talk much about this kind of medicine, but trust me that the energy signature of Gelsemium is in these pellets.''

''And these things will stop my migraine?''

He heard the disbelief in her voice. He saw the distrust in her eyes. ''Yes, it will.''

She stared at him. ''Give me one reason to trust what you say, Hunter.''

His heart ached in that moment. He knew her question grew from the way he'd made her suffer in the past; he could hear her pain in her low, hoarse tone. As gently as possible, he rasped, ''This isn't about me. This is about you and trying to help you be pain free. You don't need a migraine going into an outbreak situation. You don't have to trust me in order to take this remedy. If it works, you'll know it in twenty minutes. Your migraine symptoms will start to go away.'' Holding her challenging blue gaze, he moved his hand a little closer to her.

Disgruntled, Catt held out her palm. ''Give them to me.''

He tipped his hand. Their fingers met and touched briefly. Catt instantly jerked hers away. The white pellets fell to the deck of the tug. Ty heard her mutter a curse of desperation mixed with anger.

''Just stay put,'' he told her, unwinding and straightening to his full height. ''I've got more. I'll bring you another dose.''

Feeling foolish, Catt refused to look at him. Ty was being incredibly tolerant and gentle with her despite the sarcasm, the anger she continually aimed at him. Her fingers tingled where they'd briefly touched his. A wild flurry of heat had jolted up through her body from that contact. It had shocked her. Scared her. Feeling very stupid at jerking her hand away as if it had been scalded, Catt watched him pick up a black plastic case that looked like a small fishing tackle box. He wound his way back to her and sat down on the trunk opposite her.

Opening the case, Ty showed her some two-dram-size amber bottles with black caps on them. "I carry fifty homeopathic remedies with me all the time." Maybe if he showed her some of what he knew, she'd settle down and not be so jumpy. But Ty knew why she'd jerked her hand away. She hated him so much she didn't want to be touched by him. The hurt moving through him was as wide as the Amazon they floated on. There was nothing he could do; he felt the wound in his heart expanding. He felt his need for Catt all over again, along with the pain of knowing they could never be together again.

Taking out one bottle, he handed it to Catt, making sure he didn't touch her hand in the process. "Here's the Gelsemium. Open it and put a few pellets on the palm of your hand. And then put them under your tongue. They'll melt away real quick. They're sweet-tasting, so you'll like them."

Doing as she was instructed, Catt hurriedly re-capped the bottle and handed it back to Ty. Because she was distracted, her fingers brushed his again. This time she forced herself not to jerk away and drop the bottle.

"Look," she rasped, "I've got more work to do...."

Ty understood. He put the bottle back in the case and closed it. "No problem. Let me know if your migraine goes away?"

"Yes, sure...." Catt didn't believe for a moment it would go away because of this "energy" medicine of his. From her point of view as a medical doctor, it was snake oil or hocus-pocus at best. As he rose and left, she dragged in a sigh of relief.

Being around Ty was like being around a raging fire that was out of control. Catt was both attracted to and afraid of him. What was she going to do? How would she handle his nearness at the village? Someway, Catt realized, she had to get Ty away from her. A plan began to form in her aching head. Yes, if she could just keep him away from her and her silly, pining heart, maybe, just maybe, she could survive this time with him.

Chapter Four

"My headache's gone," Catt said grumpily. It had taken every bit of her courage to walk down the length of the tug as it chugged into the hazy sunset, and admit that to Ty. He was sitting on the rough wooden deck of the ill-kept tug, notebook in hand, writing. She stood over him, her hands on her hips, feeling tense and full of turmoil. Ty was here, with her. That fact still overwhelmed her. What sick twist of the cosmos had occurred? In all these years, Catt had never envisioned meeting with her first love again—nor had she wanted to.

Ty put his notebook aside. He looked up into Catt's strained features. Understanding what it had cost her pride to admit he was right—and he knew she had a lot of pride—he purposely remained seated before her. Right now, she was jumpy as hell around him. Ty knew if Catt could walk on water and leave this boat, she'd do it because *he* was here. The thought made bitterness coat his mouth.

Looking at his watch, he murmured, "Thirty minutes. Not bad. All your symptoms are gone?"

"Yes, even the ones I forgot to tell you about. No more nausea. My eyes aren't hurt by this light." She looked up at the cloudy sky. "Not that it's that bright, but when I get a damned migraine I want complete darkness around me." Why did Ty have to look so vulnerable to her? He sat on the gray, peeling deck, his long muscled legs bent to brace himself, his strong back and powerful shoulders resting against the bulwark of the tug. The slight breeze riffled his dark, walnut-brown hair and the naked urge to thread her fingers through those strands shocked Catt.

"Good," Ty murmured. "Homeopathy can work miracles from time to time." And then he chuckled a little. "It saved my life, and that's what got me interested in it, as I said. Dr. Donovan-Cunningham was a good teacher, too. Since then, I've used it off and on. A couple of months ago, my brother Reid was over in Africa on assignment with Casey. Did you hear about that?" He looked up expectantly at Catt. She had drawn her arms across her chest, but she didn't look as tense, so he kept up his quiet patter. In the past, his low, soothing voice had always helped quiet the highstrung tension that lived within her.

"Well, you probably didn't," he said, answering his own question. "Anyway, while Reid and Casey were staying in one of the villages there, Reid got sideswiped by a black mamba."

Catt's eyes widened. "You're kidding!"

"Nope," he said gravely, "and you know, in terms of the venom they carry, they are the deadliest snakes in the world. You don't survive a bite from them."

Rubbing her head, Catt muttered, "Yes, I'm well aware of that."

"Anyway, Reid got bitten through his pants, and only a little venom got into his bloodstream, but it was enough for him to go down for the count. Casey had him flown from Yambuku, Congo to Johannesburg, to one of the top hospitals there. Reid went into cardiac arrest a number of times on the flight, and if it hadn't been for Casey knowing CPR, he'd have died on that flight. By the time they got him to the hospital, he was in a coma. They put him on life support and told her he'd die in a matter of hours or days."

"How terrible," Catt said, her arms dropping to her sides.

"Yes, it was. She got on the first phone she could find to call for help." Ty purposely left out the fact that he and his brother both worked for Perseus, because he didn't want Catt to figure out why he was really here with her. She'd start putting things together and asking a lot of questions he didn't want to have to answer. "She told me Reid was in critical condition and expected to die. And she wanted to know if there was something I could do for him."

"Your homeopathic pills?" Catt guessed, intrigued.

"Bang on, darlin'." The moment the endearment left his lips, Ty regretted it. Damn! He shot an apologetic glance upward and saw the shock written on her features. He'd always called her "darlin'" when they had gone together. Now the word had slipped effortlessly off his tongue without him even thinking about it. He saw the tension return to Catt's eyes along with anger and hurt. "I'm sorry," he said quickly, "I didn't mean—"

"Just get on with your story," Catt said in a brittle tone. She tried to shake off the feelings that flowed gently through her because of the endearment. Had Ty done that on purpose? As she glared down at him, she saw the genuine apology in his expression and the sadness in his cinnamon-colored gaze. No, it was probably a slip from the past, that was all, she decided. Trying to steady her heartbeat, she wrapped her arms across her chest once more, feeling defensive.

Mentally chastising himself, Ty muttered, "I called Dr. Donovan-Cunningham and told her what had happened to Reid. She suggested I fly over with a high potency of a remedy called Lachesis Muta. That's venom from a bushmaster snake that lives right here in the Amazon." He gestured toward the shore of the mighty river.

"A poison to antidote a poison?" Catt murmured. "Interesting. Did it work?"

"Yeah, it did," Ty said with satisfaction. He saw the tension draining from her face once more. If nothing else, Catt had a voracious amount of curiosity as a scientist and medical doctor. Enough to help her forget his stupid slip of the tongue. The last thing he wanted to do was hurt Catt. He'd done enough to her already. "It was a sixteen-hour flight from hell, but I had the vial in hand. I met Casey in the waiting room on the critical-care floor, dissolved one pellet in a little bit of water and I immediately rubbed some on the inside of Reid's wrist." Ty smiled a little. "What happened next scared the living hell out of me."

Catt sat down on the deck of the tug about two feet away from Ty, her hands on either side to steady her. "It worked?"

"Yes, it did. About ten minutes after I'd rubbed it, he started to come out of the coma. He was flailing around, trying to rip the life support tubes out of himself. I panicked, hit the call button and yelled for the nurses to come down to his room pronto."

She saw the humor in his face. "So Reid lived because of the homeopathic medicine?"

Ty nodded. "That's right. The docs at the hospital had all said he'd die, that it was just a matter of time." His voice turned grim. "I wasn't about to let Reid die if I could help it. Rachel Donovan-Cunningham is a miracle worker as far as I'm concerned. Her and those little white pills of hers. She's married now to an EMT by the name of Jim Cunningham and they live in Sedona, Arizona. She's a world-class homeopath and when I'm in trouble, I call her, and she lets me pick her brain. Rachel's the one who gives me the correct remedy for these kinds of situations."

Rubbing her brow, Catt said, "I'd like to say that Reid's own body made him live, but if the doctors were ready to give him the last rites, this is a strong anecdotal case for homeopathy. Have any blind trials been done on this stuff?" she asked, pointing to the dark green plastic case that sat next to him, on which was printed Hahnemann Pharmacy, Advanced First Aid Kit.

"Yes, there are some going on now, as we speak,"

Ty told her. "And they clearly show that homeopathy is working." Tapping the case, he said, "I never leave home without it, believe me."

Worriedly, Catt looked down the river in the fading light. "Well, depending upon what we find at the Juma village, who knows? Maybe if we run out of options, I'll be asking you about your little white pills to help out. Does this stuff do well in epidemic situations?"

"Yes. I had Congo fever and it pulled me through."

Nodding, Catt studied his large hand, splayed across the case. It was a hand that had caressed her so many, many wonderful times. She'd wanted to forget those times, but she had never been able to. How could she? She'd loved Ty as she had no other man before or since. In fact, she'd never loved again after Ty. Hurt throbbed through Catt. She wanted to cry. It was funny how Ty always brought all her emotions to bright, burning life—the good and the bad. There was just something about him, something in his character, that made her want to relax, share everything with him and receive that nurturing quality that was usually so rare in men. That quality was still there in Ty, she realized lamely.

"Well," Ty said, "if all else fails, I can always get an idea of the symptoms and repertorize them to see if any of the remedies I have might parallel them. Like cures like."

"Do that," Catt said. "You made a partial believer out of me. My migraine's gone, and when one of those suckers gets roaring through my head, I usually have it for two or three days. And it lays me out flatter than a pancake."

He smiled a little and absorbed her softened Texas drawl, that slight Southern twist that still lingered in her voice. "I admire you for your open-mindedness despite what's happened," he told her, meaning it sincerely. He saw surprise and then momentary pleasure in her eyes. And just as quickly, it was replaced with that defensive wall again. He knew Catt didn't like him. The reality was she probably hated him. And she had every right to hate him.

Ty knew it was now or never. "Listen, before we arrive at the Juma village, which we should do in about an hour, I need to talk to you," he said in a very low tone that only she could hear.

Catt tensed. She stared at him. "About what?"

"Us. Our past. I need to clear the air so that we can work together without it getting in our way."

Savage pain scored her heart, and her mouth twisted as she held his beseeching look. "So, you didn't know you'd be working with me before you got here?"

Ty shook his head gravely. "No...I really didn't." He almost said, *even if I knew, I'd have come anyway,* but she wouldn't want to hear those thoughts. The guarded look in her eyes made him ache for her as she sat on the deck of the tug, her fingers digging convulsively into the graying wood that badly needed sanding and painting. He felt the tension coil up in her. The fear in her eyes made him feel worse than he did already. Taking a deep breath, he rasped, "I owe you an apology I never got to give you, Catt. So much was happening in my life there at the naval air station. I was a young shavetail lieutenant just out of the academy, hit with a huge assignment—to prepare security for the president of the United States, due to arrive the next day.'' He held up his hands. ''Not that it was an excuse for what happened.''

Holding her gaze, Ty felt raw pain radiating from her. He wanted to add that back then he'd wanted to shine before his superiors, to make his father proud of him. Dev and Shep were always winning trophies and being top in sports. And their successes as military men gave them center stage in their father's heart. Ty had never quite measured up to his two older brothers and that had always caused him pain. Especially since his father doted on his older sons' accomplishments. The security assignment had been Ty's opportunity to show he could successfully handle something big—to do something that neither Dev nor Shep had ever done. Looking back on it, Ty could see where his eagerness to please his father had come between him and the woman he'd loved so fiercely. He'd made the wrong choice. He should have been there for Catt—for their child....

''When you called me and told me you were pregnant,'' he continued painfully, the memories causing an ache in his chest, ''I should have done things a lot different than I did at that time. I should have come home. I should have been with you when—'' He broke off, all the sorrow from their past hitting him with renewed force. ''I know my priorities were wrong. I was young and overwhelmed with the assignment and just plain scared. I—just didn't see things clearly. And for that, I'm very sorry. You were angry and hurt and you hung up on me. I couldn't track you down for months after that and the next time I got in touch with you you told me—'' his voice broke once more ''—that you had lost our child. And that you never wanted to see me again.''

Mouth pulling in pain, Catt couldn't bear to look at Ty any longer. Her heart hurt. She ached in her lower body. It was an ache she remembered all too well and had not forgotten to this day. "I didn't *want* to be found by you, Hunter," she replied in a hoarse whisper. "And you damn well know why. You made it clear to me that your responsibilities were to the Marine Corps. I know all you wanted was to build your precious new career so you could impress your father. You wanted nothing to do with a twenty-year-old who was pregnant with your baby. No," she breathed rawly, "I got your message loud and clear. So why would I *want* to be with you after—" She stopped, overcome. Then anger filled her once more. She wouldn't cry now, after all this time. And not in front of Ty. He hadn't been there for her then. And she wasn't about to cry on his shoulder now.

Ty rested his elbows on his thighs and clasped his hands between his opened legs. "I got the message. Especially when you disappeared once again after telling me you'd lost the baby. I felt helpless. I tried a lot of different ways to track you down."

"Well, none of your methods worked because I didn't want them to work."

He studied Catt in the dusky light, her beautiful face marred with grief and pain. "Where did you go?"

"Down to the Caribbean to finish off my medical education. I then took the entrance exams to get a U.S. medical license, and passed."

This was the hardest part. Ty tried to gird himself emotionally. "And you changed your name, too?"

"Yes. I took my mother's maiden name, Al-borak."

"I see...." There was much he longed to know,
so much she had refused to tell him during that brief
phone call when she'd told him about the miscarriage. He often wondered about what she'd gone
through. Brows dipping, he said in a choked voice,
"And the baby? How—how far along were you
when—" He broke off then, knowing this was an
explosive issue because Catt suddenly stood up, her
arms wound tightly against her chest. Her eyes glittered, and he realized in the twilight it was because
they were filled with tears she refused to allow to
fall.

Hot, violent pain twisted through Catt. She gasped
at the power of her emotions as they surged up from
her abdomen straight into her wildly beating heart.
She saw the hopelessness, the utter apology, in Ty's
face. Her nostrils flared and quivered. Her words
came out clipped and filled with agony. "Days after
I called you to tell you I was pregnant, I miscarried.
I lost my baby." *I lost you. I lost everything.* She
stood there, riddled with hurt, yet still fighting the
tears that threatened.

Rising to his feet, Ty unthinkingly reached out, his
hands curving around her upper arms. He felt the
tension in Catt, saw the pain in her eyes, which were
huge with unshed tears as she looked up at him angrily. They stood tensely, like two warriors ready to
battle one another. She was breathing hard and erratically. Her lips were tight from the pain she was
feeling.

"Oh, Lord," Ty rasped, "I—I'm so sorry...I
should have been there for you, Catt." He choked,
as tears pummeled the backs of his eyes. He felt Catt

sway toward him in that instant and then he saw her catch herself and jerk out of his reach.

"Right," she spat, her pain transparent even through her anger. "Like I believe you! Don't stand there and pretend it would have mattered, Hunter. Because you're lying to me—again." She looked around realizing her voice had risen, but her team must have made themselves scarce because she couldn't see any of them at the moment. Swinging her attention back to Hunter, who stood there, shoulders sagging, his lips parted and tears in his eyes, she was caught off guard. Why tears? Fury moved through her. A righteous fury. "You abandoned me, Hunter. You made a choice. I was less important. The baby I carried in my body didn't count with you. We were number two in your life, not number one like we should have been." Catt jabbed a finger into his chest. "I don't give a damn if the president of the U.S. was coming to your silly little naval air station. Being pregnant with *your* baby should have been a helluva lot more important. But no," she breathed savagely, pinning his sad eyes with her own, "your career, the politics of climbing up the officers' ladder and getting your father's approval were your priorities."

Catt stepped back, her breath coming in choppy gasps. Wrapping her arms around her chest, she continued. "You have *no idea* what kind of hell you put me through. I damned near lost my sanity after losing my baby and you at the same time. I swore I'd never love again, Hunter. Especially after loving a man who was married to his career first. It was a huge lesson for me. I've never made that mistake since."

A scorching, fiery guilt roared through his chest

and Ty stared helplessly down at her. Her raw pain was there for him to see, to feel and to absorb. "I'm sorry I wasn't there for you, Catt. More sorry than you'll ever know...." He swallowed against a huge lump forming in his throat. Closing his eyes, Ty wished he could turn back the clock, wished he hadn't been so young, so callous, so damned stupid. Had he known the costs of his actions then...

Standing there, he felt his stomach tightening with anguish for all that he had lost. All he wanted to do in that moment was embrace Catt, hold her, rock her, care for her and take away the hurt that was clearly eating her alive. But Catt stood so stiffly, he couldn't even touch her. Choking on a lump that refused to go away, he rasped, "I really screwed up big-time with you, Catt. Apologizing doesn't seem like enough. But I never got the chance to tell you how sorry I am that you lost our baby...." And he was. Very sorry.

Lifting her chin, her eyes blazing, Catt cried, "It was *never* 'our' baby. It was *my* baby! You didn't want one, remember? You practically hung up on me because the stupid White House was calling you. Oh, I got your message loud and clear, Hunter, then as now." She made a helpless gesture with her hand. "I left. It was like everything else in my life: I had to handle it alone. At the ranch, when my father was ill, there was no one to ask for help. My whole life's revolved around that premise. Why should it have been any different when I reached out to ask you for help?" She glared at him. What Catt didn't say was that when she left, she asked no one for help when she desperately needed it during the grieving process. Perhaps that was why her driving need to be a doc-

tor—to be there for a patient crying out for help—
was the only antidote for her own, unsupported pain
and grief. Loving support had never been there for
her—ever. Not with her mother who died when she
was so young; and not with her tough-as-nails father
who felt too embarrassed to hug his only daughter
and show her he loved her. She'd never heard those
words from her father—ever. The love she held for
Ty was slammed in her face, too.

Ty wondered how Catt had handled the grief, the
loss of their child. He felt new grief blossoming in
his own heart for the child he would never know.
Frowning, he looked out at the muddy water surrounding the tug. "No...you're wrong, but I can't
change your mind on that now. I won't even try,
Catt. I thought..." He forced himself to look over at
her. She stood like a proud, tense avenging angel. "I
dreamed of our child. Over the years, I tried to find
you.... I wanted to tell you how much our child
would have meant to me, how sorry I was over the
loss." With a weak gesture, his voice cracking, he
added, "What a lousy mistake I made with you. I
should have just come home. I should have just
dropped out of that damned assignment."

Catt shook violently. "Sure...you're all hearts and
flowers now, Hunter. Frankly, I see nothing but guilt
written on your face and in your voice. It's about
time you paid a little penance for your decision, as
far as I'm concerned. And yes, you had your priorities all screwed up. Your career and your father's
opinion came first over other things, that was for
sure. And that wasn't the first time I'd seen it. No, I
got the message, believe me. That's why I disappeared for good after the miscarriage. I didn't want

a damn thing more to do with you. If you were going to put your career above more important priorities, you were the wrong person for me to think I loved."

Wincing, Ty closed his eyes. When he opened them, he saw that Catt had moved a little farther away from him. He stepped toward her because he didn't want their personal laundry aired for everyone on the small tug to overhear. "I made a mess of everything," he admitted rawly. "And there's no way to go back and change what happened." Opening his hand toward her, he pleaded, "I don't expect you to forgive me, Catt. I don't deserve it. I made a mistake I'll live with forever. And it's one that has cost us both dearly. I don't expect you to believe that it hurt me, too." He wanted to say, *I loved you. I never stopped loving you. Any woman who came into my life I held up and compared to you, and no one even came close to you, your burning, fiery way of living life.* If he admitted that, Catt would laugh him off this old, dilapidated tug. His chest ached with unparalleled grief. His baby had died. He had known that all along and yet his pain seemed more real, more raw, now that he'd finally shared it with Catt. Their child, the creation of their powerful, wonderful love for one another, hadn't lived to share their lives. He blinked back the tears. Right now, Catt was his first concern, not his own selfish emotions.

"We have to work together for at least a month or more," he told her quietly. "We needed to clear the air on our past so we could get on with what we have to do at that village. You and I can't afford to keep dragging up old history in the middle of this crisis."

"You don't get it, do you?" Catt demanded

harshly. "I didn't trust you then and I don't trust you *now,* Hunter. You abandoned me and my baby in our greatest hour of need. There is *nothing* you could do to make me think you are more reliable now, even with this epidemic raging." She shook her head adamantly. "No, you're not trustworthy, and I don't care how many times you say it, how loudly or how often. My experience with you tells me everything about you. You might be a part of my team, but I'm going to make sure you are not working with me. I'll put you in a dusty little corner to run lab samples. Out of sight, out of mind."

Anger stirred in him, along with the hurt and concern he felt. Ty grappled with his rising emotions. "You have every right to feel that way about me based upon the past, Catt. But I'm ten years older now and I'd like to think I've matured a little in that time, that I've learned what's really important in life. My career is not primary anymore. People are. You are. The safety of your team is my only priority on this mission."

How badly Catt wanted to believe him! Ty looked earnest and genuinely sincere. His voice flowed through her, soothing her anger and pain like a healing balm. She wanted to ignore that fact, but she couldn't. "Sorry, it doesn't wash with me at all." Catt jabbed a finger in his direction. "I'm the boss on this mission. You're going to be as far away from me and my team as I can put you." Her eyes narrowed. "And this is one time when you aren't going to get your own way, Hunter. I'll be damned if you're going to be at my elbow, day in and day out, as we try to save lives and define this killer."

He stood very still. It wasn't that simple, but Catt

didn't know it and he couldn't tell her. Something told him to just keep his mouth shut and not engage her on this—yet. "Let's get to Rafe Antonio's houseboat," he suggested slowly, "and assess the epidemic status. That will help you decide these issues...."

Lifting her chin at an imperious angle, Catt hissed, "I don't care *what* the status is, you are *not* going to be around me at all during this mission." The truth was, he was too close, too virile, and it was too easy for her to simply walk into his arms, to be held once again. Catt knew she could not afford to do that. But whether she liked it or not, her heart clamored for his nearness. She was too scared, too hurt to allow him that kind of access to her ever again. Once they got to Antonio's houseboat, things would change; she'd be in charge, leading the attack against an unknown danger. And that was what she'd done best since losing her baby and the man she loved: hurl herself into deadly situations with a hell-bent-for-leather abandon that scared even the most seasoned epidemic specialist on her team. She had died when she was twenty years old. Now there was nothing left to live for, to protect herself against. The living dead—that's what she was. Thanks to Ty Hunter, she was immune to any threat life could offer.

Chapter Five

By the time they met Rafe Antonio at his houseboat, it was almost dark. The Brazilian backwoodsman was in his late twenties, tall, intense looking and possessing a calm that Catt did not have at the moment. Despite the tension shimmering in the air while they off-loaded the equipment from the tug, with the tug captain nervously telling them to hurry because he did not want to become infected by the disease ravaging the Juma, Rafe seemed above it all. He behaved as if there was no crisis. Catt wished she possessed such aplomb. Maybe in some other lifetime she had, but not this one.

Catt saw Rafe go directly to Ty Hunter, saw the two men stand off by themselves, talking in low tones she could not overhear. Determinedly, she focused her attention on orchestrating where the lab tent would be set up and where all the supplies would

go near Rafe's handy houseboat, which he called
"home." The houseboat wasn't homey looking at
all. She saw a lot of holes here and there on the upper
decks and wondered if they were created by bullets.
Catt knew little of the backwoodsman except that he
was a champion of Indian rights in this part of the
Amazon, and that he was hated by the rich, who
wanted Indian land for mining or other exploitations.
He was in the employ of the state, and his bosses
were in Manaus. Basically, he was the only "law"
that stood between the inhabitants of this part of the
Amazon basin and the many who would murder, loot
and steal from them. In her eyes, the Amazon was a
Dodge City of the Old West, and Rafe Antonio the
sheriff trying to keep law and order. Catt understood
that Antonio was hated by the timber barons, mine
owners and corporate agriculturalists who wanted to
exploit the unsophisticated people living in the basin.
It was his job to see that didn't happen.

The exchange of equipment from water to land
went smoothly. Because this was the dry season,
bugs weren't around, and for that Catt was grateful.
The tug captain took his money from her and left in
a hurry.

She saw Rafe lift his head, his short black hair
gleaming beneath the kerosene lamp that he'd hung
on a pole high above the houseboat, a beacon for
them to find him. He was dressed in khaki slacks and
a white, short-sleeved shirt dampened by sweat,
which outlined his powerful chest and broad shoulders. His ebony eyes were fierce, and his gaze reminded Catt of a Texas thunderstorm just about to
strike. She decided she liked his presence, his steadi-
ness under these circumstances. Antonio was not

someone she'd want to come up against as an adversary. She was glad the Juma had him as a protector.

Going over to Ty and him, she said, "Is there any way to get into the village tonight?"

"No, señorita, there is not." Rafe lifted his square chin and studied the dark tangle of trees, vines and plants along a well-trodden dirt path that led up from the river. "It is a mile away from here. We will trek in at first light tomorrow."

His voice was deep and cultured. She was surprised that his English was excellent, although she could detect that it wasn't his first language. In fact, she learned later he spoke fluent Spanish, as well as Portuguese. "Where can we sit and talk?" Catt demanded. "I need to know the latest details so we can plan what we'll do at dawn tomorrow."

Rafe smiled slightly and bowed deferentially to her. "Of course, señorita. Come, you are my guest in my poor hovel of a home. It is not fancy by your standards, but it is clean and livable. Come."

Catt eyed Hunter as he waited for her to follow Rafe. He seemed worried. Or maybe she just sensed something different about him since they'd arrived. Whatever it was, there was a new feeling around Ty now and it caught her off guard. He was looking around, assessing everything in a sharp and alert way. She sensed a fine tension running through him. Maybe it was the narrowing of his intelligent cinnamon eyes as he scanned the area. Or maybe it was her imagination. Catt wasn't sure anymore. Ordinarily, she could rely on her instincts without fail. Since Hunter had crashed unexpectedly into her life, her emotions were in continuous turmoil, to the point where she didn't know what the hell was going on inside her.

Shaking off her thoughts, she followed Rafe and quickly caught up with him. Off to the left, her efficient teammates were already setting up a tent in which the very important lab equipment, table, slides and microscope would be set up so they could take blood, saliva and tissue samples and prepare them for transit back to Georgia, where, hopefully, they would discover what they were fighting down here.

The houseboat was old, large and in dire need of repairs, starting with a good sanding and several new coats of paint. It was a huge vessel, reminding Catt of a whale floating languidly above the muddy Amazon waters. It was tied to two huge Pau d'Arco trees with thick hemp lines. Ten black rubber tires decorated each side of the houseboat, protecting it as it bobbed slightly against the earthen bank. Rafe was right: it was a homely looking thing. She stepped gingerly on board, but not before she felt Ty cup her elbow from behind with his large, callused hand, helping her up the three feet to the deck.

Surprised, Catt glanced around once she was onboard. Her elbow tingled hotly where he'd touched her. Pleasure moved down her arm and she flexed her fingers in consternation. Catt didn't want to feel anything as far as Hunter was concerned. Scowling at him in the dim light, she turned and followed Rafe down a narrow set of wooden stairs. Above her was the deckhouse, enclosed on three sides. She saw the throttles, a wooden wheel, a radio and several maps spread out here and there across the console. As she entered the lower quarters, a somewhat homier area, the air became stuffy and close. The four small windows were closed and the humid air trapped inside had a moldy odor. Even now, Catt wished for the fresher air outside, but said nothing. Because high humidity was ever present in the basin, except during the dry season, when it was a little lower, the houseboat's wooden hull took a beating from the dampness. Wood rotted quickly in these tropical temperatures.

On the port side of the houseboat's interior was a small, square table with a faded yellow oilcloth covering it. Catt smiled a little. Rafe had picked an orchid, placed it in a chipped white coffee mug and set it in the center of the table. Though he was an incredibly masculine figure, the orchid spoke of a more gentle, refined aspect of his character. On the starboard side of the cabin was a threadbare couch in need of reupholstering and a good cleaning. Noting the spots on it here and there, Catt itched to take a sponge to the aging fabric herself. Men were *not* good housekeepers and Antonio was clearly no exception.

Rafe gestured to the couch. "Please, señorita, have a seat. May I get you some water to drink? Something to eat? Señor Hunter said you have had a very long and trying day."

Catt kept her thoughts about the less-than-homey boat to herself as she sat down. The interior of the houseboat was lit with low-wattage lightbulbs. From somewhere deep in the guts of the houseboat—the engine room, she supposed—came the chattering of a small generator, which was obviously producing electricity for them. Out here in the middle of the Amazon jungle there were no power lines, no gas stations, no nothing. Everything had to be shipped in by canoe or tugboat.

"Water, yes, please," she said.

Catt saw Hunter coming slowly down the rickety stairs, which creaked in protest with each step he took. It was on the tip of her tongue to tell him to leave. However, the dark, shadowed look on his face made her swallow her words.

Turning around in the small, cramped quarters to the tiny white refrigerator, Rafe brought out three small plastic bottles of effervescent water. "Around here," he told her congenially, "make sure that if you get bottled water, señorita, it has bubbles in it." He held up one bottle for her to observe the carbonation in it. Handing it to her, he added in warning, "If it does not, do not drink it. It could be local water filled with parasites, and you will be very sorry."

Unscrewing the top, Catt nodded. She was very thirsty. The water was cool and bubbly in her mouth. She saw Ty sit down next to her. He was close. Far too close. Choking down the water, she glared at him and moved over until she was as far away as she could get, but even that left only a foot of space between them. Rafe and Ty were big men, Catt realized as she capped the bottle of water and set it back on the table. She'd better get used to sharing cramped quarters with them.

Rafe sat down and handed Ty a bottle, who thanked him in Portuguese and drank deeply from it. Catt waited impatiently. People were dying a mile away. She itched to get into the village to start saving lives. Antibiotics would make the difference. She felt too restless to sit still. Trying to ignore Hunter's powerful presence was impossible. The air in the cabin was stifling. Catt wanted desperately to run up those stairs and get away. Couldn't Antonio see how hot it was down here and at least be sensitive enough to open the windows and get some fresh air circulating?

But Catt couldn't fool herself. What she really wanted was to run from Ty. He was too close. Her elbow still tingled warmly from the earlier unexpected touch of his fingers, which were roughened from outdoor activity. She recalled all too vividly those fingers moving across her young, untamed body. Well, she was older and wiser now. Despite her silly heart, which was crying out for her to renew contact with him in every way, Catt knew better. If she did, it would be the death of her. She could not stand to be abandoned by Ty Hunter again. Not ever.

"Can you tell us what is going on inside the village?" Catt asked as Rafe finished drinking his water. She got up and went to each of the windows, jerking them open in turn. A tiny dribble of fresh air began to circulate and she breathed a sigh of relief and sat back down.

With a nod, Rafe reached over to a small cabinet and opened it. "Yes, here are the stats I knew you would want." He laid the yellow legal pad in front of her and turned it so she could read it. "I apologize for my bad writing."

Catt smiled a little. "Looks like a doctor's writing. I can read it." She pulled the sweat-stained, yellow legal pad closer. "Go over each line of this, will you, Señor Antonio?"

"Call me Rafe," he said, smiling slightly. Pointing to the first column, he continued. "This was the original count of people in this village—one hundred and six. I've noted names, gender and ages, and the dates when each person contracted the sickness. I've also noted when they died." His voice was tinged with sadness. "Doctor, you must understand something about these figures. The Juma used to be one of the largest Indian nations here in the Amazon. Brazilians full of greed have murdered them ceaselessly. As late as the 1960s, they would come down from Manaus by boat and slaughter the Juma."

Catt looked up. "Murder them outright?"

"*Sí,* señorita." Rafe's eyes glittered. "That was, until I was assigned here. Now they no longer try to do it."

"Is that why there're so many bullet holes in your houseboat?" she wondered.

Rafe glanced at Hunter and then at her. "*Sí.* I am not popular, as you say. I am hated and feared for good reason. My job is to protect these people from gold miners, from gem marauders and from the rich who want to steal Juma land, to plow it under to create thousands of acres of cashew plantations." He gave her a grim look, his full mouth becoming a slash of stubbornness. "No, I stand between them and those who would kill them." He waved his hand toward the notepad. "Now there is another killer here in their village, one I do not understand. I am grateful that you have come. You can see by the stats that nearly fifty percent of my people have died within the last seven days."

"Half?" Catt whispered the number, frowned and intently studied the handwritten figures. Rapidly, she leafed through the pages of information.

"What are their symptoms, Rafe? Do you know? Are you medically qualified?"

He shrugged. "I am not a *médico,* señorita. I have some training, but it is in first aid only. I have done what I could to make those who are suffering and dying a little more comfortable, but that is all. Nothing I do saves them." He closed his eyes, his voice riddled with anguish. "Nothing."

"So, there are flulike symptoms?" Catt asked.

"*Sí.*"

"What happens when the fever gets high and their breathing worsens?"

Sadly he looked at her. "Within hours, usually, they fall asleep, never to awaken again. They die."

Ty noted the intensity in Catt's expression. She was now an epidemic hunter. He was seeing her professional side, and he admired her energy, her focus and the sense of subdued excitement around her. The rapt look on her face was that of a hunter stalking her prey. "Do you have any idea of what it might be, Catt?" he asked her.

Shrugging, she asked Rafe, "Any bleeding from the nose, mouth, eyes or ears?"

"No, señorita."

"Good," Catt breathed. She glanced at Ty. "From this preliminary report, we're probably not dealing with a hemorrhagic virus, which is good. That's one worry off our plate."

"You were thinking of the Saba virus, which was found here in the Amazon a few years ago?" Ty demanded.

Surprised that he knew that much, Catt nodded. "Exactly. It's a sister to the Ebola virus. Not quite as lethal, but the problem is we don't have a drug that can stop it—or Ebola either." She tapped the notes in front of her. "From all indicators, this

sounds like a bacteria of some kind." She crossed
her fingers. "And when I can get a look at those
lesions, I can confirm my professional hunch that
what we're dealing with is anthrax. But it has to be
confirmed with lab investigations by the OID."

Ty tried to hide his surprise. "Anthrax?" It was
one of the major bioterrorists' weapons. Black Dawn
could have sprayed anthrax spores over this village
a week ago. His skin crawled at the thought.

Catt saw the glint in Hunter's eyes. "Yes, anthrax.
Why?" She saw Rafe's mouth thin and a dark look
she couldn't decipher pass between the two men.
Both were on guard. It was nothing obvious, just a
subtle electric tension that sizzled through the small,
cramped space of the houseboat.

"Anthrax, señorita? Could you be wrong about
this?"

"Sure I could, Rafe."

"If it is anthrax," Ty muttered, "then we need to
take special precautions ourselves."

Catt nodded. "Universal protection for all of us."

Hunter knew that meant wearing protective gloves
and a mask that was specially designed to stop larger
viruses and bacteria from being inhaled. "How are
the villagers going to take to us coming in with
gloves and masks, Rafe?"

The backwoodsman smiled a little. "I've been
touching them, bathing them with cooling water,
holding them, cleaning up their vomit, and have not
been affected by it." He held up his long, expressive
fingers. "If this bug is infectious, then I have remained immune to it. I told the chief of the Juma
that people would be coming to save their lives and

they would wear funny-looking gear. They are prepared for you, I think.''

Catt studied Rafe. ''You've had no protection since the outbreak and you're still free of it?''

''*Sí*, señorita.'' Rafe's full mouth thinned. ''Maybe I am lucky?''

''Maybe you are,'' she murmured.

''If it was anthrax, though,'' Ty said, ''it's highly contagious and easily picked up from soil, plants or from touching an infected patient.''

Catt studied him. He was surprising her again with his extensive knowledge. When he glanced back at her, she felt warmth and worry radiating from him. ''That's true,'' she agreed in a low tone. ''Anthrax, once it gets going, is highly contagious. If you've been dealing with a lot of sick Indians and you're free and clear of it, then it's probably not anthrax.''

Ty shifted uncomfortably. He knew that the bioterrorists had cloned a new and different version of anthrax. It was a gene-spliced variety, and there was no antibiotic to stop it. Once a person got it, he or she died.

''How soon can we know if it is anthrax or not?'' he asked Catt.

Instead of answering him directly, she turned to Rafe. ''Get me into the village at first light, and I'll be able to give you a preliminary answer. Then we'll have to take samples, bring them back to the lab tent we just set up on the bank, package them up, and you'll have to run them into Manaus.''

''We have a jet standing by to take the lab specimens back,'' Ty told Rafe.

Surprised, Catt looked at him. ''*We* do?''

''Well...because I work for the federal government, I asked that they send a jet down here to help us out instead of relying on commercial flights back to the States.''

Giving him a measuring look, Catt murmured, ''I see....''

Rafe slowly unwound and stood up. ''You two need your sleep. It is going to be a long, endless day tomorrow for everyone.'' He turned and gestured to a narrow bed behind him. ''Señorita, you will sleep here.''

''Thank you, Rafe. I hope I'm not pushing you out of your bunk?''

Chuckling, Rafe said, ''No, señorita. I have a hammock that hangs between two trees. I will be fine there. The rest of the team has already set up tents on the riverbank to sleep in. Señor Hunter, you can turn this table into a bed for yourself using the cushions stored beneath. I know it is cramped down here, but at least you will have a small shower, a toilet and a kitchen. You two will sleep here for the duration of this outbreak.''

Alarmed, Catt's mouth dropped open. ''Well... wait...I don't—''

Ty stood up. ''Thanks, Rafe. You're a very good host and we appreciate your putting yourself out for us.'' He gave Catt a look that told her not to burden the backwoodsman with their personal problems.

Choking back her protest, Catt realized that their host *was* putting himself out for them. Rafe had no idea of the problems between her and Ty. Nor would he. She forced a cardboard smile. ''Thanks, Rafe. You've more than gone out of your way to help us. We're deeply appreciative.''

''Señorita,'' he said earnestly, ''I would give you

my houseboat, my life, if you would only save the Juma.'' He gestured around the small, stifling cabin. ''My home is your home. I will do all I can to help you. I will wake you at first light, eh?''

Ty moved to the center of the narrow aisle. ''That's fine, Rafe. See you in the morning.''

Catt sat there, her fists knotted. She waited until Rafe had disappeared up the stairs before she spoke. Glaring up at Ty, who stood in the aisle, his presence overwhelming to her, she said, ''*You* sleep down here. I'll sleep on the deck.''

Ty saw the panic in her face and heard it in her voice. ''And for all you know, that anthrax or whatever it is could be up on that deck you want to sleep on, too. Rafe has no way of cleaning off this old scow. If you lie on that surface, you could breathe the spores in and you know it.'' Ty desperately appealed to her medical sensibilities. If anthrax had been sprayed, then Rafe's houseboat could also be carrying the spores.

''Well…'' Catt sputtered, ''I—I just don't want to be near you! Besides, Rafe told me earlier he'd had his boat mopped with water and bleach to disinfect it, so it should be safe enough.'' Her heart was pounding. What would it be like to sleep less than two feet away from Ty once again? Anguish soared through her. He was too dangerous to her roller-coaster emotions. His nearness unsettled her, made her feel nakedly vulnerable to his gentleness, to his thoughtfulness when he chose to turn it on.

Holding out his hands, Ty murmured, ''Look, this will work. I'll go topside. You get washed up, get your nightie on and get in bed, and then call me.''

Torn, Catt felt exhaustion lapping at her senses. "Dammit, Hunter, I'm too tired to play games."

Grimly, Ty leaned across the table, both hands flat on its surface. "Listen to me, Catt," he said in a low growl, "take care of yourself first. I'm going topside now. You got your luggage here?"

He was startlingly close. She could smell the masculine odor of him and almost drowned in his intense cinnamon gaze. Catt leaned back, pressing herself against the cushion. "I—yes—it's here." She pointed to her suitcase in the corner.

"Okay," Ty rasped as he straightened up, "call me when you're tucked in."

What was the use of fighting him? With a sigh, she said, "I will...." She felt defeated. She had thought briefly about going down to the tents to sleep with the team, but the tents were small and the sleeping quarters cramped. With all the equipment that had to be stored and kept in the riverbank camp, her team had no extra space for one more warm body. She was stuck here. The outbreak was enough of a stress without this complication. The responsibility for her team was weighing heavily on her now. Her mind jumped back and forth between the symptoms Rafe had spoken about, Ty's insufferable hold over her roiling emotions, and worry for the safety of her team if it was, indeed, an anthrax outbreak.

Ty was sitting up on deck, under a night sky covered with veils of wispy clouds. A slice of moon had risen and looked like the soft glow of a lightbulb hidden behind thick gauze. Only the gauze was the constant humidity meeting the cooler air above and creating clouds that hung perennially over the Amazon basin. He heard monkeys in the distance, screaming and howling. Frogs on the banks of the mighty Amazon croaked out their songs. Other than the creatures of the jungle everything was quiet and peaceful. For now. The lull didn't fool him, however. His heart moved back to Catt, to the terrorized expression on her face when she'd realized she would be sleeping so near to him in that cramped cabin.

It hurt to think that Catt was afraid of him. How deeply he'd loved her way back when. Rubbing his chest, Ty realized all those old feelings for her were still there—alive and clamoring to be revived. She was beautiful in a mature way now. More confident and sure of herself. He smiled wearily and wiped the sweat off his broad brow. Sleeping a few feet away from her was going to be a very special hell he'd never anticipated. Yet, above all, Ty had to protect Catt. And he wanted to. At all costs and all risks to himself. He'd die for her—it was that simple. Catt would never know that, however. She hated him so much for what he'd stupidly done to her that it would be pointless to mention how he felt about her.

Well, he was getting back all he deserved. Hanging his head, he thought about the baby she'd lost. With a sad smile, he laughed bitterly at himself. For the last ten years, he often thought about what their son or daughter would have been like. In his heart, he'd wanted a daughter. Coming from a family of four boys, he figured it was a natural wish on his part. Ty had even gone so far as to think of possible names for his little daughter. His most favorite name was Christa, a variation on Catherine, her mother.

With a shake of his head, he muttered, "Hunter,

you are the sorriest bastard in this universe. You really screwed up good.''

Catt called out Hunter's name, her voice echoing up the stairway. She drew the cotton sheet in a protective motion across her. In her knee-length cotton nightgown, she felt intensely vulnerable as she heard him move cautiously down the creaking wooden steps. She shut her eyes tightly and pretended sleep. The low-wattage lightbulb was still on. To her surprise, as he came into the cabin, Ty switched it off. Relief flowed through Catt. She didn't want him staring at her, and she could literally feel his gaze rake her form as she lay tensely on the narrow bunk.

Ty forced himself to stop looking at Catt. The gauzy moonlight filtered through the narrow rectangular windows into the cabin, just strong enough to outline her soft, feminine body. He wanted to reach over and slide his hand across her shoulder. To somehow reach out and tell her just how sorry he was for her grief, her loss of their baby, and the pain she'd carried by herself for so many years. He should have been there for her. The heaviness in his chest wouldn't go away. He opened up the other bed, pulled a sheet and pillow from an overhead cabinet and placed them across it. In a few minutes his makeshift bed was ready.

The gentle motion of the houseboat was lulling to Catt, but her hearing was acutely keyed to Ty. He was trying to be quiet. When he went to the small bathroom to shower, she released a shaky breath. Gripping the cotton sheet in her fist, she opened her eyes and turned over onto her back. Looking across the aisle, she saw that he'd haphazardly made his bed. It was so close to hers! Gulping, Catt sat up. What was she going to do? She'd opened the windows, and yet there was little breeze. It was stifling in the cabin, or perhaps she was feeling trapped by Ty's larger-than-life presence.

She heard the shower trickling to life and knew Ty was washing the stink of the Amazon off his hard, well-muscled body. Groaning, Catt buried her face in her hands. Too vividly, she recalled taking showers with Ty. The way he'd sinuously lathered the soap across her arms, her shoulders, the way he'd cupped her aching breasts...

"Stop it!" Catt muttered furiously. "Just stop it, Alborak!" She felt like she was going insane. What was this seesawing back and forth all about? Why did a part of her want this no-good bastard?

Hearing the shower shut off, Catt quickly lay down again, turning her back to the aisle and to Ty when he emerged minutes later.

Pushing the dripping water off his face with his fingers, Ty kept the towel wrapped about his hips as he moved carefully out into the darkened cabin. Glancing to his right, he saw Catt still lying there, her back toward him. Glumly, he shut the door and moved to his bed. Taking off the towel, the pale moonlight bathing his naked body, Ty eased between the sheets and pulled the top one up to his waist. He was never comfortable wearing pajamas. All they did was get tangled up and knotted. He was a restless sleeper and hated anything that confined him.

"Good night," he murmured as he lay down, his arm beneath his head. The darkness felt good, the moonlight just bright enough to outline shapes within the cabin. The slight, creaking sound of the houseboat as it moved with the ancient rhythm of the Amazon lulled him.

"'Night...'" Catt muttered defensively.

Ty closed his eyes. How he ached to have Catt in his arms again. What would she feel like now? Warm? Lush? Ripe? Hot and unbridled as before? Probably all that and more. His heart and his lower body were tormenting him as possibilities floated through his mind. He heard her move around. With a sigh he realized there was a part of him that was still connected to her in some invisible way even now, and he marveled at how that connection had automatically resurrected itself after all these years. Still, he could feel distrust radiating from Catt. Her tension. Her anger. And most of all, the unrequited grief of her loss—their loss.

His mouth pulled downward. Closing his eyes, Ty rasped out into the darkness, "Catt, for whatever it's worth between us, I just want you to know how sorry I am about what happened. It was my fault you went through everything alone. I'm sorry you suffered so much. You were alone and I should have been there for you, and I wasn't...and Lord knows, I wish things had turned out different. The last thing I ever wanted to do was hurt you. You've got to believe that. Please..."

Catt choked back a sob. Ty's voice was heavy with feeling, with tears of his own. She lay tensely and felt his anguish, felt his sincerity. "Damn you, Hunter. Just shut up, will you?" She sat up, the sheet falling away to reveal the lace on the collar of her sleeveless nightgown. She saw him open his eyes and look over at her.

"Having you here is like a hot knife twisting

twenty-four hours a day in my heart and gut! I can't take it and I can't take you!'' Her voice rose with hurt. ''You have a right to feel guilty as hell. Yes, I suffered. I grieved. I still grieve for the baby I lost.'' Automatically, Catt pressed her hand against her abdomen in a protective gesture. ''You showed your true stripes then. Whatever guilt is eating you up now is yours to keep. I don't want to hear about it. Do you understand? Do you know how many years I sat with it, alone, without help? Without support? Well, it's your turn. If you think I'm going to forgive you, forget it! We might have to work together, but I want you as far away from me emotionally as I can get. Do you understand that?''

Catt was afraid. Afraid of the gentle warmth that burned in his eyes as he held her gaze. Tears glimmered in his eyes. It tore her up. She saw the suffering line of Ty's mouth and knew how much he was hurting and grieving for the loss of her baby. That shook Catt as nothing else could.

Jerking angrily at the sheet, Catt turned over, her back to him once again, and flopped down on the bed. As her head hit the pillow, she released a trembling sigh. How badly she wanted to cry for both of them. Well, what was done was done. She couldn't bring back the baby she'd lost. Nor could Ty.

As she lay there, feeling so very alone and grieving, Catt felt an ache in her womb, almost a memory of the old pain. Unconsciously, she slid her fingers across her rounded abdomen and pressed against it gently. The thought of having Ty's baby within her once again almost made her sit straight up. Where had *that* thought come from? Aghast, Catt lay rigidly and tried to ignore that fleeting thought. *No! Never.*

Not ever again! She would never allow him to touch her, kiss her or love her. If she couldn't learn from the past, then she'd deserve whatever she got. And right now, they had a deadly outbreak that would be staring them down come morning. Somehow, Catt had to force herself to sleep. But how? The father of the baby she'd lost was less than three feet away. And his anguished admission had left her more torn up and hurting. She could no longer mask her pain behind her anger. Not with Ty around her night and day.

Miserably, Catt closed her eyes. Sliding her hand beneath her cheek, she swallowed hard against a sob trying to tear from her throat.

Chapter Six

Ty had seen outbreaks before, but never one like this. At dawn they had trekked the mile back through the jungle to the Juma village. Thatched huts sat in a semicircle that faced the Amazon in the distance. The surrounding jungle, composed of a triple canopy of trees of varying heights, made the place look like a picture postcard.

But the picturesque value quickly dissolved when he saw the strain, the tears and grief on the faces of the Juma who cared for those who were dying. And the moans and cries, the suffering of those infected, grabbed at him. The people of the village had reddish skin, shiny black hair and dark brown eyes. They were a small, lithe people, Ty observed, reminding him of the small graceful people of Thailand. And they were all dressed in faded cotton clothes of the same type the beggars in Manaus wore. They were a poor people. They spoke no English, only their Juma language and some pidgin Portuguese.

Ty's duties were twofold, and he was nervous and edgy. He didn't leave Catt's side, although this morning she looked like hell warmed over. There were smudges beneath her bloodshot eyes, and her mouth was compressed, which told him she was wrestling with a lot of inner pain. His admission last night had ripped them both apart, but he had had to say it, because his grief was like a poison eating him alive. Catt had to know how sorry he really was. Now his chest felt heavy as he followed her and Rafe toward Chief Aroka's hut, which sat in the center of the semicircle.

The chief, dressed in a colorful skirt of cotton fabric that fell to his knobby knees, emerged to greet them. He was old and his hair, what little was left of it, was graying. Holding out his slender arms, he warmly welcomed Rafe with a nearly toothless smile.

"My daughter!" Aroka cried piteously as he moved to Catt. Gripping her hands, he spoke in rapid pidgin Portuguese to her.

Catt looked at Rafe as she held the old man's hands. Aroka's small, pinched features were bathed in tears as he cried out. Because of her own vulnerable state, Catt had no defense against the old man's weeping.

Ty stood off to one side. His gaze swept the area. Was Black Dawn around? In the distance, he saw a number of dead dogs lying at the outskirts of the village, and even from here, he could see large, bloody ulcers across their matted coats. Anthrax? He thought so. He and the rest of the team had come into the village wearing long-sleeved, white cotton shirts to protect themselves from infection. The latex gloves he wore made his hands and fingers sweat in the morning humidity and rising heat. The mask hung around his neck. Catt had given orders that as they went into the huts to help the sick and dying, their masks had to be worn at all times. Outside, they could take them off temporarily.

Rafe's words brought Ty's attention back to the group before him. "Chief Aroka says his daughter, Mandei, who is five months pregnant, got sick two days ago. He's begging you to help her, Catt. He says that she carries the heir to the village, that you must save her and her baby. If you save her, he will do anything—anything—to reward you."

Ty watched Catt's face and was startled by the change in her. Gone was the warrior, gone the bitterness and the assertiveness he'd seen in her since meeting her on the dock at Manaus. Her face softened completely. Her eyes grew gentle with compassion. She placed her hand protectively over the chief's gnarled ones.

"Chief Aroka, my team and I will do everything in our power to save not only your daughter, but the rest of your people. Our only reward is to help those who are sick to get well. If you can assist us by bringing in water and boiling it, and aiding my team, that is all I ask of you." She choked back tears at the desperation she saw in the man's dark eyes.

Rafe translated. He gestured to her team. "Doctor, I think everyone knows what they must do." He turned to Ty. "You and I are the only ones who know Portuguese fluently. I would suggest Maria will be needed to draw blood and prepare tissue samples from those who are ill. I can go with the rest of the team as a translator. Ty, will you accompany Dr. Alborak on her rounds?''

Catt's lips parted. She started to protest. Then she saw the dark expression on Ty's face. Her intuition told her that Ty and Rafe had made this agreement beforehand, although she couldn't prove it. ''No— I—''

''I'll help her out,'' Ty said in an unruffled tone.

Rafe nodded. ''Good.'' He lifted his hand to the waiting team. ''Come on, I'll show you those who are in the worst condition first. Dr. Alborak, I think the chief needs your help?''

Ty moved forward and picked up her physician's bag, which was wrapped in protective plastic. Cupping his hand beneath her elbow, he spoke to Chief Aroka. ''Just lead the way to your daughter, Chief, and we'll follow.''

''Yes, yes! You must hurry. She is very ill. Please, this way,'' he said, hurrying in front of them.

Catt felt Ty's firm hand on her elbow. She was too tired, too weary, to object. Whatever energy she had left from a nearly sleepless night she had to devote to the Juma today. And she couldn't deny that her heart contracted with joy as Ty moved solidly to her side. He made her feel stronger despite her distrust of him and his intentions.

The hut was dark and airless as Catt moved into the depths of it after fixing her mask in place. She saw that the windows had been covered with heavy cloths.

''Ask Chief Aroka to open up this place. She needs light and fresh air in here for starters.'' Catt wrinkled her nose at the sickly, rotten smell. The odor reminded her of a three-day roadkill someone might find on the side of the highway beneath a hot, blistering sun. How many times in the past had Catt inhaled the all-too-familiar odor of death? Her heart beat a little faster as Ty left her side. As soon as the cloths were removed from the three windows, the light revealed a young woman in her twenties lying on a pallet composed of drying palm fronds and covered with a faded pink-and-white cotton fabric, which was damp from her perspiration. The pallet lay in the center of the hut on a floor of hard-packed earth, with woven grass mats placed across the expanse.

"Have the chief change the palm leaves, too. And ask him to get another piece of cloth beneath her after we leave." She pointed to the material. "It should be changed every day. Tell him that the cloth needs to be soaped, beaten and cleaned with the bleach we brought with us. Otherwise, germs will spread."

Ty nodded as he watched her go to work. "I'll tell him."

As Catt cared for Mandei, her heart went out to her. She was a beautiful young woman, though her long, black hair was soaked with perspiration, and fever had made her huge black, almond-shaped eyes even larger looking. Her pupils were dilated and there was a wild expression in them. She lay on her side, muttering deliriously, in the clutches of a high fever. The simple cotton shift she wore, a faded lavender print with tiny white flowers sprinkled across it, was twisted damply around her knees and slender thighs.

Kneeling down beside her, Catt placed her hands on the woman's shoulder. Mandei looked up at her, a quizzical expression on her face. Catt gazed gently down at her, smoothing her hands over her shoulder reassuringly, knowing that a comforting touch needed no translation no matter what part of the world she was in. Touch was universal.

The chief knelt opposite Catt and spoke rapidly in his language to his ill daughter. Mandei tried gamely to smile at Catt, but she could not. Lifting her hand weakly, she placed it briefly over Catt's and whispered something in a shaky voice to her.

"She's thanking you for coming," Ty said grimly as he translated. "She said you are an answer to her prayers."

Catt shot a look toward Ty. "Don't I wish."

His mouth twitched uneasily and he spoke to Mandei. The young woman managed a weak smile.

"What did you just tell her?" Catt asked as she continued her examination.

"That your touch was magical."

The way Ty said it made Catt's heart ache. She vividly recalled Ty's own touch. Too vividly. Shrugging off the thought, she busied herself. Through her thin latex gloves she could literally feel heat rolling off the woman's skin. Ty knelt down on the other side of the woman, next to the chief, and Catt snapped a look up at him. He was already opening her examination bag for her. At least he was efficient, she thought as she reached across Mandei and took the stethoscope he handed her.

"Do you know how to take a pulse?" she demanded.

"Yes." Ty gently picked up Mandei's limp, damp arm and placed two fingers against the inside of her wrist.

Chief Aroka hovered anxiously nearby. "Does he know *any* English?" Catt asked under her breath to Ty as she listened intently to the woman's breathing and lung sounds.

"None," he murmured. Frowning, he placed Mandei's arm against her body. Jotting down information on a sheet attached to his clipboard, he said, "Pulse is thready and uneven. It's 150 beats a minute."

"Damn…" Catt placed the stethoscope around her neck. "Her blood pressure is high, too—200 over 100."

"Not good," Ty agreed in a softened voice as he wrote down the numbers.

Very gently, Catt turned the delirious woman over on her back. "Tell her that I must examine her," she ordered Ty. Even beneath the cloth that stuck damply to the woman's body, Catt could see large, ulcerated sores here and there. Wrinkling her nose, she lifted one of Mandei's arms and closely examined an ulcer, which was as large as a silver dollar.

"If this isn't anthrax, then I'm in the wrong business," she whispered to him tautly. Moving her latex-protected fingers around the sore, she gave Ty her medical diagnosis as she continued her examination of the woman. As Catt slid her hand across Mandei's swollen abdomen, where her unborn baby lay, she met and held the woman's gaze, her heart contracting.

Mandei moaned and reached weakly toward Catt's hand on her abdomen. She began to talk in a combination of Juma and pidgin Portuguese. Pleadingly, she held Catt's gaze, huge tears streaming from her eyes.

"What's she saying?" Catt asked quietly.

The corners of Ty's mouth drew in. "She's begging you to save her baby. Mandei says she knows she's dying. If you can save her baby, that's all she asks."

Closing her eyes, Catt dragged in an unsteady breath. She opened them, leaned over and grazed the side of Mandei's face with her fingers. "Tell her I'm going to give her antibiotics and that will save both of them. Tell her to fight back. To hold on. Tell her the drug is going to cure them both."

Ty translated and then watched as Catt drew out a syringe filled with an antibiotic. "It sure does look like anthrax."

"No kidding." Catt squirted a little of the fluid from the syringe and then gripped Mandei's arm firmly. "Well, she's going to get a third-generation antibiotic that will grapple with it."

"Does she have a chance?" he asked as she injected the young woman with the shot.

"I don't know for sure…maybe. We're catching it at a very advanced stage. But she's young and she's got a good immune system to fight back with," Catt whispered tautly as she rubbed the area with cotton and alcohol after delivering the shot. *And she has a baby,* Catt thought, but didn't say. A living baby within her. Catt couldn't remain emotionally distant from Mandei's fight to survive for her baby's sake. Oh, how well she knew that battle! Shoving back her feelings, Catt said in an uneven tone, "Tell Chief Aroka what we've done. Tell him to begin bathing her with cool water to bring down her fever. She needs fluids," she continued as she moved her fingers against the woman's tight, golden skin. "She's dehydrated. We don't have IVs. Damn. She could lose the baby just from that alone.'' Her gaze moved to Mandei's belly one more time. "Tell the chief to get her to continually sip water or fresh fruit juice. We have to get her electrolytes back up and in some kind of balance or she'll miscarry for sure under the circumstances.''

Ty scowled as he knelt opposite Catt. He saw the anguish in her eyes and heard it in her voice. Yet despite her own suffering, Catt managed to comfort the sick woman. Just her touch, her healing presence had quieted Mandei. "I'll tell the chief what you said,'' he promised her in a husky voice. The fact that the woman was pregnant was eating at Catt. Ty saw it all too clearly in her eyes. Was she thinking of her own miscarriage? The loss of their baby? Yes, she was. His heart twinged. What a helluva situation.

At that moment, Ty wished with all his heart and soul that he could get Catt out of this hut and away from this dying woman. The look of devastation in Catt's wide, vulnerable-looking blue eyes shook him deeply. Suddenly he began to imagine all that Catt had gone through without him, and questions filled his mind. Where had Catt miscarried? At her dorm? Alone? Unaided? Had she made it to the hospital? Who had held her after it happened? Or had anyone? Bitterly, Ty felt the knife of guilt twist deeper into his gut. No wonder she hated him.

In the half-light of the hut, he studied her—her hair curling from the high humidity, her face naked with emotion—and he felt a fierce, almost overwhelming urge to reach across and hold her. Catt needed holding. He felt it. He knew it. And he was the *last* person on this earth whom she would ask or allow to support her, or even try to protect her from the awful reality of Mandei's situation.

"We need to move on," Ty said gently. "I can swab her throat, take blood and—"

"No, let Maria do it later," Catt said, swiping her hair from her perspiring brow. The instant her gaze locked with his, she gasped softly. The hurt, the worry in Ty's narrowed eyes caught her completely off guard. Here was the man she'd known so long ago. The man who was gentle, who cared, who loved her so fiercely and uncompromisingly. Catt knelt there, her hands on her thighs, caught by his tender expression. The corners of his mouth were drawn in and she knew what that meant: he was suffering just as much as she was for Mandei. The raw look in his cinnamon eyes tore her heart open. His suffering for Mandei was real. This wasn't a game to Ty. He was just as caught up in the drama of her struggle for life as Catt herself was.

"Come on," she whispered unsteadily, "we've got a lot more patients to see. We've only got daylight to work by...." And she rose unsteadily to her feet.

At two in the morning, Ty finished delivering samples to the lab tent set up at the river's edge, and walked back to the village. The outbreak team was at the houseboat—all except for Catt, who had told everyone to go eat a very late dinner and catch some badly needed sleep. As he entered the community, the familiar crying, the weeping and moans, met his ears. This was a dying village. Exhaustion tore at him as he moved along the line of huts. He knew where Catt was because a number of family members were huddled anxiously at the front door. When darkness had fallen, Catt had retrieved a flashlight and continued to treat the villagers and give antibiotics to those in need. She was driven. She refused to eat or rest.

Moving through the group, Ty eased his way into the hut. Catt was on the floor, next to a pallet containing a boy no more than six years old. The boy's breathing was harsh, his body cratered with ulcers. The parents were off to one side, holding one another and sobbing. Catt had her bag open and was giving him a shot. In his heart, Ty knew the boy would die, the harsh breathing an indicator that his body was failing him.

Leaning over her as she wearily placed the syringe back into what was known as a sharps container, which held infected and used needles, Ty slid his hands around her slumped shoulder. "Catt," he rasped close to her ear, "come home…you've done all you can do here tonight…."

Choking, Catt stiffened. She felt Ty's steadying hands on her shoulders. She felt the grate of his low, gritty voice in her aching heart. He was so close, so incredibly strong when at the moment she felt so weak and useless. And then the past came back to her. Jerking away, she twisted around.

"There are still patients to see."

He stood leaning over her. The flashlight in her hand barely outlined her facial features, but he saw the darkness beneath her eyes, the strain at the corners of her soft, parted lips. "No, darlin', not tonight," he whispered gently. Opening his hand, he said, "Come on. Come back with me. You can only do so much. If you don't rest, you'll keel over, Catt, and you know it. Give me your hand and I'll help you back to the houseboat. You need to catch a couple hours of sleep.''

There was a curious mixture of hunger and firmness in Ty's gaze. In some dizzy, weary part of her barely functioning mind, Catt knew that if she didn't get up and go back with Ty, he would unceremoniously carry her out of the hut and back to the boat. She saw that glint of warning in his eyes, a red flag that he wasn't going to take no for an answer.

''All right,'' she snapped irritably, slamming her bag shut. ''Just give me room.''

Ty didn't try to shield himself from her anger. He understood it. He knew Catt too well. She was a driven woman. Driven to save lives no matter what the physical or emotional toll to herself. What mattered to Catt was to stop the dying. Backing out of the hut, he told the people in Portuguese that the team would return at dawn. The relief on the Juma's faces made him wince inwardly. Half the people in the village were either dead or dying. Would the antibiotics stop the anthrax?

Reeling unsteadily, Catt gripped the frame of the hut door until she got her bearings. Ty stood nearby watching her worriedly. She was simply too wrung out to even argue with him right now. As she stepped out past the people, who were thanking her profusely, touching her shoulder, her arm in gratefulness, Ty took her bag.

Jerking the mask off her face, Catt moved drunkenly down the path that lead back to the river. The jungle darkness silently enveloped them. She sensed Ty walking just behind her.

''It's anthrax,'' she rasped bitterly over her shoulder. ''Damn, I know it's anthrax.''

"Then the antibiotics will help," he said, moving up beside her. She wasn't steady at all. Ty almost reached out to cup her elbow, but decided not to.

"It's got to turn this epidemic around," Catt said. "It just *has* to."

There was a tree root across their path. Catt didn't see it because she was too tired, too immersed in her worry for the Juma. The toe of her left shoe caught it. With a cry, she pitched forward.

Instantly, Ty was there. He dropped the bag, threw out his arms and caught Catt just as she fell toward the ground.

"Easy," he rasped, as he brought her upright and into his arms. She was limp and weary. For an instant, he caught the wonderful perfume of her hair as she momentarily rested her head against his shoulder. Instinctively her arms went around his waist so she could steady herself. Their bodies met and touched. He felt the softness of her small breasts, that rounded quality of her abdomen where she had carried their baby, and the grazing touch of her thighs against his harder ones.

With a soft moan, Catt collapsed against him. It wasn't something she'd planned on doing; it simply happened because she was so tired. And right now, she *needed* Ty. That need flowed through her as she felt his strong arms slide around her body, drawing her into his embrace. The feeling was wonderful! Her brain was spongy. Her heart exploded with need, with a hunger that stunned her—hunger for Ty Hunter alone.

She felt his lips press softly against her temple. She heard him whisper her name like a prayer. His fingers were strong and firm as he moved them

across her tense shoulders. Somehow, her arms had
found his torso and she was clinging to him. Ty felt
so strong. She felt so weak and defeated. The masculine scent of him filled her flaring nostrils. She
drank it in greedily, starved for the feel of him, the
texture and scent of him. So many wonderful memories flowed back through Catt—of times they'd
spent at Half Moon Bay, a beautiful crescent-shaped
beach on the coast. They would go for a swim in the
sparkling blue-green ocean, ride the waves and body
surf and then run back to the white sand beach and
fling themselves onto the green-and-red plaid blanket. Like two wet, playful seals they would laugh,
touch, kiss, and then he would deliciously use his
tongue to sip the salty water from her face, her lips,
her neck, her aching, waiting breasts....

No. No, this shouldn't be happening. Catt pulled
her arms from around his narrow waist. She could
feel the hard pounding of his heart against her ear as
she remained sagging against him, relying still on his
support. How badly she needed to be held by Ty! He
was here for her this time, simply holding her and
rocking her gently in his arms. His voice flowed
across her swimming senses, his tone low, rough and
thrilling to her in every way. This was the old Ty
Hunter she'd fallen so helplessly in love with so long
ago. Oh, why couldn't everything have been different
in the past? Why had Ty thought his job was more
important than her being pregnant?

His arms were nurturing to her, and Catt hungrily
absorbed his embrace in those stunning few seconds.
The sounds of the jungle—the singing of insects, the
croaking of tree frogs—combined with the sweet,
heavy scent of orchids that hung in the branches of

trees along the narrow dirt path. Unconsciously, Catt rubbed her cheek against his chest. The white cotton shirt he wore was damp and clinging to his flesh, but she didn't care. As she nestled more deeply into his arms, she felt him groan. The wonderful reverberation moved through him and into her, like a primitive drum being played, throbbing achingly through both of them simultaneously.

"My beautiful Joan of Arc," Ty rasped as he threaded his fingers through her short, silky hair. "You fight so hard for the sick and the injured. You have a heart so large that it takes my breath away, did you know that?" Closing his eyes, he savored these moments of nearness to Catt. "Just let me hold you," he pleaded against her ear. "Let me keep you safe...let me give you some of my strength, darlin'...."

The words were coming out of him without thought. Ty was unable to stop himself. He didn't want to. Catt was in his arms and trusting him again. But the depth of her fatigue scared him. He knew what a fighter she was. Guiltily, he remembered that she hadn't slept at all last night, and that it had been his fault. Now she was drunk with weariness. She'd worked nearly sixteen hours nonstop. Placing a soft kiss against her hair, he murmured, "You do so much for so many. It's time to quit and take care of yourself for a little while, darlin'. Let me help. I can hold you. I can help you if you'll let me...." And Lord knew, he wanted to be there for Catt this time and not screw it up. Maybe, just maybe, he could prove his worthiness to her again by helping her with this outbreak now. Could Catt look at him through new eyes? Could she give him a second chance with her?

He wanted nothing more than that, he was discovering as she leaned into his embrace more securely, entrusting him with her full weight. He felt the racing of her heart in her breast, the soft firmness of her cheek against his chest. Her embrace was one of innocence, he knew. But he wasn't so innocent. Ty had been hoping an opportunity to show her he cared for her would occur because he was driven to convince her that he wasn't the villain she thought he was. He'd made a terrible mistake as a young Marine Corps officer. Couldn't she see that? Could Catt somehow, someday, forgive him for the terrible decision he'd made? His mouth compressed against the tidal wave of emotions he wanted to share with Catt. Good things. Wonderful things. Would she give him that chance?

For an instant, Ty felt hope rise in his pounding heart. And then he felt her stiffen in his arms, as if finally aware of what was going on. He knew Catt's exhaustion was making her more vulnerable, more needy, than usual. Without hesitation, he opened his embrace and, placing his hands on her shoulders, allowed her to step a few inches away from him. As he looked down, the bare hint of moonlight filtering through the canopy above them, he saw tears in her eyes. Huge, unshed tears. There was no pain in her expression, just a soft hunger in her parted lips. But questions lingered in her eyes.

"You're going to be okay," Hunter murmured, holding her steady as she gazed brokenly up at him. "You're just very tired, Catt. Come on...let me get you home, okay?"

Though Catt's brain refused to work, she couldn't mistake the burning, fierce hunger in Ty Hunter's narrowed eyes. Her body cried out for more of him. She felt her breasts tighten beneath his burning inspection. She felt a heat begin to pool in her lower body, and the ache for him intensified almost painfully. "Home?" she asked, confused. She felt like a blithering idiot. She couldn't hold two thoughts together for a fleeting second.

His smile was tender. "Yes, home...to the houseboat." He slid his hand down her arm, cupped her elbow and slowly turned her around on the trail. "I'll take you home, Catt. Just trust me...."

Trust...there was that word again. Stumbling over her own feet, Catt realized she'd pushed beyond her own stamina reserves. This time she had no mean words of anger or hostility for him. She couldn't pull up her defensive walls against Ty if she tried.

"I've got to save them, Ty...."

He heard the slight slur in Catt's speech. Falling into step with her, he shortened his stride for her sake as she wove unsteadily down the path. "I know, I know...but you can't do it at a risk to your own life. You know if you don't get enough sleep that leaves you wide open to this infection, too."

Rubbing her brow with unsteady fingers, Catt choked out, "Mandei...she's pregnant...I'm so afraid for her. I went back three times to see how she was doing...."

Wincing, Ty felt Catt stumble again. To hell with it. He placed his arm around her shoulders. "Lean on me, Catt. Just for a little while, lean on me. I'll get you home."

Wearily, she did as he asked. "You feel so strong.

I feel like a wimp,'' she muttered. Yes, he felt strong, and good and steady. Everything she did not feel presently. His fingers closed firmly around her shoulder and she smiled a little. ''You were always so strong....''

''You're strong, too, Catt, but you just don't know your physical limits sometimes.'' Hunter looked down at her. Unable to believe she was really leaning on him, he again felt that frisson of hope spring to life in his chest.

Rubbing her watering eyes with the back of her hand, she murmured, ''Mandei...I'm worried....''

''I know,'' Ty replied soothingly.

''Her baby. Oh Lord, Ty, I'm afraid she's going to die. And I won't be able to save her baby if she does....'' She sniffed. Looking up at the jungle overhead, she added, ''There's no preemie incubators out here. There's no *nothing*. It's frontier medicine, bare bones. If she dies, I can't save her baby and—''

He heard her sob once. Ty halted and moved in front of her, his hands settling on her slumped shoulders. There was such raw anguish in Catt's eyes as she looked helplessly up at him.

''Why can't medicine save them both?'' she cried. She placed her fists against his chest. ''Why?''

Shaking his head, Hunter tunneled his fingers through her hair. ''You're doing everything you can, darlin'. It has to be enough, don't you see?''

''No!'' Catt's cry was absorbed by the jungle surrounding them. ''No, I *refuse* to accept that, Ty. Dammit.'' She wiped her nose with the back of her sleeve. ''I *won't* let Mandei or her baby die! They just can't!''

''Come on, keep walking,'' he counseled her

hoarsely. Ty couldn't stop what he saw happening before his eyes. Catt was too caught up in the emotional drama of Mandei's sickness. But for the moment she moved without fighting him, and for that he was relieved. They continued down the path, his arm around her shoulders to guide and steady her.

"This village is in terrible shape, Ty," Catt continued in a broken whisper. "I've seen outbreaks before, but not like this...not to this extent. Lord, half the community has been wiped out by this—this bacteria...virus...whatever the hell it is...."

Ty let her continue to babble. He knew how worried Catt was. She of all people knew what outbreaks were capable of doing. She was no stranger to them, yet the combination of seeing him again and having to deal with dying children and pregnant mothers was too much for Catt to handle. Especially when she was dog tired like this.

Finally, he saw lights ahead and knew that they were coming to the lab tent and the houseboat. The rest of the medical team were huddled around a campfire as they cooked a late meal. Glancing down at his watch, he realized it was nearly 2:30 a.m.

To his surprise, he felt Catt suddenly pull away from him. He halted, his eyes widening. She seemed more alert now, as if getting a second wind. Her eyes were clearer, too. His heart twinged as they raked him.

"Don't you dare take advantage of me like that again," she ordered fiercely. Jabbing her finger into his chest, her voice high and off-key, she added, "You can't be trusted, Hunter. I'll *never* trust you!" And she turned on her heel and hurried down the path toward her team.

Standing there, Ty snapped his mouth shut. Catt
was so tired and out of it that she probably hadn't
realized what had happened. When she had, she'd
reacted defensively. Rubbing his chest, he scowled.
Well, what the hell did he expect? For Catt to fall
into his arms without a fight? No. It wasn't her way.
She was a Texas rancher's daughter. Ty knew of her
past, of the small, struggling cattle ranch in West
Texas where there was little water and little grass for
the animals. Her father had had a heart condition,
and after her mother had died when Catt was only
six years old, Jed Simpson had made Catt into the
son he'd always wanted but never got. She was an
only child and her father had relied heavily on her
to keep the ranch afloat and viable. Without her help,
the ranch would have ceased operating a lot sooner.

As Ty stood there, he remembered vividly her telling him one evening about her father, of her harsh
life in Texas. Catt had known nothing but a hardscrabble existence, fighting to keep the cattle alive
until they could be sold for money to pay the ranch's
heavy mortgage. Her father was a dreamer, although
he'd worked hard to make his dream come true.
When his wife died, part of him had, too. Catt was
all that was left for him. He treated her like a son
more than a daughter.

Ty had never forgotten the evening she'd told him
about her childhood. They'd lain in one another's
arms after fierce lovemaking in front of a campfire
on the beach at Half Moon Bay. She had snuggled
up beside him, naked and sipping the wine they'd
brought along. Wrapped with her in a blanket, he'd
held her close to him, feeling satiated and more
happy than he could ever recall being. As they lay

on their blanket and watched the fire lick, jump and illuminate the darkness around them, the thunder and crash of the waves not far away, Catt had told him the sad story.

"My dad..." she had begun, after sipping the fruity chardonnay from the plastic cup, "he was a fighter, Ty. You'd have liked him."

He'd glanced down at her, lifting his head just enough to catch that drowsy, fulfilled look in her eyes. "I love his daughter, so I'm sure I'd have liked him." He saw a flush steal up her cheeks and it made him love her even more fiercely. Catt was so open then, so available and vulnerable to him, to his words, to each grazing touch and tone he shared with her.

"No...really, you'd have liked him."

He brought her back into his embrace fully and closed his eyes, content as never before. "I'm sure I would, darlin'. What happened to him?"

"Oh...it's sorta sad...." Catt mused softly. She looked down at the plastic cup in her hand. "Ever since Mama died, he wasn't the same. I remember at the funeral Daddy cried. I'd never seen him cry before or after that. I just sorta stood there crying too, because I'd never seen him so unhappy." With a slight shrug, she rested in Ty's embrace. "After that, Daddy seemed to dry up and go away like water does on that Texas desert we called home. I really tried to be a help to him and not a problem. I knew he worked himself to the bone sixteen hours a day. I knew how much the ranch meant to him. He and Mama bought it when they'd first been married. It was a dream come true for them. They had talked about starting a dynasty. I was their firstborn. They talked of having a passel of kids, at least six because ranch work is so hard, and a large family would be a big help in getting the ranch operation growing.

"Daddy had lots of dreams and he was willing to work hard to make them come true. When Mama died suddenly, I did the cooking, cleaning and helped him as much as I could. About a year after she died, he started having heart pains. He never told me about 'em, but he took pills for it. Nitroglycerine tablets. I was too young to understand, I guess, but he never once asked me for help." Catt frowned and pressed the edge of the plastic cup against her lips as she stared, mesmerized, into the fire. "Once, when I was sixteen, I was out riding fence with him. It was hotter than a firecracker out there that day. The sun was blistering. It musta been over a hundred degrees in the shade. Daddy was sweating a lot. We'd find a fence post that had loosened barbed wire and we'd dismount, fix it, mount up and ride on until we found the next place where the cattle had tried to push through.

"All at once Daddy started gasping real hard. He grabbed his chest. I turned around in the saddle. He went white. I heard him cry out, and then he toppled out of the saddle. I was scared. I jumped off my horse and ran back to him. He lay there on that hard, unforgiving Texas dirt and died. There was nothing I could do. I felt so helpless.... After the funeral, I got told by the judge that the ranch would be sold back to the bank. Now, the local sheriff, Henry Brooks, took pity on me. Both my mama and daddy were orphans, so I didn't have nowhere to be sent to. The sheriff took me in as a foster child.

"He made sure that the herd of cattle was sold off

and the money from it put into an account for my college fund. I lived with him and his wife for two years and finished my schooling. What I didn't know is that he'd taken that money from the cattle and invested it in the stock market. By the time I was eighteen, I had more than enough money to get a good education and a little left over for dorm expenses.''

Ty shook his head. ''That was a hard life for anyone.''

With a tiny shrug, Catt said, ''Looking back on it, I don't think it was. My parents gave me my drive, my discipline and ability to carry through on things.''

''And that's why you want to be a doctor?'' he'd asked gently.

Nodding, tears in her eyes, Catt whispered, ''Yes...I don't *ever* want to feel helpless like that again when a human being is dyin'. I want—I *will*— make a difference next time....''

As Ty remembered her emotion-filled declaration that night so long ago, he understood even more clearly why Catt refused to lean on anyone, especially him. She had reached out to him once when he was too young, too foolish to see how much she needed him. Earning her trust again would be a challenge. A challenge Ty was more than ready to take on.

Chapter Seven

Catt twisted and turned in the bed, her dreams torrid. Ty was kissing her, melting the wall around her heart and soul. He was touching her, his fingers gliding warmly across the sensitized skin of her face, holding her at just the right angle for his mouth to descend once again upon hers. The beauty of his tender lips engaging hers made her moan. Hungrily, Catt leaned upward to meet and dissolve within his very male embrace.

A noise awakened her.

Catt groggily sat up. What time was it? Where was she? Pushing several strands of hair off her brow, she rubbed her puffy eyes. Her body throbbed with need. She felt heat pooling languidly in her lower body, that ache so familiar, so filled with desire. How long had it been since she'd felt like a thousand suns were burning so brightly within her?

Looking around, she saw that Ty had left his bed, his sheet wadded up in the corner. Glancing at her watch, she saw it was five o'clock. She had to get going! There were people to see, to help, lives to try to save. Hurriedly taking a shower, Catt dressed in a pair of jeans and a white T-shirt that had a bit of lace at the neckline, then put on her socks and a pair of sensible shoes. Running a brush through her hair, she hurried up on deck.

Dawn was barely edging away the night. Gripping the rail, Catt sleepily struggled across the graying, splintered deck. The Amazon River was a wide, muddy ribbon before her.

"What are you doing up so early?"

Catt gasped and spun to the left. Ty was sitting on some coiled rope, looking out across the moving water. Not quite awake yet, she stood there helplessly, her lips parting beneath his torrid inspection. Hunter was dressed in clean clothes, his hair gleaming from just being washed. He gave her a boyish smile of welcome.

"I thought you might be up soon. Here...." he said, pouring her some coffee from the Thermos at his side, "Drink this and relax a bit, we should wait until it lightens up a little before we head to the village."

She swallowed hard as he handed her a cup of strong, fortifying coffee.

"Sugar and cream, right?"

Dumbly, Catt took the proffered cup. Their fingers met and touched. Something good and healing flowed up through her hand. She was too sleepy to raise her shield against Ty. A huge part of her needed him right now to offset the terrible weight of grief for the Juma people that lay in her breast. It was her need of him that made Catt go to the other coil of rope a few feet from where he was sitting.

"Uh, yes...right..." She sounded like an idiot. Sitting down, her thighs apart, her hands between them holding the warm cup, Catt took a grateful sip of the hot, fragrant liquid.

Ty smiled a little as he watched her drink the very necessary coffee. This morning Catt looked more like a little girl than a warrior woman, a Joan of Arc trying to save an entire village. He saw the dark smudges beneath her sleepy-looking blue eyes. Her hair was still damp and lay in freshly combed waves around her face. More than anything, Ty felt her vulnerability. When she'd taken the cup from him, he'd felt a fine trembling in her fingers as his hand brushed hers. Ty knew she was on the edge of exhaustion.

"I've been watching the world wake up," he confided in a low tone. "There's probably about fifteen or twenty parrots across the river." He pointed to the opposite bank. "They fly up, I see a flash of red or yellow, and then they dive back down into the canopy to hide."

Catt looked around, a lot of the weight on her shoulders dissolving beneath the dark honeyed tone of Ty's voice. He could always soothe her nervousness, her pent-up tension, with just his voice. It was an amazing thing to Catt that one person could have such an overwhelming effect on her like that. No man had made her feel that way since she'd left Ty. Only him. The memory of the torrid dream that had awakened her made heat crawl into her cheeks. Catt purposely stared down at the coffee cup.

Clearing her throat, she said, "I miss the stars here. There're always clouds up there." And indeed, the gauzy film of clouds was becoming visible as daylight chased the night away. The clouds twisted and moved as if in slow motion. Strands would form, like long tentacles, and then move back into the main mass. Then more strands would form, only to be reabsorbed.

Ty nodded. "That's the only bad thing about the equator area of the Amazon."

"In a way," Catt said wistfully as she watched the clouds, "this place reminds me of a birthing incubator of sorts—it's hot, humid, moist and so alive, so pulsing, with life."

Nodding, Ty said, "Rafe works closely with a woman named Inca, who is known as the jaguar goddess here in Brazil. He was telling me yesterday that Inca is worshipped as a goddess in the flesh around these parts. The Juma are one of the tribes that she tries to protect from marauders. He was saying that Inca has told the Juma that the Amazon basin is really the womb of Mother Earth." He met and held Catt's drowsy gaze. "I liked the way she described this region. And it looks like you and Inca are on the same wavelength about this place."

Catt wanted to drown in Ty's soft cinnamon gaze, which burned with such tenderness—toward her. She was aware of that special look he gave her. It made her feel cherished, nourished and loved. Loved? Instantly, Catt rejected that notion. Cradling the cup between her hands, her voice still husky from sleep, Catt whispered, "How do you see this place?"

Ty was pleased and delighted that they were talking like they used to. He yearned for a white flag of

truce between them. One corner of his generous
mouth lifted. "Well, I'm a little prejudiced about it,
Catt." He gave an appreciative look around. The
cape of night was drawing back. To the east the dull
glow of day was being birthed on the horizon. "I've
spent a lot of time in South America over the last
six years. For me, this is home away from home. I
like coming to the Amazon. It's a special place—a
place where mystery and magic combine, and sometimes, if you're in the right place, you can physically
see some of that magic."

She smiled softly and held the cup next to her
cheek as she observed him. Ty's face was free of
tension, and he was so handsome to her. His was a
face filled with character, with the scars of life im-
printed upon it. She couldn't help letting her gaze
fall back to that very male mouth of his, now twisted
slightly in a half smile of wonder at the beauty surrounding them. Just hearing that low, roughened tone
as he spoke of the sense of mystery he had experi-
enced in this place made her feel incredibly tender
toward him.

Sipping her coffee, Catt pulled her gaze from him
and stared out across the slow-moving water. "Can
you give me an example?" she asked. "What have
you seen that seemed magical and then turned into
reality?"

Chuckling, Ty sipped his coffee. He saw a number
of emotions on Catt's face. He still saw wariness in
her glorious blue eyes, but there was something else
he couldn't quite decipher. He'd seen that look from
her before, long ago, however, when he would love
her senseless and then simply hold her for a long

time afterward in his arms, talking, touching and enjoying the closeness they shared.

"Inca would be a good example of it."

"The so-called jaguar goddess?" Catt said with a hint of derision.

"Don't be so fast to condemn her status among the local Indians," he cautioned. "Inca has earned her reputation here. The Indians believe all things are alive, all things have spirit. They believe that spirits can manifest, turn into human form, into birds, reptiles or whatever. Because I've spent so much time down here, I'd often heard from various sources about the jaguar goddess. Like you, I shrugged off the legend about her."

"What is the legend?" she asked, curious now. She had always enjoyed his stories. Ty was a good storyteller and she poignantly recalled the hours they'd spent in one another's embrace as he'd shared memories of his childhood growing up in Colorado.

"That she is a member of the mysterious Jaguar Clan." He raised his hand and pointed to the south. "It is said that the clan has a village known as the Village of the Clouds. It sits somewhere at the edge of the Amazon jungle on the border between Brazil and Peru. It is said to exist between jungle and mountain, always covered in a continuously rolling bank of clouds so that people who aren't supposed to see it won't. Those who are allowed to view it are guided into this village to be healed. Near the village itself is a place called the pool of life. People from around South America travel to that region to find it."

"Do they?"

Ty shrugged. "This is where the magic and mystery that is only South America, that is only the Amazon, comes in," he warned her warmly with a smile. He watched as Catt responded to his teasing. There was a flush in her cheeks, a softness in her halting smile.

"I've met a number of people over the years who swore they went to find this place when they were sick and dying. When they found the pool they were healed of their illness. They also said they had met members of the Jaguar Clan. A clan member would give them information on why they were here on this earth, and what they should try to do now that they were healed, for the betterment of all humans and animals."

Catt relaxed and closed her eyes. She rested her chin carefully on the rim of the cup she held. "Then this place is sort of like Shangri-La? Only it's in South America and not in Tibet?"

Chuckling, Ty said, "I suppose it's a good parallel."

Catt opened her eyes and gazed at him. The lapping of the water against the houseboat was soothing to her. In the distance, more and more birds sang as the day grew brighter. "And have you seen the Village of the Clouds?"

Shaking his head, Ty murmured, "No. People who have gone there and were allowed entrance swear that it's real, though. They all describe the pool of life in similar terms. And they don't know one another, so I've got to think there's something to it. These are village folk who live hundreds of miles from one another, with no transportation except by donkey or by foot. And they don't have telephones, either. Their descriptions match, Catt. I can't think they'd be lying to me about how sick they were before they went. When they speak of the Village of the Clouds, their eyes all light up. They become very animated and it's like this light begins to glow around them.'' He held up his hand when he saw her brows dip. "Honest…their faces light up. They become so excited and impassioned about what happened to them. Every time I've met one of them over the years, each person who had this experience has come back to his or her own village and done good for others. That person might have been a bastard before, but going there changed them—made them become better human beings, kinder, more loving and helpful instead of destructive.''

With a sigh, Catt whispered, "I wish I could bring the pool of life to this Juma village then…''

"Rafe said he was trying to get ahold of Inca, to let her know what's going on. He thinks she might show up here. If she does—'' he smiled a little ''—she's got one helluva reputation for laying hands on a dying person, or holding a very sick baby and giving it life again.''

"You mean…a hands-on healer?''

"It's more than that, from what I understand. Rafe's seen Inca in action. I haven't. She always comes into a village unannounced because the Brazilian army has a fifty-million-cruzeiro price on her head, dead or alive. She's wanted for thirteen murders in Brazil. She's always on the run, and she travels alone. No one knows where she'll show up or when.'' Ty looked up as a flight of red-and-yellow macaws sped in fighterlike formation across the river. They winged directly over the houseboat, their feathers colorful and decadent in contrast to the grayish dawn.

"Inca has a reputation for coming into a village, laying down her rifle and other weapons at the edge of it, and sitting on a chair provided for her by the officials. The people then bring their sick, their aged and especially those who are dying to her for healing. They stand in a long line, waiting patiently for hours for her to touch them. If it's a child or baby, she's known to hold him or her against her breasts for a long moment. When the child is released, it is no longer suffering from whatever it had before."

Catt saw the awe in Ty's expression. "Rafe's *seen* this?"

"Yes, many times. He's worked with Inca off and on for nearly a decade. Inca considers all Indians to be under her protection and jurisdiction. She'll do whatever it takes to protect them from the gold miners, the greedy businessmen and the timber barons who want to destroy the forests her people have lived in for thousands of years in harmony and peace."

"She sounds like a cross between a healer and an environmentalist."

Ty nodded. "Better add warrior to the mix. Inca's also got a fierce reputation for protecting Indians and killing anyone who would dare harm them."

"Hence the thirteen murder warrants hanging over her head?"

"Yes, but Rafe says that the Brazilian government is after Inca on trumped-up charges. That fact doesn't matter much though, because she's a dead woman if they ever find her."

"That sounds unfortunate," Catt murmured, finishing the last of her coffee. "The Indians love her. The government hates her. Inca sounds like a woman of conviction. Not someone I'd want to run up against as an enemy." She stood up, though she longed to continue their talk. How much she enjoyed and craved Ty's conversations. She always learned something from him. He had such an interesting and diverse background.

Ty watched as Catt slowly unwound. "The Juma call her a green warrior. She's considered an eco-warrior for Mother Earth and all her children." He gestured toward the village. "These are Inca's people."

"Maybe she'll show up." Worriedly, Catt stared in the direction of the village, which was hidden by the dark jungle. "Because if those antibiotics don't start working, we're going to have a lot of people dying today...."

He saw her fingers close tightly around the cup, her knuckles whitening as she stood there, looking so alone and embattled. The set of her lips told him of Catt's personal stake in this unfolding drama. Life was fragile and should be lived as fully as possible each day, as far as Ty was concerned. "You're worried about Mandei, the pregnant woman?"

Softly she replied, "Yes...."

"Rafe is on his way to Manaus with those slides and tissue samples. He left early this morning. He will wait there until he hears from OID on exactly *what* you're battling down here before he comes back."

Rubbing her furrowed brow, Catt murmured, "I know. He's been indispensable to us."

"But you're already fairly certain it's anthrax?"

"I'd bet my reputation on it." Lifting her chin, Catt turned and gazed down at where he sat. Relaxed as he was, Ty looked part little boy in that moment and part virile male. He'd always had those two engaging qualities about him. The urge to simply move toward him and ask him to hold her once again as he had late last night nearly tore her heart open. Such a huge part of her wanted to be close to him. And right now, for whatever reasons, she was feeling terribly vulnerable. Her mind moved back to Mandei, to the unborn baby she carried, and she felt her heart squeeze. Mandei *couldn't* die! She just couldn't.

"I've got to get going," Catt said abruptly. "I need to see how Mandei is doing."

Quickly rising, Ty rasped, "Hold on, I'll go with you."

The darkness was complete when night fell once more. Catt moved from hut to hut checking on her many patients. Her whole team had worked as feverishly as she had all day and she had sent them home to have dinner and get a good night's sleep. Her head swam with fatigue. Her hand shook as she held the flashlight trained before her on the red clay earth as she headed, almost with dread, to Mandei's hut. All day long the condition of the young mother-to-be had been worsening. Catt had given her the absolute limit of antibiotics in order to try to save her life.

"Catt?"

Stumbling to a halt, she felt a warmth flow through her. It was Ty. Right now, she needed him. Dread was suffocating her with every step she took toward that hut that held the mother and unborn baby. She saw his large bulk emerge out of the darkness. When he came closer, she saw that he was no less stressed from the day-long activity than she was.

"You're going to check on Mandei before we call it a night?"

"Yes." Catt gazed up at him. When he placed his hand on her upper arm, it no longer made her recoil in dread. Something had happened out on that boat deck this morning. Maybe it was part of the magic and miracles Ty had spoken about. Catt wasn't sure. She wanted to take that step and move into those strong arms she knew he would open for her. Though Ty's features were shadowed, she saw the worry, the anxious look in his eyes. His fingers closed firmly on her arm.

"Let me go with you?" He saw Catt's expression, the longing for him, and it surprised him. Ty knew how weary she was. She'd gotten only three hours of sleep the night before. And once again, she'd worked herself relentlessly throughout the day and evening, without rest. Earlier he'd shoved a sandwich into her hands and forced her to stop for fifteen minutes to eat, and drink a little water. She was a tireless worker in the midst of the carnage of this epidemic.

"Yes, I'd like that," she whispered, her voice low and off-key. And then she blurted, "I'm afraid, Ty. Afraid…"

Releasing a sigh, he rasped, "I know you are. I know how much she means to you."

"The baby…" Catt looked forlornly at the hut in the distance.

Ty winced, his hand tightening momentarily on her arm. He wanted so badly to just hold Catt and protect her from the inevitable. "I'll go with you, darlin'.…"

This time his endearment filled her with hope, if

only for a moment. Catt looked up at him, a twisted smile on her lips. "I just can't figure you out, Hunter."

He matched her wry smile. "Don't try. Just let me help you all I can. Okay?"

"Okay...." And she turned unwillingly toward Mandei's hut.

Ty tried to gird himself for what would happen. He saw the reality in Catt's face. She knew the woman would die and so would the baby she carried. Sensing Catt's utter frustration, he walked at her side, his hand firmly around her arm. She was almost staggering from fatigue. This time she did not fight the contact. This time, it seemed, she almost welcomed him at her side, and his heart took off on wings of sunlight.

Just as Catt approached the hut, she heard a man's wailing scream. A number of other voices began that same, animal-like sound from within the hut. Catt clenched her teeth. She tore loose from Ty's grip and ran toward the structure. Jerking the cloth away from the front door, she flashed her light across the earthen floor. Mandei lay on the pallet, her father beside her rocking back and forth in agony. A number of relatives sat off to one side, all of them wailing and sobbing. Aroka was holding the limp hand of his daughter, while her other hand was protectively resting against her swollen belly beneath the cotton shift she wore.

"No!" Catt cried softly. She fell to her knees and pressed her fingers to Mandei's neck. A pulse! There had to be a pulse! No...there was none.

"No..." Frantically, she searched for other signs of life from the mother.

"She has died! She has died!" Aroka wept. Kissing his daughter's hand, he howled, "Aiiiee, she has died. They have taken her soul. They have taken my grandchild...aiiiee...." He covered his face with his other hand. The relatives followed the father's lead and began to weep harder. They sat crouched together, rocking back and forth, praying and crying for Mandei's lost spirit.

Catt sat there, stunned. Mandei was dead, her body ravaged by the deadly disease. Automatically, Catt put her hand across Mandei's, which lay across her abdomen. There was no way to save her baby. No way! With a moan, Catt leaned forward, her brow resting against her hand as it covered Mandei's. No, she just couldn't die! Why hadn't the antibiotics worked? Why hadn't they saved this valiant woman's life? The life of the baby she carried?

The sounds of grief swelled and filled the hut. Catt lifted her head and sobbed, "I'm sorry, Aroka. I'm so sorry.... I tried to save her...and your grandchild. I thought the antibiotics would save her...oh, Lord...."

Ty leaned down. "Catt, come home. Come with me." He curved his hands around her shaking shoulders as she wept unashamedly, huddled over Mandei. He knew there was nothing else to be done. Ty understood as no one else in this hut the devastating effect this would have upon Catt. She'd lost her own baby. Now Mandei was dead, and her baby, too. Gently, he lifted Catt upward. She sagged against him, inconsolable. Curving his arm around her shoulders, he rasped, "Come on, darlin'. Let's get out of here. You've done all you could do. You fought hard for her, Catt. I'm sorry." And he was.

Tears blinded Catt. She staggered into Ty's arms. He felt so comforting to her now, when her heart was ripped open and bleeding because of the mounting losses. He led her out of the hut and walked with her across the village. She was crying so hard, her hands pressed to her face, that she relied on him to guide her.

Catt's weeping struck Ty profoundly. She was shaking and trembling against him as they slowly made their way down the path. Soon the jungle and the darkness enclosed them completely, absorbing the sound of her sobs. He was glad to be alone with her.

Ty felt like crying himself—for Catt, for the loss of their baby, for not being there for her in her greatest hour of need. Bitterly, he shoved away all his guilt. Right now he had to deal with Catt. He wanted to attend to her needs and be here, this time, to support and help her through this awful situation.

The rest of the outbreak team was already asleep in their tents on the shore of the Amazon by the time Ty got Catt to the houseboat. By then she'd stopped weeping. He guided her to where they'd sat that morning and asked her to sit down on a coil of rope.

"Stay here," he urged. "I'll get us something to drink and be back in a minute, all right?" His narrowed gaze met and held her tear-swollen eyes. "Catt? I'll stay if you don't want me to go."

Miserably, she wiped her nose with her sleeve. "No...you can go...."

When Ty returned, Catt felt his hand on her shoulder. Absorbing his quiet, strong presence, she rested her elbows on her thighs and pressed her hands against her damp face. For several minutes she sat there, trembling like a leaf in a storm as his hand moved gently and slowly back and forth across her shoulders.

"You did everything you could," Ty rasped as he set the tumbler aside after she had taken a drink. He knelt on one knee beside Catt, one hand on her shoulder, the other wrapped around her arm. "You never gave up on Mandei," he told her in a broken voice. "You did everything humanly possible to save her, Catt. Don't blame yourself for what happened. Please..."

Lifting her face, she cried out, "I should have saved her, Ty! I should have! Why didn't the antibiotics work? They should have!" Her own voice cracked. "Dammit, those are third-generation antibiotics. The best we have. They didn't *faze* that damned bacteria! None of the people treated with the antibiotics lived, do you realize that?" Huge tears rolled out of her eyes and down the taut planes of her cheeks. She saw the agony in Ty's narrowed gaze and in the tight set of his mouth. In frustration, she opened her hands, her voice cracking. "*Why* didn't they work? Why? I know we're up against anthrax. The medicine should have worked! What the hell's going on here? I don't understand it! I just don't!" Catt sobbed in angry helplessness.

Reaching up, Ty threaded his fingers through her hair. "I wish I had answers for you, Catt. I really do, but I don't. I agree with you, it's anthrax. It should have responded to the antibiotic, but it didn't. We'll have to wait to hear from Rafe, from OID, to understand all this. Don't take it personally, please. You're so damned tired. You need a good night's sleep...." And he wanted to add, *I'll sleep with you. I'll hold you. I swear I won't take advantage of you or the situation. I just want to hold you and heal you, Catt. I know I can do that for you....* He remained silent, however. He knew she'd never acquiesce to his request because of their own shattered and grief-stricken past. And worst of all, she had never reached out to ask for his help one time during this epidemic. Why should she? He hadn't been there the last time when she'd pleaded for his help.

Miserably, Catt wiped her eyes with shaking fingers. "Sleep..." she muttered. "Maybe if I sleep..."

"That's right," Ty urged as he helped her to her feet. "Come on, let's get you down below. Take a shower and go to bed. You'll feel better in the morning."

Catt allowed him to guide her to the stairway. Gripping the rail at the top, she uttered hoarsely, "Nothing is ever going to make how I feel go away...." She tottered unsteadily down into the dimly lit hold.

As he began to follow her down the steps, she looked up at him. "Please, I—can you give me a few minutes? I—I need to be alone." More than anything, Catt needed to escape his strong presence. The thought of being in that small cabin with him tonight when she felt so vulnerable frightened her.

Ty stood there for a long time, hands on his hips, the suffering moving through him in unrelenting waves of agony. He felt every emotion Catt was feeling, and now he was getting a taste of the kind of grief she had gone through by herself when she'd lost their baby.

"Son-of-a-bitch," he whispered hoarsely as he turned on his heel and went over and sat down on a coil of rope. Catt had been like this before—and he hadn't been there for her. Why would she want him around now? What kind of idiot had he been back then? The worst kind of man, that was for sure. He'd chosen his job, his career, over Catt's need of him. That one phone call was the worst possible mistake he'd ever made in his life, affecting not only him, but Catt, whom he had loved with every cell of his being.

As Ty sat there, enveloped by the night, hot, unwilling tears welled up into his eyes. Hanging his head, he no longer fought them off, but let them roll down the stubble on his cheeks and tangle in the bristle of his dark beard. In the darkness, he felt all of Catt's pain. All her grief. All her isolation and the pain of being abandoned in her time of need. But he also remembered how lost he'd felt—how helpless when he hadn't been able to find her. As he sat there alone, he remembered all those nights he'd lain awake wondering where she was, *how* she was. He knew the loss of the child had devastated her, and seeing her sorrow tonight proved to him just how much pain she was in, then and now.

As he sat there alone, he realized something else. Then, as now, she'd run from help. He remembered how she'd told him that day on the dock in Manaus that he hadn't been able to find her because she hadn't wanted to be found.

"Once bitten, twice shy," he muttered to himself as realization dawned. He understood now that his hesitation—his damned foolish mistake in not coming home to her at the news of the baby—had made Catt run for cover. She wasn't one to ask for help. Hell, her whole life was spent helping others—her

father, her patients. What would it take to win her
trust again, to let her know that he would be there
for her—that he would have been there in the past,
if only she'd let herself be found?

Chapter Eight

Catt lay in the bed, her arm across her eyes. She ached with grief and pain, though when she'd heard Ty come down, she pretended to be asleep. As he took a shower and went to bed, she lay there listening, desperately needing him, needing his touch and his arms around her. *Why?* her brain screamed. *He abandoned you when you needed him most!* Yes, that was true—then. But now…oh, Lord, he'd been so solicitous toward her and incredibly caring each time she'd wanted his support. Perhaps he was right—with age he'd matured. And with maturity, he was able to anticipate her needs much better than he had in the past. Turning onto her side, she opened her eyes. The moonlight shining through the houseboat windows revealed that he was lying on his back, his hands behind his head. She knew he wasn't asleep, either.

Her heart won out. Catt pulled the sheet aside and slowly sat up. Her hands were damp and she wiped them nervously across her thighs, which were covered with the thin cotton nightgown.

Ty heard the bed creak and moved his head slightly to the right, acutely aware of the noise. Catt was sitting up. His heart began to beat a little harder in his chest. The moonlight exposed the suffering lines of her face. Just the way her mouth was pulled in told him everything. He knew how much she needed him—and he knew that her stubborn determination to harbor her pain alone would keep her from reaching out to him. It was up to him to let her know he was there—but he had to be careful with her, or she would run from him like she'd run before.

"Catt?"

Ty's voice was like low, rumbling thunder throughout the cabin. The sheet fell away and exposed his naked upper body as he sat up—he'd worn a pair of pajama bottoms to bed out of respect for Catt. Now, with his hands resting on the sides of his mattress, he studied her tear-filled gaze. She was trying so hard to be brave. To not cry. But he knew she was grieving for the past as well as the present.

She tried to speak. Opening her hands helplessly, Catt forced herself to look directly at Ty. His eyes burned with tenderness. It gave her the courage to speak in a wobbly tone. "I—I need to just be held for a little while, okay? I know it sounds stupid. I know our past. But—if you could—"

Before she could say anything else, Ty had moved across the aisle and settled down beside her. A sigh escaped Catt as the warmth of his near-naked body brushed against her left arm. She felt the strength of his embrace as he drew her toward him. A small cry of relief escaped her lips and she turned and moved fully—completely—into his awaiting embrace. It was so easy to surrender once she had silenced her screaming mind, which told her she was a fool twice over. Her heart, however, sang with a quiet joy within her breast.

"That's it," Ty rasped against her hair as she settled against him, "just let me hold you, darlin', if only for a little while...." Shutting his eyes, he pressed his lips to her damp hair and felt a shudder of old fear moving out of him as Catt surrendered effortlessly to him. She slid her arms around his naked torso, her cheek pressed between his neck and his broad shoulder. The feel of her soft but firm breast against his burning flesh, separated only by the thin barrier of her nightgown, made him tremble inwardly.

"Just let me hold you...." he whispered, and began to gently rock her back and forth in his arms as he had so many times before. Somehow, the slight rocking motion always helped Catt relax. He felt the tension begin to bleed out of her as she leaned more fully against him. She was trusting him—finally. Ty realized he had a chance to salvage what he'd once destroyed between them. Though his mind wasn't functioning at all, his heart, which was thundering in his chest over Catt's unexpected invitation, was guiding him now. He grappled with his escaping emotions. Trying to listen to the wisdom of his head and not this vast, overflowing cauldron of feelings for Catt, which were now moving wildly through him, was impossible.

Catt sighed again. How good Ty felt to her! She

nestled more deeply into his arms and savored the
male scent of him mixed with the soap he'd used
while showering. He was strong and yet held her so
gently, as if she were a fragile cup that might break.
Here she felt safe. Finally, safe. The word circled her
aching heart and made it soar with a joy that
thrummed through her as she felt his warm, moist
breath against her cheek.

"Better?"

She nodded, unable to speak. Reaching up, she slid
her hand across the roughened stubble of his jaw in
response. Words were foreign to her right now. Instead, she luxuriated in the safety of Ty's embrace
and the gentleness that she'd once fiercely loved
about him. She was starved for what he effortlessly
gave to her. Why, oh why, had he abandoned her
before? *Yet,* her heart whispered, *he's not abandon-
ing you now. He's here holding you and trying to
make you feel better.* That was true, and Catt allowed
her sensitive fingers to move upward, following the
curve of his cheek. She felt Ty stop rocking her, felt
tension sizzle through him.

The grief was making her crazy, Catt decided, but
she felt helpless to stop the flow of feelings she had
for Ty. Just getting to touch him in such an intimate
way began to dislodge a little parcel of grief from
her heart. Was touching him that healing to her? Catt
closed her eyes and continued to gently move her
fingers across his cheek, following the hard line of
his jaw. She was remembering. So was her heart.
And so was her body. That wonderful warmth that
always lay in her lower body whenever Ty was with
her in the past was back now, for the first time in a
long time.

Catt marveled at her physical body. It did, after all, have a mind of its own. A wonderful heated sensation throbbed throughout her abdomen, and like the brilliant light of a million suns, radiating fingers of pleasure began to move upward through her and downward toward her toes. The feeling was delicious, and Catt moaned softly as she unconsciously pressed her lips to Ty's strong, broad shoulder. Her fingers trailed down his jaw to the thick column of his neck.

Ty didn't know what to do. He knew what he wanted to do, but was it wise? Was it the *right* thing? Catt's fleeting touches haunted his heart, reawakening feelings for her that had never died. Should he make love to her? That was what she was asking in the way she was touching him. His skin burned as if branded where her lips traced a path across the naked flesh of his shoulder. Her fingertips glided from the column of his neck up to the hard line of his jaw again. There was no mistaking what Catt was asking of him now. Torn as never before, Ty closed his eyes and shuddered as she pressed herself more insistently against his chest. He felt himself hardening to such a degree that it was almost painful. He wanted her. All of her. In his heart, he knew that if Catt would allow him to love her just one more time, he could begin the healing between them, ease the burden in her heart and the grief she'd carried so long by herself.

Somehow, Ty sensed and knew that loving Catt was the most right thing in the world at this moment, but it had to be her call. *She* had to initiate that choice, not him. And whatever it took, he had to go slowly, not make any moves that might destroy her leisurely, exquisite exploration of him. But it was hell to sit there quietly with Catt in his arms as she slowly reached out to him in so many silent, satisfying ways. He'd never been more afraid in his life as in this moment. One wrong move, one wrong decision, and he would turn Catt off. She would shut him out of her life forever this time. Fear shuddered through Ty, setting his heart pounding in response.

Catt felt Ty tense as she moved her fingertips from his neck to trace the outline of his shoulder. She was lost in a haze, a hinterland between grief and joy. There were no words, nothing that she could say to him. Each time she touched him, pressed a small, exploratory kiss here, one there, on his damp, tense flesh, it was releasing her from a dark prison she'd lived in for nearly a decade. Somehow, Catt knew he would understand her silent exploration. She had no idea if she was making a mistake, she was simply driven by the spreading warmth that throbbed in her lower body, and the yearnings of her heart, which cried out for Ty's presence, his touch and his tenderness.

Because her grief was boundless, Catt sought refuge in the joy that moved through her each time she touched Ty. Rubbing her cheek against his neck, she allowed her fingertips to move with delicious slowness downward from his shoulder to his heavily muscled upper arm. She felt so many tiny scars here and there as she moved her fingers outward in continued exploration. At his elbow, she felt a welt of a scar and wondered briefly how Ty had received it. She knew it hadn't been there before, when she'd known every inch of his hard male body. This puckered scar was recent. It hurt Catt to think of the pain he'd endured before it had healed.

Sighing, she closed her eyes and continued to trace the rest of his arm. There was so much dark hair covering his forearm that she smiled a little to herself. Ty's massive chest was covered with a thick, dark carpet as well. Inhaling his male scent, she felt her senses blossom. As her fingers trailed languidly along the back of his wrist, she felt him turn his hand over. Her fingertips grazed his palm and he drew in a deep, ragged breath. He was holding himself tightly in check, she knew. Catt appreciated his control, for she needed that right now. More than anything, just reacquainting herself with him, with his magnificent male body, was a gift that was assuaging her grief. She could no more explain it to him than to herself. Right now, Catt was following the dictates of her overburdened heart. Right now, the powerful masculine qualities of Ty, who had once loved her, were a safe place to lose herself within. He was a wonderful harbor in her present storm of life.

As her fingers glided tentatively across his large knuckles, Ty gently threaded his fingers between hers. Catt was utterly relaxed against him. She was exploring him like a wide-eyed child. He recalled the first time they'd made love—on a beach at Half Moon Bay. They had lain in the light of the moon that night on a blanket, listening to the waves crash and foam before being absorbed by the sandy shore. Catt had never had a man before him. And she was his first. But he had had enough experience to know that she had to initiate everything. Ty recalled how he'd patiently allowed her to divest him of all his clothes, how she'd looked at him, savoring him, gliding her fingers across every inch of his body. In exploring, Catt had lost her fear of him. When she was done, she had moved to his side and asked him to love her. He'd never forgotten that incredibly beautiful and tender night. Not ever.

It was the same now, Ty realized. She was retracing an old pattern of introduction with him once again. That realization made his heart soar with hope. Somehow, the grief of Mandei and her child's death, as tragic a loss as it was, was also paving the way for a door deep in Catt's heart to be opened after it had been so painfully shut and locked all those years ago. Humbled by her strength, by her courage, Ty rasped, "Come here, let's get more comfortable...." And he moved Catt easily around until he lay on the bed with her, at his side, so that she had full access to him. As Catt lay beside him, he gazed upward and saw the desire in her eyes, the warmth, the need of him burning in them. Her lips were parted, just begging to be caught, tamed and kissed, but he placed steely control over himself. As her hand moved gently across his chest, he sucked in a ragged gasp of air. Eyes shuttering closed, Ty worked to stop another response, but it was impossible. Catt would clearly see his need of her, there was no doubt. If only he could quell his own needs—but hot fire licked up through his lower body. Pain throbbed, along with his hunger to have her in every possible way.

Just moving her fingers through the coverlet of silky, thick hair on Ty's chest sent tiny tingles of joy up through her hand and arm. Catt felt him tense as she explored his massive, well-sprung chest, but she could not help herself. Right now, she felt as if she were caught in a web of some extraordinary heat and joy. Her heart was opening rapidly, ravenously. All she could do was follow the dictates of it, follow her own animal senses as they filled her with a bright, bursting demand for life.

Leaning over, her body meeting and touching his, she felt her breasts brush across his chest. She wanted to kiss Ty. She needed to feel his mouth against hers. He could take away her pain. He could take away her grief. Eyes closing as she leaned over him, she felt his hand come to rest on her shoulder. Yes, to kiss Ty was what she wanted more than anything else. As her lips glided against the hard line of his mouth, Catt felt his fingers dig deeply for an instant into her shoulder, not painfully, but hungrily. Joy spiraled through her. She felt his lips soften, accepting her exploration of him. How strong his mouth was, she thought, as she pressed her own more surely against his, feeling the power of him and savoring it completely. Catt wanted that power. She wanted to sip and take it into herself.

The pain in his tight lower body was excruciating as her lips grazed his. With a groan, Ty opened his mouth. He felt helpless beneath her ministrations, her seeking, and when she moved the tip of her tongue across his lower lip, he groaned again. Mindlessly, Hunter moved his large hand against her slender shoulder. He could feel the strength of her, the femininity of her as his fingers slid along and captured the back of her neck, bringing her down more surely against his mouth. He heard Catt moan, but it was a moan of pleasure. That drove him over the edge as her mouth blossomed hotly beneath his powerful, returning exploration. Her tongue met his, touched

fleetingly, and he captured her and drew her more
deeply into him. The brush of her taut breasts against
his chest, the way her hand slid down the line of
dark hair in the middle of his belly, her fingers seeking and finding entrance beneath his pajama waist-
band, told Ty what she was asking of him.

Catt drowned in the splendor and power of his
capturing kiss, as he shifted her onto her back. She
willingly lay beside him, her arms around his shoulders, her mouth clinging hotly to his. Yes, she
wanted him in every possible way. Nothing mattered
anymore—not their past, not their fragile present.
The driving force within her was to create life, to
feel alive and no longer allow death to hold sway on
her. As she felt Ty's hand move commandingly
down to her shoulder to remove the strap of her
nightgown, Catt accepted that whatever they shared
between them had never died. It was alive. It was
wonderful, and she lay in awe of the volcanic explosion of feelings her heart released as he removed her
gown easing it over her legs and allowing it to drop
to the floor. As he stretched his long, hard body
against hers once more, he smiled down at her. It
was a smile of welcome, filled with tenderness. She
met his burning, narrowed gaze and smiled tremu-
lously in return.

As his hand came to rest alongside her firm breast,
Catt moaned. Then his thumb moved upward to en-
circle the taut nipple and she cried out softly, pressing herself wantonly against him. His smile was one
of a man who knew his woman, knew what she
wanted and knew what she liked. It was so easy to
close her eyes and surrender to Ty in every way.
Tonight, Catt knew, she was safe with him. Tonight

he could love her and she could return that love, which had, miraculously, never died.

Ty felt her hand move boldly beneath the band of his pajamas as he lay above her, her head resting on his forearm. He saw the sparkle in her slumberous eyes, and liked the softness of her now pouty, well-kissed lips. She had always been a bold lover and was no less so now. Glorying in her assertiveness, he felt her tugging at the material. Leaving her side for a minute, Ty removed the pajamas.

The instant his hardened body met and touched hers, Catt moaned and closed her eyes. She felt him slide his arm beneath her neck and shoulders and bring her fully against him once more. It was a possessive gesture. Just the burning touch of their damp flesh meeting made her sigh raggedly with need. Reaching out, Catt slid her fingers downward across his hard, flat abdomen. Instantly, Ty tensed. As her fingers slowly, deliciously, curled around him, she heard him growl. It was a growl of warning, of pleasure, and she lifted her chin upward. She was not disappointed. His mouth fell upon hers in a plundering, commanding motion. Within moments, she felt his heavy warmth settling above her. It was so easy to open her thighs to him, to feel his knee nudging between them, opening her even more for that sweet assault. Yes, this was what she wanted. Needed so desperately that the ache in her lower body was becoming almost painful in its intensity.

When his lips tore from her mouth and settled on the hardened nipple of her breast, Catt cried out. Instantly, her fingers dug deeply into his bunched shoulders. As he began to suckle her in slow, deep motions, her hips automatically lifted to receive his thrust into her.

A cry of joy tore from her parted lips. She threw her head back. Her spine arched to receive the power of him as he plunged deeply into her hot, slick depths. His suckling of her combined with the lightninglike bolt of fire that jolted through her, and all she could do was moan with pleasure, surrender to him and meet him with equal fervor and driving need. Her fingers ranged upward and she gripped his hair as he teethed her nipple gently, his mouth sending wild fluttering sensations throughout her. She felt him groan as she closed her legs over his and captured him with her femininity. They were joined. They were one once again. In that glorious, heated moment, Catt knew without a doubt that she loved Ty. The love they'd had, had never died. He was deeply within her body now, and the driving force of his hips, the ragged breath near her ear, the powerful movement of him as a male taking her, capturing her, was all she wanted.

Within seconds, Catt released his hair and grasped his long, powerful torso. His flesh was damp, trembling, hard, and she met and matched his driving thrusts. Their ragged breaths joined in tumult. Their hearts slammed in unison. Their flesh gleamed and they slid wildly against one another in an out-of-control, ravenous hunger. Catt felt like the jaguar Ty had mentioned the other day. Her blood pounded hotly through her as if with a raging fever, as they breathed together with gasps of pleasure. Their moans mingled. One of his hands gripped her shoulder and he slid the other beneath her hips, lifting her at an angle. Instantly, heated pleasure exploded through her. She could do nothing but cry out, helpless beneath the power of her own surging womanhood as desire burst and moved powerfully through her. She felt him tense and continue to thrust into her, holding her in that position so that she could enjoy the explosion of pleasure now shimmering through her like hot, dappled sunlight.

Her world collided with his. The brilliance of the heat within her body was like molten, life-giving energy. She felt him growl, a reverberation like that of a wild jungle cat, moving through her like a drum. He gripped both her hips and thrust even more deeply into her. She arched to meet him, experiencing once again the thunderstorm, the sunlight and the rainbow of pleasure and beauty that came with them. His lips pulled away from his teeth; he froze above her. Catt knew how to increase his pleasure and, smiling softly, began to move, to tease and drain that masculine power from him into herself. The moment was magical, mystical, for her. They were joined; they were together as they had been before. And now her heart sang as she moved her fingers in silent joy across the frozen planes of his face and he released his life into her.

With a groan, Ty collapsed beside her in the aftermath. He heard Catt sigh raggedly as she moved to her side next to him. Just the small, fleeting touches of her fingers upon his spent, damp body made his heart sing. All the years, the wondering, the guilt and the grief of losing her melted away in those beautifully spun moments. Moving his arms around her, Ty drew her against him. He kissed her flushed cheek and gazed deeply into her blue eyes, now filled with golden dapples of happiness. This was the

woman he loved. That woman was back. He knew
he'd fulfilled her by the soft part of her glistening
lips, by the flush in her cheeks and, most of all, by
the tender look she shared with him.

With a sigh, Catt rested her head on his shoulder
and languidly curved her arm against his torso. How
wonderful it felt to be in Ty's arms like this. How
much she had missed him all these years! If anything,
he was an even better, more attentive lover now. Just
the way he grazed her hair with his trembling fingers,
touched her dampened cheek and outlined her lips
made her feel deliciously worshiped. She couldn't
get enough of him, of his touch. They'd been one
once again. Catt felt like a satiated female jaguar that
had been driven by primal lust to find her mate. Well,
Ty was her mate, for better or worse. Her body
throbbed with heat, with his power and energy deep
within her, and Catt lay weakly in his arms, spent
and happy.

Ty saw the joy and rapture in her vulnerable expression. Her eyes were closed, but he saw the soft
play of her lips, the way the corners lifted, and knew
that he'd given her pleasure. Catt had given him no
less. His body tingled, and although he felt satisfied,
what he felt more than anything else was the over-
powering feelings he held for Catt alone. No woman
had ever matched her fierceness during lovemaking,
her boldness or her incredible ability to give all of
herself to him on every level.

Instinctively, Ty moved his hand across her abdomen, his darkly tanned fingers splayed out against
the pearl-like whiteness of her flesh. Once, she'd held
their child in this wonderful belly of hers. A remorse-
ful ache moved through Ty as he saw her hand come

to rest on top of his. Her eyes were still closed and he saw her expression change just a little. There was a haunting tenderness to her face now. Did she wish she was now with child—his child—once more?

Startled at his train of thought, Hunter furrowed his brows. They had used no protection. Catt could become pregnant—again—with his baby.

Ty had no desire to break the beauty of this moment with Catt. She needed the safe haven of his arms, and he chose to offer his healing strength rather than worry her with other concerns right now. Moving his hand from her belly, he slid his fingers upward to cup her breast. She moaned a little, and barely opening her eyes, she smiled up at him.

"You are so beautiful," he murmured, and then he leaned down and gently engaged her mouth once more.

Just the warmth, the nurturing male tenderness he shared with her as his mouth met and captured hers, was all Catt needed. Ty was warm, strong and caring—as he always had been in the past. Catt was too satiated, too weary to think—she could only feel. She was hungry for the touch of Ty, for the feel of his lips moving commandingly across her mouth and taking her once more to that place of joy, of sunlit brightness once again. Despite her fatigue, she gloried in his gentle assault upon her lips, his tongue outlining her lower one, his teeth gently grazing her mouth. Everything he shared with her was done with such incredible tenderness. Her scarred heart absorbed all of Ty, without judgment, without prejudice, and she moaned softly as his mouth left hers and settled once more on the hardening peak of her breast.

The suckling motion made her moan again, and she pressed herself to him and let him know how much she enjoyed it. His mouth left her nipple and he trailed a series of small, exploratory kisses down the center of her torso. When he kissed her belly and moved his hand gently across her, tears suddenly burned in her closed eyes. They had lost so much! And yet he was here with her now, loving her, taking care of her and in some way trying to atone for past mistakes. Catt felt his sorrow. Felt it eating at him. Gently, she turned and wrapped her arms around Hunter's shoulders.

The movement wasn't lost on Ty. He smiled a little, sighed and brought her deeply into his arms. She was very tired. "You need to sleep, darlin'. Just close your eyes and I'll hold you while you dream."

The roughness of his voice moved gently through her. "Yes...I'm so tired, Ty. So tired..."

He heard the weariness from the depths of her fatigued soul. "I know you are," he whispered, and pressed a kiss to her hair. "Just sleep. I'll hold you and keep you safe...."

She reveled in the sound of his voice, his protectiveness. Tonight, as no other, she truly needed Ty in every way. And he knew it and was responding in kind. Despite their jaded past, which was riddled with grief and pain, he was here for her now as never before.

Hunter felt Catt relax completely against him, trusting him. How long he lay there in the darkness, with shreds of moonlight stealing silently through the cabin, he didn't know, nor did he care. His life's treasure was here in his arms right now, and nothing else mattered. For the moment, it wasn't important that death was all around them—a lethal, mysterious disease they didn't know the cause of. His brow furrowed as he lay there with the woman he loved so fiercely. His senses were still molten, like newly freed lava from an exploding volcano. There was no right or wrong in loving Catt again. Ty hadn't believed it could ever happen. And yet a miracle had occurred.

How many times had he lain awake at night wondering how she was? His brows dipped. His mouth compressed. Somehow, Ty wanted to create a bridge of trust with Catt. He wanted a future with her. But would she give him a chance? Just because they had lain here and made love didn't give him any claim to her at all, and he knew it. No, this night was special. Catt was hurting so badly that her heart had finally overridden her head, and, for the moment, she'd forgotten her past experience with him. Gently dragging his fingers across the cooling flesh of her arm, he could feel Catt's breathing change. She was sleeping now. Deeply—perhaps for the first time in years. Ty hoped Catt's dreams were good, for she'd always been a vivid dreamer. He recalled all the times when they'd slept together, how she'd reel off three or four of her dreams the next morning to him. Hell, he never remembered his, but they always had fun talking about hers, what they might mean and the symbology behind them. Ty found it interesting, and he'd learned a lot about Catt from her vivid dream world.

Well, tonight, I wish only good dreams for you, darlin', because no one deserves them more than you. Ty closed his eyes and released a ragged sigh. He had no idea what tomorrow would hold. Catt

could wake up hating him. She could spurn him and
take her rage out on him—not that he didn't deserve
it. At least this time she could not blame him, because she'd initiated it all. No, he thought. He knew
Catt well enough to realize that she wouldn't throw
tonight in his face. She had integrity. She had a right
to be angry and hurt by his past mistakes, but he
seriously doubted she would blame him for what
they'd shared hotly tonight.

If nothing else, it was a beginning, Hunter hoped.
A second chance. He knew he didn't deserve it, but
he loved Catt with a fierceness that had never died,
that had transcended a decade without her. As sleep
pulled at him, Ty smiled a little. Catt was in his arms,
where she should be. Always…

Chapter Nine

Ty awoke with a jerk. Voices! Instantly, sleep fled. Gray dawn light filtered into the cabin. Reaching for Catt, he discovered she was gone. He relaxed when he realized the voices were familiar to him: Catt and Rafe talking quietly on deck. Memories of the night, of loving Catt, slammed back to him as he hurriedly got out of bed. Throwing the rumpled sheets aside, he climbed into a pair of khaki pants and a white cotton polo shirt, pulled on some socks and put on his roughout boots.

Climbing the stairs, he raked his hair into some semblance of order. His heart was still beating hard. At first he'd thought it was Black Dawn terrorists, the threat of their presence never farther away from him than the beat of his heart. Gripping the wooden rails, Hunter lifted himself up on deck. Heads bowed,

Rafe and Catt were standing near the coils of rope, looking at a set of papers Rafe held between them.

So much rushed back to Ty in those seconds as he hesitated at the gangway. His heart became suffused with yearning the instant Catt lifted her chin and looked in his direction. Heat pooled restlessly in his lower body as he recalled being one with her and loving her wildly and without reserve. The moment their gazes met and locked, Ty knew without a doubt that he loved Catt; he'd never stopped loving her. And last night was a gift beyond any he'd ever been given.

The look in her gaze was one of vulnerability, clearly etched with fear, desire and so much else. As he slowly walked toward them he wondered if Catt thought last night had been a mistake. His eyes raked over her as he moved closer. She was dressed in a pale pink tank top, a pair of jeans that outlined her slender form, and her red hair, recently washed, lay gleaming and damp around her face. He saw the glorious blue of her gaze, and even now, as he approached, he saw gold highlights in her eyes. He knew what that meant—that Catt was happy. About them? Was there really a chance for them? Ty felt an ache settling in his chest. Never had he wanted a second chance with Catt more than now.

Rafe looked up. His face was set with worry. "Morning, Ty. I just got back an hour ago with the results of the testing from OID. Come take a look. You aren't going to like what you see."

Scowling, Ty halted less than a foot from them. When Catt moved away, the ache in his heart intensified. Her body language spoke to him clearly and it wasn't what he'd hoped for. Swallowing his disappointment, he took the papers Rafe handed to him.

"Are we dealing with anthrax like Catt thought?" Ty rumbled as he perused the figures.

Catt felt shaky. Her voice trembled slightly when she answered, "Yes and no." She saw Ty shoot a glance at her. "The good news is it's anthrax. The bad news is that it's the newer, genetically engineered kind against which we have no vaccine, nor any countermeasure."

Catt tried to handle all her escaping feelings as she watched Ty study the report. He looked deliciously vulnerable this morning. His beard darkened his features, making the hollow of his cheeks even more pronounced. It gave him a dangerous look. His hair was disheveled, and she longed to reach over and slide her fingertips through it, taming it into place. He looked so achingly approachable, her heart urged her to move toward him and simply be near him, for he gave her the silent measure of protection, care and nurturance she found she had been starving for since they'd broken up so many years ago.

"Damn them," Ty rasped as he flipped over to the second and third pages of the report. "They finally did it."

Trying to table her own needs, Catt asked, "Who's 'them'?"

Rafe grimaced and shot Ty a warning look.

Ty saw it and rapidly perused the rest of the report, then handed it back to Catt. The moment their fingers touched, he saw her lips part and go soft—with need. Despite her wariness, Ty recorded her reaction. She tried to quickly hide it, but it was too late. She wasn't sure of him. That gave him hope. That she wouldn't run from him just yet. What a helluva time to discover Catt again—in the middle of a damned outbreak.

Rubbing his eyes, he muttered, "We need to sit down and talk—just the three of us," he said.

Catt eased herself down against the wooden railing of the houseboat. She placed her hands on either side of her, resting them on the grainy surface of the deck. "About what?" She looked at Rafe, who stood with his hands on his hips, his gaze locked on the peeling deck. There was something they knew that she didn't. "Ty, what haven't you told me about this outbreak?" Catt gave him a challenging look. Her heart beat once in anxiety of the unknown. All along, she'd suspected there was some hidden reason why Ty had been sent along with her team. It was out of the ordinary for Casey to do something like that.

Catt held her breath as he walked over and sat down on a coil of rope no more than a foot away from her. Rafe joined him and sat on another coil of rope nearby.

"You're going to have to inform your team once they wake up," Ty murmured in a low tone. It was barely dawn, the gray half-light hovering over the triple canopy of the jungle and the muddy Amazon.

"I'm all ears," Catt said.

He heard the derision in her tone and didn't blame her for her anger at not being given some very important information. "I was sent down here by OID and Perseus."

"What's Perseus?"

"A supersecret government organization. It's a part of the CIA." He saw disbelief explode in her eyes.

"CIA?"

"Yes."

"What the hell is going on that the CIA would send *you* with me and my team?" Catt demanded hoarsely. She glanced toward the Juma village. "What's going on here that we don't know?" Her heart was racing with trepidation. She saw the apology in Ty's eyes as he held her demanding gaze.

"Have you ever heard of a terrorist organization known as Black Dawn?" he asked her softly.

Catt reared back. Her lips parted, then closed. "Bioterrorists?" she asked in a choked voice.

Ty nodded. "I got called into this particular outbreak situation because it was suspected that Black Dawn had initiated it."

"Oh, no…!" Catt whispered. She placed her hands momentarily against her lips. Staring at Ty, she saw the seriousness of his expression, the way his mouth compressed into a thin slash, holding back the anger he felt. "But how—when?"

Rafe held up his hand. "A week ago, a small, single-engine airplane flew over this Juma village several times. Chief Aroka told me later, after I'd visited their village just by chance, that he saw the plane spitting on them. He's not familiar with a plane spraying something or having the ability to spray. He said it was like rain falling from the sky, settling all over the village area. Shortly after that, within forty-eight hours, many people began to fall ill. I got here two days after the spraying occurred."

"Rafe called us," Ty said, "and at the time, we had thought Black Dawn was going to try and steal some Ebola virus over in the Congo, so a team was sent there to stop them. It was a ruse," he told her

heavily. "It was designed to pull us off track."
Glancing at Rafe, whose face was dark with anger,
Ty said, "We think they struck here, instead."

Catt gasped. She studied the backwoodsman.
"You know this for a fact, Rafe? Has the plane been
identified? Traced? It had to have numbers on the
fuselage."

"Chief Aroka said he only saw a blue-and-white
bird with an engine. He doesn't read English, Dr.
Alborak. And he saw the plane so briefly that he
couldn't tell us more. I'm sorry."

"Ty? What do you think?" Her voice shook. All
the beauty of their lovemaking last night was dissolving as terror for the people of the village over-
took Catt. Who had carried out this murderous attack?

Sighing heavily, Ty held her demanding gaze. He
saw the fury in her eyes over the outrageous act.
"With test results coming back from OID confirming
the genetically altered anthrax material, I'm confident it was Black Dawn." Looking sadly toward the
Juma village, he added, "A hundred and six innocent, unsuspecting people were used as guinea pigs
for this bioterrorist group to see if spraying of the
material worked."

"It did," Rafe concluded unhappily.

Fingers digging into the cool, damp wood of the
deck, Catt rasped, "And that's why our antibiotic
treatment didn't work worth a damn. That's why
Mandei and her baby died." She hung her head and
felt tears surge into her eyes. Pushing them away,
she looked up and gazed at Ty. "No wonder..."

"I thought we might be working with the genetically altered anthrax, but I couldn't be sure until the test results came back," Ty told her apologetically.

Catt stood up, her hands tense on her hips. She looked out at the river and then back at them. "Medically, we're useless here, except to keep them comfortable and watch them suffer and die. We have no advanced medical facility. We have no IVs and we can't run fluid drips. We can do *nothing* except witness the horror of what crazed men do to innocent people."

Hearing the hopelessness, the rage in her husky tone, Ty slowly unwound his limbs and stood up. "Maybe..." he began.

Rafe stood up in turn. "Maybe what?"

"It's a long shot," Ty murmured pensively. Turning his attention to Catt, who had a confused look on her face, he said, "Remember when you started getting that migraine headache on the way out here?"

"Yes. But what does that have to do with the situation these poor people are in?"

His mouth twisted a little. "Hear me out, okay?" He knew Catt's tendency to jump to conclusions sometimes. "Remember what I used to make your headache go away?"

Catt's eyes widened. Suddenly, hope thrummed through her. And then disbelief. "You aren't saying your homeopathy can help in this situation, are you?"

He held up his hands. "We've got to try it, don't we? I've never used it in an outbreak situation before. According to Dr. Donovan-Cunningham, in the mid-1800s in America, when they had outbreaks of cholera, yellow fever and malaria, homeopathy handled the situation just fine. People who had cholera lived instead of dying. I know from historical reading that homeopathy *has* dealt with life-and-death epidemic situations. For instance, in 1918, when the Spanish flu swept across the world and killed twenty-two million people. Remember that outbreak?''

Catt nodded. ''Every virologist knows about it,'' she muttered.

''Here are the facts,'' Ty said. ''In the U.S., half a million people died of the Spanish flu. Rachel said it was homeopathy's shining hour. She showed me some old magazine reports from that time, printed shortly after the flu epidemic. People who were treated with allopathic, or traditional, medicine died eighty percent of the time. People who went to a homeopath, and took a remedy, lived eighty percent of the time.''

Catt studied him in the tense silence that followed. ''You're *sure* about this?''

''As sure as I'm standing here.''

''Then why didn't I read about it in our scientific literature? I'm quite well versed in the outbreaks of the last two hundred years, in the U.S. and around the world.''

''If you had read the homeopathic medical literature of that time, facts and figures from the federal government health department are all there. A lot of people survived that epidemic because they took a homeopathic remedy.''

Rubbing her lips with her fingers, Catt studied Ty. The enthusiasm in his voice was reaching out to her. She saw the burning belief in his eyes that this alternative medicine could help.

''I wish I had those medical reports....''

"I can supply you with the names and everything, and even get you copies of them once we get home," Ty said fervently. "Right now, Catt, don't you think we should try and save who we can with homeopathic medicine?"

Helplessly, she said, "How do we use it? You're the only one who knows anything about it."

"I can do what I did with you and your headache. Remember how I took all your symptoms, checked them in my book, called a repertory, and found the remedy that cured you? I can do the same here. I can take the symptoms of five people and come up with a remedy. You can test it out on those five, okay? Decide for yourself whether this will work or not. I know for a fact that homeopathy was used in Europe in the 1900s on anthrax cases and cured it. It wasn't the genetically altered variety, but it still might help."

Rafe cleared his throat. "That's a good plan, Ty, but we also need to be on the lookout for Black Dawn. We don't dare devote all our attention to the epidemic and forget that we've got terrorists lurking around somewhere. Somehow, they must be monitoring this situation, too."

Catt nodded. "You're right."

Ty said, "Let's get to the village. I'll take those five cases. It won't take long. Rafe, you play guard dog in the meantime. Catt, can you get your team up to speed while I do this? I'll give the five people the remedy indicated and then you and your team can monitor them through the day. How does that sound?"

What choice did she have? Catt knew that the medicine she'd been using so far was useless. Homeopathy had cured her of a migraine that would have normally laid her out flat for three days, with no relief. She saw the burning excitement in Ty's eyes. She felt fear at the cold-blooded terrorist attack on the Juma. Rage mingled with hope and other feelings she was afraid to admit to as she held Ty's gaze.

"All right," she whispered, "it's the only plan around. We'll focus on the people who are dying. We need to do anything and everything we can for them." Turning her head, she saw a few of her colleagues onshore. "I'll inform my team. Ty, once I'm done, I'm coming into the village to watch you operate. If this works, I need to understand as much as possible what you're doing."

Nodding, he said, "Sure." More than anything, Ty wanted time alone with Catt. They needed to talk. But in the next few hours, anyway, that would be impossible. Rafe looked worried, and Ty knew the woodsman was tense about Black Dawn lurking somewhere nearby, waiting and watching.

For just an instant, before Catt left the houseboat, Ty saw her eyes soften. But only for a split second. What did that softening mean? Did it involve him? Did it have to do with what they'd shared last night?

Catt sat on a log near a fire in the village. Nearby, a Juma woman who had never caught the anthrax was making stew in a black pot hung over the smoldering coals of the fire. It was early afternoon, and the heat and humidity were bearing down on the jungle as they always did at this time of day. Wiping her brow with the back of her arm, Catt removed her protective gloves and dropped them into an awaiting plastic biohazard sack. All these specially made sacks would be burned tonight to kill whatever spores the medical team had picked up in their examination and care of the victims.

Unscrewing the cap on her bottled water, Catt drank deeply. The water was lukewarm and highly chlorinated, but she didn't care. It still tasted good. Recapping the bottle, she saw Ty emerge from one of the huts nearby. Her heart picked up in beat. She felt fear. She felt desire. Most of all, unsure of herself and him, she felt confusion. Her body responded powerfully to him as he spotted her, changed direction and walked toward her. His face was grim looking. No wonder. Last night, ten more people had died. They'd all been given high doses of life-saving antibiotics, but it had been a useless gesture. At least now they knew why.

"Mind if I sit with you?" Ty asked, motioning to the large log she was sitting on.

Catt shook her head. "No...come and rest. You've been at it full bore since six this morning." He looked exhausted. But then, they hadn't slept half the night. Just looking at his wonderfully shaped mouth and recalling it moving hotly upon her own hungry lips made Catt go shaky with desire again.

Grateful that she didn't tell him to go to hell or get lost, Ty sat down, leaving a good foot of space between them. He took off his protective gloves and dropped them into the specially marked sack. "I just repertorized the last person and gave him the remedy," he told her. Catt passed him the bottle of water and he took it. "Thanks."

A tremor of joy raced through her at the intimate look he gave her as she handed him the water. She relished the feeling of his fingers touching hers. This

time the contact gave her hope. For a second, it put
out the fires of fear and distrust toward him. But only
temporarily. As he tipped his head back, his throat
gleaming with sweat, his Adam's apple bobbing as
he gulped down the water, Catt could not tear her
gaze from him. Her heart was devouring him, while
her leery mind screamed at her to run.

The woman at the kettle smiled at them and then
rose and slowly walked away. Catt took advantage
of the fact to speak. Her voice was strained and low
when she said, "We have to talk, Ty—about last
night—about what happened."

Gravely, he lowered his head and capped the water
bottle. Handing it back to her, he said, "Yeah, we
need to talk, but there hasn't been much time to do
that."

One corner of her mouth lifted. Where to begin?
What to say? Catt had rehearsed a hundred times
throughout the day, and each time, it hadn't sounded
right to her. "No, there hasn't...."

Hunter placed his elbows on his thighs, his hands
clasped between them. "What do you want to say to
me?"

Just the gentleness in his low tone reassured Catt
enough to speak. "I'm in a quandary, Ty. I'm not
sorry for what happened last night, but I'm scared. I
didn't plan on anything happening. I...just...well, I
never thought..."

He smiled at her. "It surprised me, too, but I'm
not sorry it happened, darlin'."

The endearment touched her and she absorbed the
tenderness in his expression. Opening her hands nervously, Catt rasped, "Look, I think it happened because I was so grief-stricken over Mandei's

death…the loss of her baby. It hit too close to home for me, brought up a lot of unresolved grief I've had about the loss of my own child.…''

Ty reached out and captured her hand. "I understand that."

Catt saw that he did. The strength of his fingers around hers sent a wave of stability through her. He released her and she breathed a sigh of relief. "What happened was just a fluke. I know I initiated everything. I take responsibility for that." She lowered her gaze and couldn't look at him. "And you let me come to you.… You held me, let me cry and let me grieve.…''

His mouth twisted, then tightened into a slash. "A decade too late, wasn't I?"

Catt winced as she heard the anger toward himself for his actions. Forcing herself to look at him, she saw the naked guilt and grief etched clearly in Ty's face. More than anything, she saw the suffering line of his mouth. The tension lengthened. Finally, she whispered unsteadily, "Look, I'm confused about a lot of things right now. I can't sort out anything. I'm a mass of emotions. I'm worried sick over the Juma. I'm afraid of the bioterrorism, of the possibility of another attack. This isn't a good time to try and sort through issues regarding you and me, Ty. Frankly, what I needed last night was to feel alive after Mandei's death. What's more appropriate than making love to someone in order to feel alive?"

Ty was very careful not to reveal his reaction to Catt. She wasn't ready to hear how he felt toward her. Indeed, he sensed that if he told her he wanted a second chance with her, she'd run and he'd never see her again. His gaze moved down to her rounded abdomen. Had it crossed her mind yet that they'd had unprotected sex? Where was she in her cycle? Could she become pregnant? These were things that he wanted to talk to her about, but now was not the time.

"What you're saying is logical," he agreed gently. "The last thing I want to do, Catt, is make you feel pressured. I'm willing to let what happened last night stand on its own merits. I'm not going to read anything into it. I'll respect how you feel about things." *Liar,* he thought to himself.

He saw relief come to her eyes instantly. Sitting up, Catt released a tremulous breath of air. "Good... because I don't want you to think that—"

"You initiated everything last night, didn't you?"

"Yes."

"Then that's the way it will be between us, Catt. I won't make a move toward you unless you want me to. Fair enough?" Ty saw even more relief in Catt's expression. They had to sleep a few feet away from one another in that houseboat every night. She was afraid he'd take advantage of her, of the situation. That hurt him, but he didn't say anything. They needed time. And she didn't need that kind of unspoken pressure placed upon her right now.

"I'm so glad you understand," Catt said. She felt her fear dissolving. Just the look on Ty's face told her he was a man of his word. He always had been before.

Looking around, he said in a grim voice, "We've got enough to worry about without our personal problems or needs getting in the way."

"I'm glad you see that," Catt said. How badly she wanted to throw her arms around Ty's neck and simply embrace him and thank him. Memories of his molten, capturing mouth upon hers made her go hot and shaky inside once more. He wouldn't touch her. He would not pursue her. If she wanted more, wanted him, she would have to initiate it. Never had Catt felt more in control than now. She felt badly, because she recalled Ty's spontaneity with her in the past. She understood what it was costing him because she sensed as well as saw that he wanted her again and again. For him, the past was over. It didn't matter. He was more than willing to have some sort of relationship with her. That was obvious. But she wasn't ready. And probably would never be. Catt just couldn't let go of the past. Of her loss.

"Well," Ty murmured as he slid his hands over his large, hard thighs, "in the next forty-eight hours, we'll know if this homeopathy is going to help or not."

Catt nodded. "I hope it does," she said fervently.

Rafe met them on the trail that evening as they trudged wearily out of the village. Darkness was falling, the grayish light such that Catt could barely see the path ahead of her. Ty was walking behind her, and she was grateful to him for giving her the space she'd requested earlier in the day. Not once had he reached out to touch her. No, he'd kept things friendly. Her heart missed the intimacy, but her head did not.

As Rafe approached, a dark shadow out of the night, the clean features of his handsome face marked by the deepening dusk, Catt saw worry written in his eyes and mouth.

"Hi, Rafe. What's up?" she said in greeting as she came to a halt.

Ty stopped at her shoulder. He saw the warning look Rafe gave him. "Black Dawn?"

Halting, Rafe said, "No. The Valentino brothers. That could be worse than Black Dawn."

Frowning, Catt said, "Sounds like a movie duo. Who are they?"

"Local cocaine dealers. They're part of a huge South American drug cartel." He gestured to the north of them. "They've got manufacturing sites all over in the Amazon and they make cocaine and other drugs at these places. They enslave local Indians, force them to work in the buildings, and if they don't do it, they put a bullet in their heads, rape their women and girls, usually destroy their villages. Believe me, they are dangerous."

"And they're around?" Ty demanded.

"I just got off the radio," Rafe said. He shrugged. "My radio is an on-again, off-again proposition. Sometimes it works and sometimes it doesn't. Down here, the humidity and moisture just eats up the wiring. Anyway, I was talking with the local constable in Manaus and he said that a number of cigarette-class boats were seen on the Amazon downriver from us by about ten miles. Those boats are fast and powered by some of the biggest engines around. They can go sixty miles an hour real easy. The Valentino brothers use these boats to carry their coke up and down the river. Manaus is their major airport facility. From there, it's flown around the world to drug dealers who buy it from them."

Catt sighed. "Like we don't have enough problems right now. What does this mean, Rafe? Are we in danger?''

''It means we stay on guard. I don't know if the Valentino brothers are involved with Black Dawn or not. Usually, I don't see them on the river because I'm in one of the hundreds of side channels, checking in on tribes under my jurisdiction. I've run into the Valentinos a couple of times and equal firepower is the only thing standing between them and me. They're the most powerful drug lords in this area. Inca has been after them for years. I wish she was here now. We really need her and her abilities.''

Catt looked up at Ty, who had stepped closer to her. She saw the serious set of his mouth and the flash of concern in his eyes. She felt protection emanating from him toward her. The feeling was delicious. ''Is it unusual for them to be operating in this area?''

''Yes,'' Rafe said. ''I've tried for years to map out all their manufacturing sites. Inca has done most of the ferreting out. Between us, we've put together a pretty comprehensive picture. I'm just about ready to send it to the Brazilian government. Once they get it, the government can send in troops to destroy these sites and set the Indians free. But it's going to take a massive undertaking. Inca and I can't do it by ourselves. It will take a lot of money and a lot of government help to pull it off. I've run into the Valentino brothers and their drug soldiers too many times, and they're cold-blooded killers. The fact that they're nearby doesn't sit well with me. I don't know of a manufacturing site around us.''

''Is it possible they're carrying a load of cocaine to Manaus?'' Ty asked.

Running his fingers through his short black hair, Rafe muttered, "Maybe. But I think we need to move the lab site, the tents and even the houseboat out of sight. We don't need to expose ourselves unnecessarily to drug runners on their speedboats. They're well-known for throwing grenades at local Indians who fish the Amazon. They use them as targets and shoot at them with their weapons. We don't want to become their latest target practice. No, we need to move now."

Sighing, Catt shook her head. "This is a nightmare. It just keeps getting worse."

"Well," Rafe said, "you and your team will probably be staying here at least another three or four weeks, so I need to ensure your safety as much as possible."

Reaching out, Catt gripped Rafe's long, lean hand. "I know, and I'm very grateful for your being here, believe me. We'll move, Rafe. Don't worry. I don't want to be a sitting duck, either."

Ty nodded. Grimly, he followed them back toward the houseboat, his mind going back to the suffering people in the village. It would take a week to know for certain if the homeopathic remedies would help. In the next forty-eight hours, they'd get their first indicator. If it worked—and he knew it would—then the next week was going to be a very busy, but productive one. His biggest worry was for Catt and her team.

His heart pounded briefly in his chest to underscore the molten feelings he held for her. She was right: this was a mess. For more reasons than one.

Chapter Ten

"Hard to believe three weeks have passed," Ty said casually to Catt as they walked slowly down the dirt path that led to where the houseboat was tied in the channel. Above, the sun peeked briefly out of the humid, ever moving clouds, though its rays never reached the leaf-strewn jungle floor through the dense canopy of trees.

"I know...." Catt murmured. She absorbed Ty's closeness as he walked at her side. So much had happened since the night they had loved one another. The last three weeks had been some kind of slowly evolving metamorphosis of her attitudes toward Ty. They had never really talked about the past—yet— but Catt was on the brink of broaching the topic with him. Now as she studied him, she decided she liked the soft way his mouth curved when he looked at her. Their arms swung and sometimes their hands inadvertently touched. Catt didn't draw away as she had before. Now she looked forward to those priceless moments, for touching Ty was a pleasure and very necessary to her.

"At least the homeopathy is helping," he said.

"More than a little. I'm having Maria write up a full report on it. The rest of my team is examining each person who has survived because of it." With a shake of her head, Catt marveled, "I'm so glad you were here. Without you, these people, I'm sure, would have died like the others did."

"I'm kinda happy I'm here, too." And he was. Ty didn't know what was happening, but he sensed a miracle was in the works with Catt. She had grown almost indescribably beautiful since he'd made hot, unexpected love with her nearly a month ago. Her skin practically glowed. The look in her eyes held him prisoner. There was gold sunlight in her wide blue eyes, and a new sense of calmness about her. She seemed softer, too, her former edginess replaced with a newfound serenity. She no longer had that hard, defensive wall in place as when he'd met her on the dock at Manaus. Maybe she'd only put it up there to protect herself from him.

At a fork in the path, they moved down a new trail, widened daily by the team members walking back and forth on it. It led to their new camp and laboratory site, on a channel about a hundred feet wide. Rafe's houseboat fit snugly along the bank, and the placid, muddy-looking water that surrounded it teemed with unexpected life. They were safer here, Rafe had told them, from Valentino's cigarette boats, now plying the Amazon with their cocaine cargos, headed for the Manaus international airport. Catt had breathed a sigh of relief when they'd moved, because she didn't want to have problems with those well-known, murderous drug runners. Chief Aroka had told her in broken Portuguese through Ty, that the brothers were dark and evil. And only Inca, the infamous jaguar goddess, had held them in check. Inca fought to free the enslaved Indians who were ripped from their villages and forced to work in chains in their jungle factories to manufacture the deadly drugs. When a man or woman was kidnapped from a village, they were rarely seen again. Too many times, Aroka told Catt in warning, they would, while on hunting trips, find the bodies of those Indians, and sometimes their own people, shot in the head and thrown away by the drug lord's roving bands of soldiers who raided the villages. If anyone refused to work at a factory, it was sure death. Without Inca's considerable threat and influence, the brothers would have taken the Juma people, as well, Aroka told her. Without the green warrior, the woman who lived in and called the Amazon her home, the Juma would be enslaved as a nation, or what little was left of their once great nation.

Ty was about to say something when he heard the sound of a plane's engine coming their way. Reaching out, he gripped Catt's arm.

"Hold it..." he rasped, and he jerked his gaze skyward. It was hard to see much of anything through the triple canopy.

Gasping, Catt listened. "Oh, Lord...a plane... Is it them? Black Dawn?" Her heart skittered with fear. Automatically, she moved into the safety of Ty's embrace. She wasn't disappointed. Instantly, his arms

wrapped around her snuggly, as if to protect her from
the unknown.

"I don't know," he replied, waiting tensely. Every
cell in his being was aware of Catt's body pressed
against his. He felt her fingertips digging into his
forearms as they waited in fear and trepidation. The
engine grew louder and louder. Was it Black Dawn
terrorists? Had they come back to spray their lethal
germs over the Juma once again? This time, if they
had, he and Catt would be sprayed, also. The houseboat was half a mile away—too far to run for cover.
No, all they could do was wait and pray.

Catt's eyes widened as she saw the plane. "It's
blue and white!" she cried.

Hissing a curse, Ty pushed her up against a tow-
ering Pau d Arco tree, its branches wide and shielding. He saw flashes of the single-engine Cessna as it
puttered overhead. Eyes narrowed, his breath held,
he tried to see if there was any spray coming from
the plane.

Catt followed the path of the plane as it moved in
a lazy circle about a thousand feet above the canopy,
before moving toward the river. The engine sounds
began to fade away. She forced herself to release the
tight grip she had on Ty's arms. His face was a stony
mask. His entire body was hard and tense. She was
getting a taste of his Marine Corps side, the military
warrior, for the first time. Studying the harsh, narrowed look of his eyes, the thin line of a mouth she
had once kissed and been kissed by in return, Catt
felt a tremendous surge of protection emanating from
him. He hadn't eased his arms from around her and
she felt pinned.

"Is…did they spray anything? I couldn't see if they did," she mumbled, her voice wobbly with fear.

Ty shook his head. He eased his grip and allowed her to move away from the trunk of the tree. "No…I didn't see any aerosol spray coming from the plane, but we have to be sure." Grasping her by the arm, he said, "Get back to the houseboat. Take a bleach shower and throw the clothes you've got on into the firepit and burn them. We're not taking any chances."

"My team—" Catt protested.

"I'll find them and tell them to get back here and do the same thing," he growled ominously. "Go on, Catt. Don't fight me on this. We've got to take every precaution."

Nodding, she moistened her lips, her heart still beating erratically in her breast. "Yes, okay…and you? What about you?"

Ty stepped away from her. He saw the fear in her eyes and heard it in her voice. "I want to find Rafe. We'll do some checking and then we'll come back here to be with you and your team." He jabbed his finger at her. "You do as I say, Catt. No heroics on this, okay?"

Holding up her hand, she whispered, "Don't worry, I'll stay put." She was too fearful—and too exhausted—to argue. The truth be known, she was feeling very tired of late for no apparent reason. She usually got an ample night's sleep. Still, her body felt loggy, and in the afternoons particularly she had this overwhelming desire to just lie down and take a nap. That was highly unusual for her. Last week, Catt could barely keep her eyes open as she made her late afternoon rounds to her patients.

"Get back to the houseboat as quickly as possible." Ty lowered his voice. "Just stay safe, darlin'."

She smiled weakly. From time to time, Ty would use that endearment. Absorbing the burning look in his eyes, that incredible tenderness that he was able to share with her, she whispered, "Stay safe yourself, Ty…please.…"

"For you, I will." And he turned and jogged quickly down the path, heading toward the Juma village.

Halfway to the houseboat, Catt suddenly became nauseous. To her great surprise, her roiling stomach revolted completely. She found herself bending over, holding her stomach and throat as she got rid of everything. Her mouth stung and burned afterward. What was going on? Had the plane sprayed something? Had she picked it up this fast? Worriedly, Catt hurried to the houseboat. She stripped, threw her clothes off the boat, moved into the cooling spray of the shower and scrubbed herself with a cloth soaked in bleach as never before. When Ty came back, she'd know more. As she stood beneath the weak, tepid stream in the tiny shower stall of the houseboat, Catt was worried that she'd inhaled whatever the plane had sprayed. She could die. They could all die.

As Catt sat on the deck of the houseboat, she told everyone what had happened. Her colleagues had all showered, burned their old clothes and put on clean ones, and were now gathered together discussing this latest wrinkle. The look in Ty's eyes made Catt ache and feel terror at the same time.

Rafe murmured, "I was in the clearing of the village. I got a good look at the plane, and I memorized the number on the side of it.'' He looked down at Catt. ''But I didn't see any spray.''

''Could it be just a reaction based on fear?'' Maria wondered. She smiled a little and placed her hand over her heart. ''I can tell you how scared I was. In fact, my heart's still pounding over the possibility that we could have been sprayed by Black Dawn.''

''Chief Aroka saw the plane,'' Steve noted gravely. ''He said it was the same one as before, but that it wasn't spitting anything on them this time. He said last time it fell like a fine rain from overhead.''

''And we gathered a lot of soil and plant samples to check,'' Maria said. ''I'll get busy with the microscope and see if we can detect any residue on them.''

''I don't think you'll find anything,'' Rafe said. He reached over and patted Catt's shoulder. ''Frankly, I think it was just a fear reaction. Concern for your team, Doctor. You care deeply for everyone, I've found out.'' His smile deepened with respect.

Catt shrugged. ''I feel a little stupid,'' she said apologetically. ''I've never done this before. You're probably right, Rafe.''

''We need to stay on guard,'' Ty warned. ''We don't know if Black Dawn is in cahoots with the Valentino brothers or not.''

''Yes,'' Rafe said heavily. He surveyed the medical team. ''Above all else, we need to stay on alert.''

Maria moved toward the ramp of the houseboat with the samples in plastic bags in her hand. ''Let me look and see what I find. At least we can know for sure if there was spray or not....''

Everyone left the boat except Ty and Catt, who sat down heavily on the coil of rope. She saw Ty approach, seating himself on the coil of rope next to her and placing his hand on her shoulder.

"You okay? You look pale."

Managing a weak smile she didn't feel, Catt said, "I'm fine. Just scared, is all. Isn't it funny, Ty? I can jump headlong into an epidemic outbreak with an unknown enemy. Yet seeing that plane and knowing that it could be spraying a deadly germ into the air just tore me up." She rubbed her mouth with her fingertips and gave him a quick look. "Maybe I'm getting old?"

Chuckling, he moved his hand gently across her shoulder. He could feel the warmth and strength of her body beneath the pale yellow cotton blouse she wore. "I think Rafe's right—it's your care of others, your worry for everyone else that probably triggered your reaction."

"I hope so," Catt said fervently.

Something was wrong with her. Catt slowly got up off her hands and knees after vomiting, again, for the fifth afternoon in a row. Yet Maria had confirmed that there was no residue on the soil or leaves last week. Though she didn't understand her condition, Catt had started carrying a damp cloth in a plastic bag and a canteen of water. Now, as she sloshed the water around in her mouth, spit it out and wiped her mouth with the cloth, her stomach roiled threateningly once more.

She stood up, trying to recall where this reaction, this symptom, had occurred to her before. As she placed her hand on the trunk of a nearby tree, a memory slammed back to her: she had been pregnant with Ty's child! Gasping, her eyes wide, she stared down at her slightly rounded belly. Instantly, Catt placed her hand protectively across that region. No! It couldn't be! Or could it? Her mind raced back. It had been exactly four weeks since they had made unprotected love with one another. She hadn't had her menses; it was two weeks late.... *Oh, Lord, no! Could it be?*

Fear shot through her. Shaky now, Catt headed toward the houseboat. It was midafternoon and everyone was at the village conducting their rounds. In the medical supplies she always brought with her were pregnancy test kits. On trembling legs, she hurried up the gangplank and moved down into the tiny cabin below. Her hands shook as she riffled through the bag that contained all the pregnancy items. Locating a test kit, she stared at it, her heart racing wildly.

What if she *was* pregnant with Ty's child? With a soft moan, Catt closed her eyes. She threw out her hand to stop from pitching to the left as dizziness assailed her. There was only one way to find out.

An hour later, Catt sat on a coiled rope, sipping tepid liquid from her water bottle and staring out across the muddy channel. She saw a great white heron land no more than fifty feet from where she sat, hunting for its favorite meal of frogs or small fish that swam in the shallows. Clenching the water bottle, she felt reality wash over her once more, shattering her peace. She was pregnant. She'd run the test twice. Both times, the indicator showed she was carrying a child. But it wasn't just any child—it was Ty's.

Gently and tenderly, Cat slid her fingers across her

abdomen. This explained her general tiredness, for she remembered that early on in her other pregnancy she could barely keep her eyes open during afternoon classes at the college.

Every time she thought of Ty now, her heart warmed and she felt a flood of joy move through her. What would he do if he knew she was pregnant? Would he walk conveniently out of her life again as he had before? Would his career take precedence over her and the baby again?

Grimly, Catt felt a powerful surge of protectiveness. No matter what, she was going to keep this baby this time. There was no way she was going to jeopardize this child's life. Should Ty even know? she wondered. Catt tried to find the right answer to that question. Everything hinged on the fact that he'd abandoned her before. Even though Ty was obviously more mature at this age, could he be trusted with such information? In the past month, he'd never spoken of loving her. True to his word, and at her request, he hadn't tried to take advantage of her or their situation.

Yet Catt felt his care of her. She saw it every time Ty looked at her. She knew that the tender flame in his cinnamon-colored eyes spoke volumes to her. Catt bowed her head, feeling unsure. "What a helluva mess you've gotten yourself into, Alborak," she muttered to herself.

Her quandary was interrupted by the sound of voices. Raising her head, Catt saw her team coming toward the boat. Rafe and Ty were with them. Happily chatting and laughing among themselves, they were carrying medical equipment back from the village. That meant they'd finished up their work. They could go home now. Catt slowly rose. She felt weak, and unsure about telling Ty anything. She wanted to tell him and ask him for his help. Yet, Catt realized as never before her own weakness in refusing to ask for help when she needed it most. Asking made her feel stripped and vulnerable. He was looking for her now, and she avoided his sharpened gaze and moved toward the gangplank to join her team by the tents pitched on the channel bank.

Ty frowned as he watched Catt come down the gangplank. Damn, but she was looking bad. What the hell was wrong with her? His mind raced. She was thinner, and he was sure she'd lost a good five or so pounds this past week. Yet her skin glowed like sunlight, and there was a soft flush in her cheeks. Maybe it was just the demands of her work getting to her. Maybe it was him being around that was wearing her out. Guilt niggled at him. He couldn't deny the joy of simply being with Catt. Perhaps his presence was weighing her down in a way he didn't realize or anticipate. After all, she'd never spoken of love to him. The past had remained buried between them, unexplored and unopened. How badly he wanted to open it up now, to talk at length with her. No one wanted a second chance more than he did with Catt, but from the looks of things, he was a pestilence to her, not a healthy influence. Hurt moved through him as they halted and met Catt at the bottom of the gangplank.

"I'm going to take you and Ty by motorboat back to Manaus," Rafe told Catt. "You're all wrapped up here." He smiled a little and gestured to the tents and the rest of the team. "Once I get you two to Manaus, I'll motor back here. By the time I return, your team will have gotten everything on board the houseboat, and then I'll bring them back on it.'' He reached out and patted her shoulder. ''And from the way you look, I think a few days in a nice five-star hotel with good food, a firm bed and plenty of sleep, would do you good, Doctor.''

She tried to smile. ''Thanks, Rafe. I think I'm ready for it, too.'' She noticed Ty was assessing her from the rear of the group, his eyes narrowed and questioning. Catt felt panic. Did Ty know she was pregnant? How could he? That was impossible. No, right now, she had to keep the secret to herself.

''Excellent!'' Rafe said. ''Ty will help me load your personal luggage on board my small aluminum boat, and we'll be off. I should be able to get you to Manaus by twilight.''

Ty waited until everyone had dispersed. Catt was pale looking, the shadows beneath her eyes pronounced. Ty felt anguish. She was distancing herself again. The skeletons of the past were alive once more. He felt helpless. She was shutting him out again as she had done all those years ago. He'd never get close to her if she didn't allow these protective walls around her to dissolve. The love and care he wanted to share were stifled. He followed her down into the hold, to their cabin. At the bottom of the steps, he reached out and gently curved his hand around her upper arm. Instantly, she gasped. He released her.

Catt turned around and nearly stumbled. He reached out and caught her by the arm again. Once she was upright, she pulled free of his grip.

Was his touch so unwanted that she reacted to it

this violently? More hurt moved through him, but he tried to keep his personal feelings out of it.

"You're looking ill. What's going on?" he asked.

Heart hammering, Catt closed her eyes for a moment. She gripped the bulkhead to steady herself. "Oh…nothing. I'm just tired, Ty, that's all. It's been a helluva run, you know? I'll be glad to get back to civilization this time." She saw the glitter in his eyes. He didn't believe her. Catt swallowed convulsively.

"Look at you."

Alarm spread through her. Instantly, her hand went to her belly. "What?" Her voice was off-key.

"You've lost weight," Hunter noted, gesturing toward her body. "If I don't miss my guess, at least five pounds, maybe a little more."

"I, uh, just haven't felt like eating much lately. It must be the humidity, Ty. You know I don't do well in humidity."

He nailed her with a dark look. "As if Atlanta, Georgia, doesn't have the same humidity as down here?"

Heat swept across her cheeks and Catt refused to look at him. "Well…it's just everything," she whispered.

"Us?"

Wincing, Catt chewed on her lower lip. Truthfully, Ty had been wonderful, and she felt partially healed by the turn of events between them. She didn't want to lie to him. The silence strung tautly in the cabin.

"I thought so," he rasped harshly. "It's me. It's our past." He knotted his fists, feeling impotent to change it or to change Catt's mind about him. It was on the tip of his tongue to say, *We could have a future, a beautiful future together if you'd just let me*

*in. If we could just talk about the past and get it out
in the open…* But one look at Catt's averted features,
and Ty felt a horrible sense of hopelessness wash
over him. This reemerging love was one-sided, his
only. She didn't love him. She never would allow
herself to because of his very stupid, unthinking mistake so long ago. He'd never win her trust again.

"Okay," he said in a low tone, "I understand.
Come on, I'll help you pack. Maybe getting you back
to Manaus will help you feel better. I hope so."

Catt sat at the bow of the twenty-foot aluminum
motorboat, the humid air racing past her. Rafe sat in
the rear, his capable, guiding hand on the rudder. Ty
sat between them. They were going home. Even Manaus sounded good to her! Still, her heart was heavy.
Catt felt badly about Ty thinking her physical condition was due to his presence. Somehow, when they
reached Manaus, she would have to let him know it
wasn't due to him. But right now, she couldn't tell
him more—the thought of sharing the news gripped
her with fear. Confused, she sat rigidly on the aluminum seat as the boat hugged the shore of the river.
They were a good half hour into their trip back toward civilization.

"Look out!" Rafe's warning carried over the
noise of the motor.

Catt twisted around in surprise. To her horror, she
saw two black-and-red cigarette boats barreling up
behind them at high speed. She heard Ty curse.
Without warning, gunfire winked off the deck of the
nearest boat, which was less than a quarter mile away
from them. The pinging of bullets hitting water

sounded around the boat, sending up geysers of spray.

"Pull ashore!" a voice on a bullhorn demanded in Portuguese.

Ty jerked a look at Rafe. "Do it. We don't have weapons on us." The Brazilian government forbade foreigners from carrying weapons. Rafe had a rifle, but it would be no contest with the heavier, more powerful weapons aimed at them.

Rafe nodded, held his free arm high in the air to let the drug runners know he'd heard their demand. He swung the boat toward the shore.

Ty leaned forward. "Keep your mouth shut. Let Rafe do the talking," he whispered fiercely to Catt.

Frightened, Catt saw that the men aboard the two boats were armed with assault rifles. Obviously they were drug runners. As Rafe's boat hit the shore, she felt Ty lift her upward. Together they stepped out of the boat onto solid ground. The deep, throaty engines of the speedboats filled the air as the leader, a man in an army fatigue uniform, moved arrogantly to the bow of the closest one. He was in his early thirties, his face deeply pockmarked, his skin tobacco brown and stretched tightly across his high cheekbones. The thick, black mustache could not hide his sensual, full lower lip, and his ebony eyes were slitted and fierce looking. Catt shuddered as his gaze raked the three of them standing onshore, their hands in the air.

"I am Juan Fernandez," he crowed, striking his chest. "You are my prisoners. You and you, climb in. And you, woodsman, you go to the other boat."

Catt gave Ty a wild look. Could they run for it? The jungle was only fifty feet away. Yet she knew the drug runners would follow them and kill them.

Oh, Lord, her baby! At all costs, Catt realized, she must protect the baby she carried deep within her body. Her mouth went dry. Catt could barely hear above the adrenaline-charged beat of her heart. When Ty's hand settled on her elbow and propelled her forward, Catt went without a fight. They climbed up a small ladder at the back of the cigarette boat. Rifles were shoved in their faces, reminding them that they were now prisoners.

Once on board, they were frisked for weapons. Rafe's rifle was thrown into the river by one of the guards. Then Fernandez strolled toward them and jumped down into the cockpit, the butt of his weapon riding on his narrow hip. He smiled savagely at them, disdain written in his hard features.

"We know who you are. Dr. Alborak, yes? And her assistant, Señor Hunter? Yes?" he asked in broken English.

Catt nodded convulsively. She cringed as the drug leader strutted over to her. His gaze provocatively raked her body, lingering an excruciatingly long time on her breasts before moving down to her crotch, where it stayed for the longest, most humiliating time of all. Slowly, he looked up again, his gaze meeting her wide eyes. "You, señorita, are *mucho* woman. Very pretty." And he reached out and placed his hand on her cheek.

Before Catt could cry out, she heard a commotion behind her.

"You son-of-a-bitch!" Ty snarled. He lunged forward, regardless of consequences, and slapped Fernandez's arm away from her.

Pain split through his head. He saw white, flashing

light, and then darkness. The last thing Ty heard as he fell to the deck was Catt's scream of terror.

"Uhhh…"

"Don't move, Ty. You've probably got a concussion."

Catt's voice was low and strained.

The pain in his head made him groan again. Raising his hand weakly, Ty touched his skull. He forced his eyes open. Where the hell were they? How much time had elapsed? As he slowly looked around, he realized they were no longer on the boat, but in a small room. Catt was sitting on the edge of the bed, a cloth in her hand, gently dabbing the top of his skull. Her face was blanched, her eyes dark and fearful.

"What—where…" he grunted, and tried to rise. Catt instantly placed her hand on his shoulder and forced him back down on the thin, dirty mattress.

"Stay still…." She took the cloth, leaned over and placed it in a small, chipped bowl that held bloody water. "Fernandez took us to a villa. From what I could pick up from their English, it's one of the Valentino brothers'." Wringing out the cloth, she again placed it gently against the gash in his skull. "We've been here about four hours, Ty. You were cold-cocked from behind by one of those assault rifles." Catt swallowed hard and held his pain-filled gaze. "You're damned lucky you survived it. I thought they'd killed you, they hit you so hard. You damned fool."

Tears glittered in her eyes, and Ty forced himself to try and think straight. Little by little, the events were coming back to him. Anxiously, he reached out, wrapping his fingers around her lower arm. "Are you okay? Did they hurt you?"

Catt shuddered. "I'm fine, Ty. Fine. I think Fernandez was scared when you suddenly lunged at him. After that, they threw us in the hold of the boat. We must have been on the move for about half an hour, and then they docked in a channel by this villa. It's a fortress here in the jungle, about a quarter of a mile from the channel where the boats are tied up. They carried you here and I walked at your side. We're prisoners. Fernandez spoke in English for my benefit, so I was able to understand everything they said." Catt dabbed at his wound and examined it gently. The bleeding had finally stopped and the blood was coagulating. She knew Ty must have one hell of a headache.

"They knew all about us. Fernandez was bragging that they were just waiting for us all along. Apparently, once one of the Valentino brothers gets here, they're going to ransom us to the U.S. government. They're going to ask for ten million dollars for our release."

With a groan, Ty sat up. He gently touched his aching head. "Our government won't pay it. We're on our own," he told her as he dragged his feet across the bed and onto the floor. Catt got up, giving him more space. The room they were in was small. Bars stretched across the only window, which gave them some air and provided a small relief from the humidity that lingered heavily. Still, the room was stifling with leftover heat from the afternoon, Ty realized, when he saw it was almost dark outside.

"What about Rafe?" he asked, his voice raspy. It hurt to talk. It hurt to think. His heart was pounding with relief that Catt was all right. He'd known from the look on Fernandez's face that he was planning to rape her. Ty wasn't sorry for what he'd done. He'd die trying to keep Catt safe. Studying her now, he saw that she was very pale, her hands trembling as she washed the cloth out in the bloody water.

"I don't know," she whispered wearily. "I asked but they just laughed at me."

Ty held out his hand. "Come here, let me hold you?"

Tears stung her eyes. Catt allowed the cloth to drop from her fingers. Hunter's voice was low, strained and filled with care. The raw look in his eyes made her slowly sit down next to him once more. Welcoming his arm around her shoulders, Catt released a ragged sigh and sank against him. Burying her face against his neck, she murmured, "Oh, Lord, Ty, I'm so scared...so scared for you...for—" She choked as she moved her hand gently across her belly.

"I know, I know...." he rasped, and pressed a small kiss meant to make her feel safe on her silky red hair. Just the way her arms wrapped around his waist made him groan with pleasure. Without thinking, Ty slid his other arm around her so that she was completely within his embrace. Catt did not fight him; she acquiesced to his unspoken demands, his need of her. They were in trouble. Serious trouble.

Terror moved through Catt as she sat there wrapped in his arms. Yet the sense of protection, of love emanating from Ty soothed her fear for their lives. He had to know, she realized. It was only fair under the circumstances. They could die at any time. Ty had to know she was with child—his child.

"I have to tell you something," she whispered unsteadily. Catt gripped his heavily scarred hand and looked into his dazed eyes. "You need to know this, Ty.... I only found out just recently...." She stopped.

Puzzled by her reaction, by the fear he saw in her wide blue eyes, Ty reached up and touched her flushed cheek. "What? What are you talking about, Catt? What's wrong?"

Choking back a sob, she slid her hand over Ty's, which lay against her cheek. "Not what's wrong, what's right.... Oh, Lord, Ty, I'm pregnant. That night we made love, I got pregnant. I—I'm carrying your baby again...."

Chapter Eleven

Ty felt the blood drain from his face. It felt as if someone had pulled the floor from beneath his feet. He saw the tears in Catt's eyes, her uncertainty over what his reaction might be. It felt as if a bolt of lightning had ripped through him, through his heart and chest. In its wake was an incredible sense of agony followed on its heels by joy.

"A baby?" he rasped unsteadily, his fingers closing tightly over her hand. "Our baby?"

Sniffing, Catt murmured, "Yes...again...I'm sorry, Ty...I—we...just didn't think." She pulled her hand from his and wiped the tears from her eyes.

He gave her a shocked look. "Sorry? I'm not sorry, Catt. Why would I be?"

Now it was her turn to look stunned. Catt studied his pain-ravaged face, the tears swimming in his narrowed eyes. The line of Ty's mouth spoke of suffering. The sound of his low voice moved through her like a storm on a quiet spring afternoon. "Well..." she mumbled hoarsely, "you didn't want the first baby—"

"*No*...that's not true!"

Her lips parted. She reared back at the anguish in his tone; it was almost a moan of pain. "But—"

"Listen to me," Ty growled harshly as he placed his hands on her slumped shoulders, gripping her firmly and holding her wide gaze with his. "I made the worst mistake of my life that day, Catt. I wasn't unhappy you were pregnant. I was elated. Yeah, I was scared. I was fresh out of the academy. I was trying to show my superiors I could handle a tough assignment. I tried too hard to please the wrong people for the wrong reasons," he told her bitterly, his fingers digging more deeply into her shoulders. "You've *got* to believe me on this. I *never* meant to send you running away like you did. I tried—" He swallowed hard, looked away, trying to gather his wildly fleeing feelings.

Ty felt his lower lip tremble. It took everything in that moment not to cry. Fighting the feelings, the tears, he looked at Catt, who had an incredibly pained and tender expression on her features. "I tried to find you. You have no idea how long I searched, how many phone calls I made, how often I drove up to Stanford to try and find you. I finally hired a detective and he tried to trace you. I spent the next six months of my life in a hell I never want to go through again. I thought you might go to another university or college to complete your medical education. I wrote letters. I made phone calls. When I could, I would fly to a campus, rent a car and just drive around with your photo and ask people at the dormitories if they'd seen you. This went on for almost two years, Catt, until I finally realized that you would have graduated, and I had no idea where you would go after that.''

Wearily, he sighed and allowed his hands to drop from her shoulders. Gathering her hands, Ty stared down at her long, capable fingers. ''I gave up, but I never forgot.''

A sob choked Catt. She pressed one hand against her mouth. Hot tears flowed across her fingers as she stared at him through a veiled, blurry mist. ''Oh, Lord...I didn't know, Ty. I'm so sorry...really I am....'' And she was. At the agony in his eyes, the way his mouth was set with suffering, Catt began to realize that he, too, had suffered as horribly as she had.

Whispering his name, she moved into his arms, throwing her arms around Ty's shoulders. Wildly pressing herself against him, her fingers sliding into his hair, she held him with all her womanly strength. The tension in him was explosive. It was only then that Catt realized it was grief that had never been released, grief for the loss of their first baby. She sobbed softly, her face pressed against his neck. His arms went around her, tight and sure. The air rushed from her lungs as he held her as if he'd never embrace her again.

''I didn't mean to hurt you like this, Ty, I really didn't,'' Catt whispered brokenly. ''You made it clear that you didn't want a family right away. Remember? I asked you how you felt about getting married and having a family. It was out at the beach, about a month before I knew I was pregnant.''

Hunter nodded, his eyes tightly shut. Just feeling Catt's strength, her slender, giving body against him was all he needed. The knowledge that she carried his baby deep within her was more than he'd ever dreamed of. "Yeah," he managed to answer in a low, bitter tone. "Believe me, I remember every conversation we ever had, Catt. Over the years, I played them again and again in my head. And I remember that night. We'd made love and we were wrapped in a blanket by the fire, drinking wine afterward. I remember you wistfully asking me about how I felt about having a family. I remember telling you that I wanted a family, but not right then. I was a young lieutenant fresh out of the academy. I wanted a couple of years to get my feet on the ground and to establish my career." He lifted his head, framed her face with his hands and looked deeply into her tearful eyes. "I had *no* idea you were pregnant. We'd taken precautions...."

Sliding her fingers over his, she tried to smile but failed. "I guess the IUD I was wearing didn't do its job. I really didn't want to be pregnant at that age. I wanted to finish medical school and then have a family. I remember that, at the time you told me, I really felt your commitment to your career. I could tell from your tone of voice you meant it. And I couldn't disagree with you, Ty, at the time...until, well, I found out I was pregnant. And then—" Catt's voice lowered "—then I was scared. I remembered that conversation when I picked up the phone to call you. I was so frightened. I was making ends meet with the money left by my father's will, but I had no way to support a baby. I knew I'd have to leave med school. I wasn't sure how you'd take the news. I loved you. I knew you loved me. But I wasn't sure if you wanted to commit to living together and raising a baby.''

Taking her hands into his, Ty held her grief-stricken gaze. ''You had every right to be scared at the time,'' he told her gravely. ''It was me that screwed up, Catt. I should have told that White House secret service agent to wait, that I'd call him back. I was scared, too—the captain was there in the room with me. He was tracking my calls and what I did. I knew he was rating me, judging me on my performance.'' Ty shook his head. ''Hell, if something like that happened now, I'd tell the White House to wait and I'd tell you that I'd call you right back. Then I'd get out of that room to somewhere more private, where we could talk without that captain looming over my shoulder.''

''I didn't know....'' Catt moaned softly. ''I'm at fault in this, too, Ty. I didn't have to overreact like I did. I assumed a lot of things that weren't true at all. It was a knee-jerk reaction from my past. I never asked for help after Mama died. I just got used to doing everything for myself.'' Miserably, she held his gaze and said, ''It's not all your burden to carry. I have a share of that load to carry myself. I ran away instead of asking for your help. I'm so sorry....'' Achingly, she whispered, ''Can you forgive me?''

Reaching out, he grazed her flushed cheek unsteadily with his fingers. ''Forgive you? Can you ever forgive me?''

''In a heartbeat,'' Catt sobbed.

Closing his eyes, Ty pulled her into his arms more firmly. A sheet of weight that had felt like a lead apron around his shoulders miraculously dissolved as she whispered those words of forgiveness. Pressing Catt gently against him, he buried his face in her soft, mussed red hair. Breathing in the scent of her, the scent of a woman he loved so fiercely, Ty rasped, "There's nothing to forgive you for. You were young. You came out of a tough past. You had no parents. And you were struggling hard to make something of yourself, darlin'. I admired your guts. Your courage." He smiled brokenly as he moved his hand along her shoulder. "You made the best decisions you could at the time, that was all. Neither of us were mind readers. If I were in your shoes, and I'd got that response from me, I'd have thought the same thing—that I didn't care if you were pregnant, that you were not that important to my life and career."

Kissing her damp cheek, Ty placed his finger beneath her chin and forced her to meet his gaze. "I loved you too much throughout the years, Catt, to blame you for whatever choices you made after that phone call."

He loved her. She blinked through her tears. "Y-you...loved me?"

"I still do," Ty told her helplessly, a slight, boyish smile softening the grim line of his mouth. "I never stopped loving you, darlin'. *Ever.*"

The words felt like soothing rain across the heat of her parched, starving heart. Gripping his hands, Catt gazed into his vulnerable eyes. "You never stopped loving me?"

"No...never." Ty looked around the small, darkening room. "Maybe that's why I could never get married. Oh...I had some affairs, but when it came time to get serious, I just couldn't do it. I remembered you, Catt. I remembered very well what we had. The laughter on the beach. Sitting by the fire roasting marshmallows—dumb things, but important things...."

"I never realized...." she admitted painfully. "I just put you in the category of another hotshot military officer whose eye was on making general someday. I thought the women in your life were strictly secondary." Rubbing her furrowed brow, Catt admitted, "I really screwed up." Her mind whirled with what-ifs. What if she had stuck around and been there when Ty came to her dorm room? What if she hadn't run and stayed instead to work it out with Ty? Would she have miscarried? Catt had no way of knowing. But the fact that he'd come all that way up to San Francisco from his naval station to find her hours after that phone call told her *everything*. If only she hadn't bolted like she did. If only she hadn't been so afraid to trust his love.

"All my life, my dad rejected me because I was a girl and not a boy. I wasn't his son, Ty, and I felt like being a girl was second choice. Second best. When I fell in love with you, I felt like I was the most important thing in your life. I felt like number one and not number two. Rightly or wrongly, when I called you and got the message loud and clear that I was number two again, something inside me broke. It just broke...." Catt touched her breast. "I loved you so much. You were my first and only love.... I soared on wings of happiness when I was with you. You treated me like I was some marvelous gift in your life...every time we were together."

With a ragged sigh, Catt whispered, "Why, oh,

why didn't I see it then? Why didn't I ask you for help? If only—"

"No," Ty said, "don't do this to yourself, Catt. Let the past die a quiet death. We both know the rest of the story now. What's important," he murmured, "is what we do from this moment onward."

Looking around the room, Catt said, "We're in trouble. We could die. That's what I'm seeing."

Ty's hands tightened around hers. "Listen to me. And listen very closely. I will do everything in my power, with every breath in my body, to see that you and our baby get out of here alive. Do you understand me, Catt?"

The way his eyes drilled into hers sent a shiver of terror through her. Catt saw the mercenary in him now. She saw the marine. She felt the warrior, prepared to protect and defend her and her baby. His mouth was set hard. There was no mistaking the look in his eyes, either. Suddenly, she became very scared.

"Don't you do anything foolish, Ty! Damn you! Don't do something stupid in trying to save us." Catt gripped his thick, massive shoulder and shook him as hard as she could with her womanly strength. "Don't you *dare* give your life away to save ours! I just found you again," she sobbed. "I don't want to lose you! I couldn't stand it. Not again…oh, Lord, not again, Ty. Please don't do anything that would rip you away from us.…"

Her plea tore through him. "Hush," he ordered harshly. Gripping her by the arms, he gave her a small shake, just enough to get her full attention. "Stop it. Stop all the possibilities here." His breathing was ragged and short. "Dammit, Catt, hear what I'm saying. I love you. I love the baby you're carrying. I'm not going to see anything happen to you or the child again. This is my second chance. I've been praying for a long time for this opportunity to make peace with the past, to undo what I did to you.''

''You're not going to throw your life away!'' Catt cried. She pulled out of his arms and stood beside the bed. Wrapping her arms around herself, trembling, she repeated hoarsely, ''You're not going to die for me...for the baby! Don't you *dare!*''

Ty gave her a stern look, as she stood there wavering, her chin held high, her eyes blazing with unshed tears, her lower lip trembling. ''Why not?'' he asked.

''Because I want a life with you, that's why!'' Catt cried. Looking toward the door, she tried to lower her voice. Leaning over, she jabbed him in the chest with her finger. ''How thickheaded are you? I'm carrying your baby. I want the father to be around. Does that compute with you, Hunter? Or do I have to spell it out on this damned stucco wall for you?''

He stood. The pain in his head was voracious, but he ignored it. ''What are you really saying, Catt?'' He was afraid to say it. He was afraid to suggest it, afraid to think it. Could she love him? Could she see him back in her life? It was almost too much for him to hope for, and Ty stood there, feeling raw and naked as she glared up at him through the tears burning in her narrowed blue eyes. He saw the stubborn set of her chin, the way her delicious mouth compressed. She was breathing hard, too. They stood like two prizefighters squaring off with one another, tense and rigid.

''Oh! You are thick as a damned block, you know

that?'' Catt claimed. ''And don't give me that naive look. Don't you realize I love you, too? Did it ever occur to you that I never stopped loving you, either, through all these years? Did it? Of course not! Sometimes men are thick as bricks!''

Ty felt a tremendous surge of relief tunnel through him. His heart banged hard against his ribs. Joy suffused him as he held her angry look, studied that petulant set of her kissable lips. A silly smiled tugged at one corner of his mouth. The tension began to drain out of him. ''You love me?''

Catt rolled her eyes. ''Of course I do!''

The other corner of his mouth lifted a little. ''You really do love me?''

''Isn't it *obvious?*'' Catt breathed angrily. Jabbing her finger toward the door, she hissed, ''Why do you *think* I'm so upset that you might throw your miserable life away on us? Men! They just drive me crazy sometimes!''

Humility avalanched through him. Hunter stood there in those silent moments just looking at Catt, at her righteous fury, at the bravery in her heart and the courage it took for her to admit her feelings to him. ''Darlin', you're a hellion. You know that?''

Catt glared at him. ''Where I come from, Texas women don't mess around with diplomacy, Hunter. You and I love each other, so let's figure out how to get out of this fine mess we're in. You're the father of my baby. I *want* you around.'' She moved her hand across her abdomen. ''Our baby wants you around. So don't you try anything stupid like getting your head blown off, okay? Don't play hero. Heroes get killed. I—'' Her voice cracked and all the anger went out of her. ''I couldn't *stand* to see you killed.

I almost lost it when they hit you on the head with that rifle butt. I thought for sure your skull was cracked and you had a cerebral hemorrhage...."

"You have a wild imagination," he chided with a silly, boyish smile, "but I love you, anyway. My head's too damn hard to break."

Catt stood there, feeling suddenly weak, happy and frightened. Ty towered over her and looked so strong, confident and powerful when she felt just the opposite. The joy in his eyes was something she desperately needed at that moment. He *wanted* her. He wanted the baby she carried. Suddenly, life was very precious to her.

Lifting her hand toward the door, she said, "How can we escape?"

Ty moved over to her and placed his arm around her. "First things first," he rasped, taking her into his arms. This time, he brought her gently against him. This time, he felt every soft, firm touch of her body meeting and melting against his tall, hard frame. She came willingly and surrendered herself utterly to him, to his protective, shielding body, to his powerful, embracing arms. There was such unspoken beauty in her surrender. Lifting her chin, Ty slid his hand across the slope of her cheek.

"I love you, Catt Alborak," he breathed, leaning down and kissing her parting lips.

His mouth was tender as it moved across hers. Catt felt the warmth and moisture of his breath flowing against her as he spoke those beautiful words to her once more. Moaning his name as his mouth met and clung to hers, Catt slid her arms around his shoulders. Just the way his strong mouth glided against hers sent an ache of fire through her belly. Every cell within Catt cried out for the effortless love he was now sharing with her as his mouth rocked her lips open even more to taste her, to relish her, and most of all, to worship her as the woman he loved and wanted in his life.

Within those heated, vulnerable moments, the past dissolved, and with it, the sense of abandonment Catt had always felt. His mouth was tender, searching and filled with the promise of a bright tomorrow. As their breaths mingled and their heartbeats thundered in unison, they eagerly tasted the wonderful differences between them in that deepening kiss.

Ty eased his mouth from her soft, glistening lips. Her eyes were drowsy with desire, with love—for him. It made him feel strong and capable once more. It made him feel a kind of masculine power he'd been missing ever since Catt had fled from his life. Now it was surging back through him, making him feel even more protective of her and his baby, more confident to face the future, though it promised only death.

"I love you, darlin'...."

His words rumbled through her like a rainbow after a terrifying thunderstorm. Only the storm was fear for their safety, for their lives. Catt reached up and slid her hands across the dark stubble of his beard. She caught and held his fiery, narrowed eyes. "And I love you...more than you'll ever know. But I want to spend the rest of my life showing you—"

At that moment, the doorknob jangled. Catt jerked her head to the left. Hunter tensed. In seconds, he had placed her behind him. The brass doorknob moved again. Moonlight filtered in between the iron bars and gave them just enough light to see across the room.

Catt held her breath. She clung to Ty's arm, held out in a protective gesture. The movement at the door was gentle this time. The knob twisted again. The latch clicked. The door was open. Catt's heartbeat soared. What would happen? The Valentino brothers were known to be cold-blooded murderers. Catt was all too familiar with them raping women and then killing them. Shuddering, she worried about their baby. Could she talk them into not raping her because she was pregnant? Rafe had told her terrible stories of these two drug kingpins. They raped pregnant women, little girls and old women. They were heartless. Life meant nothing to them. Catt dug her fingers into Ty's damp shirt, her gaze riveted upon the door. Oh, Lord, they were coming for her and Ty!

Slowly, the door opened, creaking several times in protest. Ty stood on guard. At first he saw a hand slide around the edge of the door. Stymied, he stared at it. Damned if it didn't look like a woman's hand! But then, maybe the Valentinos had women mercs in their employ. He wouldn't be surprised. The hand was long, artistic and a golden color. Then he saw a slender arm, and finally a figure clothed in darkness eased into the room. With one fluid motion, the stranger closed the door as quietly as she'd opened it.

Ty's gaze narrowed upon the shadowy figure. It *was* a woman; there was no doubt. She was tall— damned near six feet if he didn't miss his guess. And she was a soldier. She wore a sleeveless, olive-green T-shirt that showed off her firm, well-muscled arms.

Across her chest were two criss-crossed bandoliers
of ammunition. On the web belt around her slender
waist he saw a pistol, grenades, a knife and a first
aid kit. As his gaze moved down, Hunter took in the
camouflage fatigues she wore and the unpolished
black G.I. boots. Swinging his gaze upward, he saw
the assault weapon resting on her hip, her right hand
wrapped comfortably around the stock. As she
moved silently out of the deep shadows, her features
were revealed.

The woman had an oval face, with high, angular
cheekbones, and her willow-green eyes slightly
slanted at the corners, giving her the look of a lethal
jaguar, an animal Ty had come upon twice in his
time in South America. Her face was a golden color,
attesting to her Indian heritage, yet her thin nose
hinted at nobility. And she could very well be nobility, Ty thought, for it was no secret that in South
America, the land barons of old often took peasant
women as lovers.

This woman in battle garments, whoever she was,
was clearly of mixed heritage. Her long black hair,
which shone in the moonlight, was captured into a
long braid that fell across one of her proud shoulders,
offsetting the lethal power of the bullets draped
across her body. As she turned toward them, he saw
a leather strap across her shoulder. On her back was
a leather scabbard that reached to her waist. The dull
gleam of an emerald-handled machete was lodged in
the heavily scarred leather sheath.

For a moment, Ty said nothing, for the power
swirling around her was stunning. He blinked. Was
he seeing things? She seemed to be there in the room,
and yet he could see the door *behind* her. Impossible!

He was seeing things! Blinking again, he no longer saw the door behind her as she stood gazing at them with an expression of mild curiosity laced with irritation. The glittering look in her eyes stunned him. Ty vividly recalled where he'd seen it before: on a jaguar ready to pounce on its prey. Her mouth was full and soft looking, yet the corners were pulled in, almost as if she was laughing at something. Them? He wasn't sure.

Her gaze moved languidly from him to Catt. Ty tensed as he felt a shift of almost palpable power around this unknown warrior woman. He saw her eyes narrow briefly and her mouth curve faintly as she lifted her left hand and pointed at Catt.

"You are with child."

Catt gasped. She had no idea who this woman was. How could she know she was pregnant? Stunned by the ferocity of power throbbing around her, she felt battered by waves of invisible energy. As soon as the woman uttered the words in stilted English, Catt felt the invisible pounding cease. Gasping again, she stared at the stranger, who stood aloof and relaxed near the door.

"I am sorry," she informed Catt.

Her voice was low and husky, reminding Ty of a cat growling. Ty remembered facing a big male jaguar once on a trail deep in the jungle. The growl of warning was just like this woman's voice.

He frowned. "Who are you?" he asked, trying to brace himself for the fact that she might well have been sent by Fernandez to kill them.

Her mouth puckered and she moved her glittering gaze to him. "Inca."

Shocked, Ty stared at her. His mind whirled. The

green warrior. The jaguar goddess. So this was the
woman Rafe spoke about in such glowing, worship-
ful terms. Now Ty could see why. He didn't know
if she was real or not. Again, he saw the door through
her. It was as if she were a holographic projection,
not really there with them. He had to be crazy. No,
she was very real. He saw the gleam of perspiration
down the long column of her throat. He saw the pulse
at the juncture where her proud shoulder connected
with her neck.

"You're…Inca?" Catt asked, slowly easing
around Ty's arm. "You've come to help us?"

Inca smiled mirthlessly and allowed the assault rifle to move off her hip. She held it confidently in her
right hand, the barrel pointed toward the floor. "*Sí*,
señorita. I heard my brother's call for help."

"Brother?" Ty said. And then he realized she was
talking about Rafe. "Rafe? Is he all right?"

"I have already released him. He is on his way
out of the area as we speak." She lifted her hand
sharply. "Come, it is time to go. You are in danger.
If we do not go now, we will all be killed shortly.
Fernandez is a murderer. I have read his mind." Inca
gestured toward Catt. "He lusts for you. He is going
to send two soldiers here, one to put a bullet in his
head—" she gestured toward Ty "—and the other
to bring you to him." Her upper lip curled and exposed her strong, white teeth. "I enjoy making Fernandez unhappy. One day he and I will meet one
another and only one of us will walk away from that
meeting."

Shocked and fearful, Catt gazed over at Ty. He
was assessing Inca, as if he was trying to decide
whether or not to trust her. Catt recalled Rafe talking

about this legendary woman and as she studied the huge white claw hanging from a leather thong around Inca's neck, she remembered how Rafe had told her the claw belonged to Inca's jaguar guardian, an invisible being from another dimension who was at her beck and call, who would attack and kill anyone who tried to threaten Inca's life.

Swallowing hard, Catt gripped Ty's hand. "Listen to her," she rasped. "We've *got* to trust her!"

Inca's laugh was low and filled with derision. She turned and twisted the brass doorknob. "Why is it always the woman who knows best? This is no time for wondering if I am leading you into a trap or not, Señor Hunter. Follow me and do not hesitate! If you do, you and your pregnant woman will die." Her eyes glittered in warning as she met and held his shadowed gaze, which was filled with distrust. "Is that what you want, señor? Or do you really want that second chance you have been praying for to the Great Mother Goddess for long? Eh? She has heard your prayers. She has sent me to get you to safety. Now, come! No more doubts!"

Chapter Twelve

The night swallowed them up. Catt gripped Ty's hand as they walked quickly through the jungle, away from the villa. How could Inca see anything? As Catt's eyes adjusted to the blackness, tinged faintly with moonlight filtering through the trees, everything around her took on dark, threatening shapes. Ahead she could see the proud, confident green warrior striding forward, her rifle in both hands, prepared for combat. Inca walked as if it were daylight. And she was soundless. Breathing through her mouth, Catt tried to remain silent. She was grateful for Ty's hand on hers. Several times she stumbled across unseen tree roots. And each time, Ty stopped and caught her before she fell to her knees.

Where were they going? How had Inca gotten into the villa? There had to be armed guards. How had she evaded them? Or had she killed them? Catt recalled the bloody stories of Inca's ability to murder those who stepped into her path. There was such power around her! No wonder people stood in awe of her and called her the jaguar goddess. She seemed almost unearthly to Catt, who wasn't easily impressed by anything or anyone.

Without warning, they reached the bank of the channel, and Ty suddenly halted. He half turned and placed his hand on Catt's shoulder, swiftly forcing her into a crouch. Ahead, he saw Inca crouch as well. Luckily, they still had some jungle foliage to camouflage them on this murky night. Eyes slitted, Ty breathed raggedly. His heart was pounding unrelentingly in his chest. He kept his fingers dug into Catt's shoulder as she huddled next to him, breathing hard. He could feel her trembling beneath his hand. She was scared. So was he. Though his senses were acute and his night vision excellent, he was forced to trust this woman with their lives. He studied her as she stooped like an unmoving stone on the shore, halfway to the dock where two cigarette boats bobbed gently. There was a guard at the end of the wooden pier. What was Inca going to do? If she fired that assault rifle she carried, it would alert the entire villa. And then all hell would break loose.

He wished mightily for a weapon himself. He didn't like trusting Inca. She was too cocksure of herself, acting almost as if this were a game. Did she seriously consider that real people's lives were at stake? Catt was pregnant and carrying his child. Above all else, Ty was going to protect her this time. He wasn't going to lose her or his baby again. No, somehow he had to protect her even if he had no weapon. The guard, obviously not on alert, stood smoking a cigarette, his rifle slung across his left shoulder. Ty thought about leaving Catt's side, slipping into the water, coming up behind the guard and jumping him.

Instantly, he received a sharp command to remain where he was. Stunned, he heard Inca's growling voice reverberating inside his head.

You fool! Do not move. My guardian will take care of him. Be patient a moment longer!

An explosion of pain ripped through Ty's head. He fell to one knee to stop himself from keeling over. It felt as if someone had physically slugged him in the side of the head. Lifting his hand to his aching brow, he watched Inca, who remained unmoving ahead of them. She had spoken to him, and yet she hadn't moved or said anything out loud. What the hell was going on?

As he focused on Inca's long, lean back, with its criss-crossed bandoliers, he thought he saw a dark movement off to her right. The darkness seemed to waver, like invisible heat rippling and rising off the hot asphalt of a desert highway. Blinking several times, Ty watched intently. What was near Inca? He saw a darkened form begin to appear. The moonlight shifted through the thick, dense clouds that hung above the treetops. As the light faded, he could see something shadowy near her right side. Whatever it was, it was large. Very large. And it was an animal. But how...? He hadn't seen any four-legged creature come waltzing out of the jungle.

Hunter's throat closed with tension. He saw Inca lift her right arm very slowly and slide it across the animal's broad, short back. What the hell was it? The darkness seemed to deepen until he could barely make out her form, much less that of the creature at her side. The hair on the back of his neck stood up. Ty felt a terrorizing sensation rip through him. Moments later, he heard a low, guttural growl. And then something dark and powerful moved swiftly toward the unsuspecting guard.

Ty gripped Catt's shoulder hard to prepare her. He saw the creature leap upward. The guard let out a sharp cry. In seconds, he slammed to the sandy bank of the channel.

Move! Now! Follow me!

Inca's voice careened through Hunter's head. This time, there was no mistaking that it was a telepathic command. This time there was no pain associated with it. Ty didn't hesitate. Inca stretched lithely to her full height and dug her booted toes into the sand. She sprinted toward the downed, unmoving guard at the dock.

Grabbing Catt by the arm, Ty hauled her upward. "Come on," he rasped.

Catt ran hard at his side. The sand sucked at her feet. Breath tearing from her, Catt suddenly heard a shout behind them. *Oh, no!* She heard more cries of surprise and alarm. Several rifle shots were fired. Instantly, Ty pushed her ahead of him. He was protecting her. Catt had no idea if they were being shot at or if the firing of the weapons was to alert the villa personnel that they had escaped.

Ahead, she saw Inca pull the limp guard away from the entrance to the dock. As Inca turned, Catt saw the frozen expression of rage on her face. Her eyes were slitted and her gaze was pinned behind them. In an instant, she had locked and loaded her rifle.

Stepping aside to allow them passage, Inca called to Ty, "Hunter, the keys to the boat are on board. Take the boat on the left. Hurry! They know you are gone. I will try to stop them, but it will not be for long. Go!"

Inca dropped to one knee, the rifle butt jammed against her shoulder. She took careful aim toward the path that led from the villa. Ty hauled Catt past the woman warrior and pushed her forward. Their footsteps echoed eerily on the wooden deck, which was in bad need of repair. Ahead on the left was a red-and-white cigarette boat, its sleek, high hull gleaming in the moonlight. To the right was a blue boat. Noting the controls located in the cockpit at the rear of the vessels, Catt knew these racers were high powered and could attain speeds of over sixty miles an hour with their mighty inboard engines.

A series of rifle shots rang out. Catt instinctively winced. She felt Ty lift her up and over the edge of one of the boats. Her feet made contact with the deck. Quickly, she moved aside as he leaped into the cockpit. Turning, she saw Inca firing systematically toward the path. Catt heard several cries, then more gunfire erupted.

"Get down!" Ty snarled as he groped for the key on the ignition panel in front of him. When he twisted it, the deep-throated engines coughed, sputtered, and then roared to life. The instrument panel became illuminated. He had to get both lines untied from the dock, Ty noted. Making sure Catt was lying down in the cockpit, Ty leaped back onto the pier. Heart thundering, he saw two soldiers running toward them. Inca was flat on her belly in the sand, coolly firing at them. Both men fell with screams and

began writhing. Ty jerked at the first rope holding
the boat to the dock, several rounds of bullets whis-
tled past him. He heard more cries. *Damn!* Racing
back toward the rear of the boat, he jerked the second
rope free.

Leaping back into he cockpit, he grabbed the
wheel. The throttles, two of them, sat just to the right,
and his hand fell over them. Jerking the steering
wheel, he pushed the throttles forward. The boat was
only a few feet from the bank. He couldn't take time
to go into reverse. Instead, Ty gunned the massive
engines. The boat's bow, because of the enormous
horsepower unleashed, lifted high. At the same instant, the sharp rudder movement to the right caused
the boat to arc upward out of the water a good ten
feet and dip to the port side, causing water to spill
into the cockpit from the violent maneuver.

Ty held his breath. If he didn't do something fast,
the boat would run aground on the sandy shore.
"Hold on!" he yelled at Catt. He jammed his right
leg downward to compensate for the torque and
movement of the huge boat.

Catt bit back a cry. She clung to the deck, her
fingers gripping one of the gunwales. The boat shuddered with power as it suddenly leaped upward and
to the left. Water splashed in across her. Suddenly
they were out in the channel and free. They were
free of the bank! Gasping, Catt lifted her head. She
barely caught a glimpse of the shore, but she saw
Inca's shadowy form sprinting back toward the jungle. The heavy hail of rifle fire was all around them.
Catt heard the water pinging and a dozen small geysers erupted around them. She saw Ty jam the twin
throttles forward. Hurled suddenly to the back of the

boat, Catt uttered a cry of surprise. Gravity pinned her in that position for a good five seconds as the boat lunged forward like a wild horse released from its tether. Muddy channel water arched like two high, thin sheets—rooster tails—on either side of the boat.

Wind tore at Ty's face as he grimly guided the powerful craft down the channel. He had to be careful. He had no idea where the hell they were and the darkness didn't help matters. Which was north once the channel joined the Amazon? His head spun with options. He was still dizzy from the blow he'd received earlier. Was Catt all right? Risking it, he glanced momentarily across his shoulder. She was struggling to get up on her hands and knees. Her face was white with terror.

"Stay down!" he roared, and jerked his attention back to the channel, which curved to the right. He slowed the boat and tried to control its power. One wrong move and he could send this speedboat up the bank.

"They're behind us!" Catt cried. "The other boat! It's coming after us!"

Damn! Mouth tightening, Hunter zigzagged through one turn after another. He could hear the other vessel racing down upon them, the noise deafening. The driver of the other boat knew this channel, knew its curves and just how fast he could take the boat through them. Ty did not. And because he wasn't powering the boat at high speed—he didn't dare risk it—the other boat was advancing rapidly upon them.

"See if there're weapons on board this thing," he shouted to Catt. "Get into the hold. There!" And he jabbed a finger at a door that led to the cabin below.

Their lives were on the line. Catt scrambled to her feet. With shaking hands, she tried the door. It opened! Lurching inside, she made her way down the ladder. There was light inside the cabin and she blinked her eyes. Gripping the rungs as the boat jerked to the right, then the left, she hurriedly glanced around. Her eyes burned from the sudden bright light. There! Two rifles were suspended on hooks from the port bulkhead. Slipping and nearly falling as the boat made another unexpected sharp turn, Catt reached out for the first assault rifle. Throwing the sling across her shoulder, she made a grab for the second one. Hurrying up the ladder, she climbed back out on deck. The humid night air slammed into her.

"Hold on!" Ty warned her. "We're hitting the river."

Just ahead, the channel opened up. And finally Ty spotted a compass on the console in front of him. Now he knew which way was north. North toward Manaus. Toward possible safety. Bracing himself, he jammed both throttles to the fire wall. Instantly, the roar of the engines thundered around them. The boat shook wildly and the bow lifted. They hit the wide, dark Amazon River at full speed. Ty gauged the turn. He was still learning how to handle this beast that begged to run. It was a huge boat, nearly fifty feet long, slim and tapered. It was built for high speed on a smooth, safe surface. But the Amazon wasn't safe at all. Logs routinely bobbed along, barely visible above the water's muddy surface.

Moonlight peeked from behind the ever-present clouds. Hunter could see nothing ahead of the boat except when a slice of moonlight illuminated the water momentarily. Risking everything, he steered the boat to the center of the wide river. Behind them, he heard the roar of the second boat. Their pursuers were coming out of the channel after them. Gunfire began. He knew that in a matter of moments, the drug soldiers would be upon them if he didn't race up the Amazon at full speed. But in doing so, he risked colliding with a floating log, which would rip the guts out of the boat and send them to their deaths. What choice did he have?

"Stay down," he yelled at Catt.

She nodded and knelt down on the deck, a rifle in hand. Stabilizing herself as best she could, Catt made sure there was a full clip in the weapon. There was. With shaking fingers, she found the safety and flipped it off. For once she was glad her father had taught her about all kinds of guns as a child growing up. Pressing her left shoulder against the side of the boat and using it to steady the rifle, she sited toward the other boat, which was steadily gaining on them.

She saw winking red-and-yellow gunfire from the other craft. Bullets were humming and singing around them. The boats were within range now, with barely a mile separating them. If they got within a thousand yards, a good marksman could kill them. Trying to steady her breathing, Catt took aim. They only had two clips of ammunition. She had no idea if there was any more or where it would be kept on the boat. She didn't have time to search for it. No, each round she fired would have to count. The boat skimmed wildly across the muddy, sluggish Amazon. The humid air slapped at her. On either side of them, an arc of water lifted nearly ten feet high. Catt had no idea how fast they were going, but it seemed like a dizzying speed.

A number of bullets sang near her head and she ducked. From where he stood in the cockpit, legs spread, Ty was an open, easy target. They would try to kill him first. *No!* Suddenly, life became more precious than Catt could ever remember it being. Her mind spun. She didn't want to kill anyone, but she had to do something to protect them. The engine! Of course, why hadn't she thought of that before? Swinging her rifle slightly to the right, she took her bead on the center of the boat that was pursuing them and slowly but surely gaining ground. With one methodical shot after another, Catt tried to place a bullet into the hull of the boat and hit the thundering engines. Destroying them would effectively halt their pursuit.

Ty heard Catt firing back. *Good!* Ahead, he saw a dark object coming up rapidly. *Damn!* It was a huge log. Swerving to the right to avoid it, he almost capsized the boat in the maneuver. The speedometer on the console read sixty miles an hour. At that speed, the boat roared around the log and came almost completely out of the water from the sharp movement.

Catt was thrown to the deck with a cry. The loose assault rifle flew out of the boat. She grabbed for it. *Too late!* The rifle disappeared over the side. Sobbing with anger, she felt the gravity pin her once again to the deck. Ty wrestled with the boat as it skimmed along, almost out of control. They were heading sideways toward the opposite bank of the Amazon. Her eyes widened. A scream lurched up her throat. She saw him jerk the wheel back and yank at the throttles.

At the very last moment, the boat steadied and slowed down tremendously. Once he got the bow pointed upstream once again, he slammed the throttles to the fire wall. Braced this time, Catt felt the breath being torn out of her by the speedboat's lunge forward. Then she managed to look up and her blood went cold.

Screaming out a warning, she saw the drug soldiers' boat aimed directly at them, no more than a hundred feet away.

"Hold on!" Ty yelled. He saw the boat careening down upon them and knew their pursuers were going to try and ram them. He had only fifty feet of maneuvering room between himself and the shore. Trying to control the wild machine, he jerked the wheel to the left. He knew the drug soldiers were expecting him to move to the right, to try and escape.

The maneuver stunned the soldiers. Ty braced himself. They were going to collide! There wasn't time to warn Catt. Grabbing the wheel, he kept their boat moving at an angle toward the other vessel. Within seconds, a loud, ripping sound joined the howl of the engines. Ty was thrown heavily to one side. Pain arced up his arm and shoulder. He saw the amazement, the terror, on the faces of the soldiers in the other boat. Moments later they were flying in all directions, weapons one way, bodies another.

Catt screamed as the boats collided and she was thrown against the bulkhead. She heard the cries of men, the sickening sound of one hull being slit like a can opener by another. Within moments, it was all over. She was thrown again, this time to the opposite side of the cockpit. The gunwale at the rear raced at her. Trying to protect her head, Catt threw up her hands to shield herself. Too late! The boat leaped forward like a startled deer and the roar of the engines thundered through her as she fell semiconscious on the deck.

The last thought she had was of her baby. She was going to lose her baby because of the severe trauma to her body.

Ty couldn't look back to see if Catt was all right or not. He wasn't sure of anything in those moments after the collision. The drug boat was dead in the water; he saw men swimming all around it in the moonlight as he jerked a glance back across his shoulder. Amazingly, it seemed that his own craft wasn't taking in water. Maybe he'd gotten lucky and hit the other boat at just the right, glancing angle, incurring only minimal damage himself.

Swinging the boat back toward the center of the wide, dark Amazon, he concentrated on getting them away from the sinking boat and drug soldiers. All his attention was focused on avoiding floating logs, which seemed to be all over the place. As quickly as he could, he steered a course among them. When he was a good mile from the collision site, he finally throttled back. Turning, he searched for Catt.

Pale and unmoving, she lay on her back behind him, one arm thrown outward. To his shock, he saw blood oozing from her right temple. She was bleeding heavily. *No! Oh, Lord, no!* Desperately he searched for a side channel. He had to put distance between them and the drug soldiers; he didn't dare land too soon or the men could run down the bank, find them and kill them. Ty's heart ached with fear. It was impossible to handle the boat and race to Catt's side at the same time.

Heart pounding, he risked stopping at the next channel opening he saw. They were a good three miles from the drug soldiers by now, far enough away to risk stopping. Hauling back on the throttles, he nosed the boat into the channel. There was no way to dock it, so he put the engines on idle and let the boat slowly come to a halt against the bank. Turning, he devoted all his attention to Catt.

"Catt?" He knelt at her side. Ty knew enough about medicine not to move her. She could have a spinal injury, a fractured vertebra, and if he moved her, she could become paralyzed for life. Anxiously, he searched her face. Her breathing was slow and shallow. But it was the dark red ribbon of blood dripping from her right temple that scared him the most. He saw the gunwale she'd struck.

"Catt? Can you hear me?" he called, bending to place his lips near her ear. She was so terribly pale. And their baby? Terror ate at him. Picking up Catt's wrist, which dangled nervelessly between his fingers, he felt her pulse. It was thready. That wasn't good. Very quickly, he ran his shaking hands across her body to check if she was injured anywhere else. No...nothing. Just her head. One of the most vulnerable parts of a human body.

Hurrying down below, Hunter located blankets and pillows. Plenty of them. In the next few minutes, he did what he could for her. She was in shock. He placed several blankets over her to prevent further heat loss. She had a head injury, so he didn't elevate her feet, fearing that more blood would rush to her brain and put pressure on it. If there was hemorrhaging going on inside her skull, that would only hasten her death. With several pillows on either side, he

braced her head. Finding some duct tape, he quickly
used it to stabilize the area, just in case she had a
spinal injury as well.

Getting to his feet, he hurried back to the console
and put the throttles in reverse. The boat eased out
of the channel. As carefully as possible, Ty moved
the boat close to shore and shifted the throttles forward. He had no idea how far they were from Manaus, only that this was the right direction. Catt was
unconscious. In a coma? Would she die? And their
baby? *Oh, Lord, no…no! Please, please let her and
the baby live. I'll do anything You want, just let her
and the baby live….*

As he steered the boat up the dark river, with the
night being eaten away by sifting shreds of moonlight, Ty tried to concentrate on watching for floating
debris. He wanted to hurl the throttles forward and
make swift time to Manaus, but he couldn't risk hitting a log. If they did, Catt could be killed. He had
to move slowly, keep his intense focus on the river
and get her to the hospital as soon as possible.

Tears burned in his eyes as the humid air tore at
him. Ty stood braced at the wheel, his legs slightly
apart to compensate for the movement of the mighty
boat. Would Catt survive? What if she didn't? The
thought tore at his heart, shredded his composure.
They'd survived so much! Had they lived apart for
ten years, only to come together and then lose one
another? *No! It couldn't happen! It just couldn't.*
Grimly, his mouth thinned, he gripped the wheel
even harder, his knuckles whitening. All around him,
night shifted to a gray netherworld. He felt as if he
were trapped in a surreal nightmare. He kept glancing back at Catt every minute or so. She remained

unmoving. Dread filled him. *Just let us get to Manaus. Let me get her to a hospital....*

The world slowly came into view for Catt. She heard beeps and sighs. Her nose told her she was in a hospital, for the smell of antiseptics was familiar to her. Her body felt very weighted and heavy. When she forced her eyes open to bare slits, she saw that a number of blankets covered her. For a moment, her mind was fuzzy. How had she gotten here? What had happened? As she lay there in the silence, her blurred vision steadily became more focused, and bits and pieces started to take shape in her returning consciousness. She remembered the drug runners... Fernandez grinning darkly at her as if she were a prized slave captured for his own pleasure. And Inca...and... Her eyes widened slightly. *Ty?* On the heels of that thought, she moved her hand toward her belly. Her right arm had an IV in it. Her baby? Terror seeped into her awareness. *Ty? The baby?*

Catt parted her lips, but only a rasp issued forth. Her lips were chapped and dry. Her energy was slowly returning as her hand rested on her belly. Pain stitched across her right temple. The sensation didn't stop. Instead, it intensified. Catt remembered hitting something. Her head was aching fiercely. Closing her eyes, she tried to remember more.

A noise caught her attention—a door opening and closing. Lifting her lashes, she saw Ty Hunter enter the room. He was holding a white plastic cup in his hand and his clothes were rumpled, dirty and sweat stained. The haggard look on his face—the darkness of a beard that was at least two days old and his bloodshot eyes—made her cry out, her voice a hoarse croak. But he was safe! He was alive!

She saw his eyes widen even though he looked utterly fatigued. Placing the coffee on the bedstand, he leaned over her. "Catt?"

She tried to smile, but found it impossible. Just his fingers wrapping around her hand made her feel incredibly joyous. "You're—okay...." she managed to murmur.

Skimming her from head to toe with his eager gaze, Ty couldn't keep the tremble out of his voice. "Yeah, I'm fine...fine...and you? Are you okay? You've been unconscious for nearly forty-eight hours."

The urgency in his tone made her sigh raggedly. Weakly, she returned his grip. "I hurt like hell. I mean...my head..."

"You took a nasty spill in the back of the boat when we collided," he told her apologetically as he eased himself down on the side of the bed, facing her. She was so pasty looking. From the dark blue shadows beneath her eyes and the way her cracked lips parted, he knew she was in pain. "The doctors said your X rays showed a concussion on the right side of your head. They weren't sure how bad. They didn't detect any bleeding in your brain, and they were hoping you'd wake up pretty soon."

He was unable to control the flood of emotions tunneling through him. Leaning down, Ty brushed her mouth gently with his own. The moment his lips glided against hers, he heard her sigh softly. Catt tried to return his welcoming kiss, but she couldn't. She was still too weak. Lifting his head away, he met her drowsy, confused-looking blue eyes. Her right pupil was still slightly dilated, indicative of the concussion she'd received.

"Ty..." Catt gripped his fingers as hard as she could "...our baby?" Her heart pounded wildly in her breast. Terror ate at her as the news of her condition slowly sank in. As a medical doctor, she knew that a baby could easily be miscarried in such a traumatic ordeal.

Grazing her pale cheek with a finger, he smiled a little. Tears flooded his eyes. "The doctor said you haven't miscarried." His mouth pulled into a trembling smile as he carefully cupped her cheek and held her gaze, which rapidly blurred with answering tears. "You're still the mother of our baby, darlin'. All I want you to do is lie there, sleep and get well. You hear me? You've got our baby to care for, so I want you to do what the docs say."

The words fell over her in a heated cascade of relief. An incredible happiness spiraled through Catt. "Oh!" she whispered brokenly, "Oh, thank you...thank you! I love you so much, Ty...so much...." And she weakly tried to raise her arms and slide them around his broad, capable shoulders. He smelled of sweat. He was dirty. But she didn't care. She loved him with every breath she took. Ty had saved their lives.

Gently, he caught her arms and folded her hands into his. "Just lie there and get your strength back, my woman."

His woman. The words sounded wonderful to Catt. She felt an incredible sense of tiredness stalking her, however. How badly she wanted to talk further with Ty, but she felt a seeping heaviness pulling at her. "I—I'm so tired, Ty.... Sleep...I have to sleep...."

He sat there and watched her thick red lashes rest against her pale cheeks. Squeezing her hands and resting them across her belly, Ty rasped unsteadily, "Sleep, darlin'. Sleep for yourself and for our baby.... I'll be here when you wake up, I promise. No one's going to leave you or abandon you this time...." He choked back a sob that had lodged deep in his throat.

Ty sat there holding her hand and watched her drift off into a much needed, healing sleep. Catt's bright red hair looked shocking against the white of the pillowcase she rested upon, against the pallor of her skin. Still, he felt warmth coming back into her once cool, limp fingers. Just the way the soft corners of her mouth lifted told him of her joy that she was still carrying his baby. *His* child. Trembling violently, Ty looked around the private room of the hospital, situated on the outskirts of Manaus. Light leaked in around the blinds covering a small window at one end.

They had so much to look forward to. So much. But first things first. Ty didn't want to, but he eased off the bed. Leaning over, he pressed a tender kiss to Catt's cheek and then straightened up. Morgan Trayhern had flown down to Manaus upon hearing what had happened to Catt and was in the waiting room. The man had stayed with Ty the last twenty-four hours. Morgan had had a head-injury specialist from Houston, Texas fly down with him. Dr. Rona Peters was known to be the best in her line of emergency medicine, and she was in charge of Catt's care. Ty was grateful that the doctors at this hospital had worked willingly with Peters to give Catt the very best chance to pull through.

Opening the door, Ty took one last look at her. How badly he wanted to be home, to be back in Atlanta with her. He wondered what her place looked like. There was so much catching up to do. So much discovery lay ahead of them. And now their prayers were being answered. Easing out of the door, Ty shook his head. Maybe the mysterious and enigmatic Inca was right: the Great Mother Goddess of them all had taken his request to heart and given him a second chance at love, at life, with Catt. And on top of it all, she'd given the added, unexpected gift of a baby, created out of the aching passion of love that had simmered, unknown to either of them, for nearly a decade. No, all he wanted now was peace, quiet and time to share with Catt. That was all.

Moving down the hall, Ty met Morgan Trayhern in the visitors' lounge. His boss looked decidedly haggard, his dark blue suit rumpled, his white shirt open at the throat, the tie removed and hanging over one of the plastic couches. Ty smiled wryly, realizing he probably looked even worse than Morgan did. But Trayhern's care for his people was refreshing to Ty, and he was deeply indebted to the man for many things, especially for the neurologist he'd brought in for Catt. What corporate boss would do something like that for one of his employees? Not many, that was for sure.

Morgan lifted his craggy head. "Is she better?" he asked in a rumbling tone.

"Much," Ty said. "She's conscious now. I think we're over the worst of it." He halted near the couch and casually placed his hands on his hips. "Have you made contact with Rafe yet?"

A slight smile pulled at Morgan's mouth. "Inca

got him back to his houseboat safe and sound. He called me just a few minutes ago to report in. I guess the Valentinos' boys beat him up pretty good. Inca had released him from the room in the villa where he was imprisoned, but he was suffering from a concussion and got disoriented out in the jungle after he escaped. If Inca hadn't found him, he might have gotten recaptured. They went downriver to a Catholic mission, borrowed a boat and she just got him home."

"That Inca woman is something else."

"Isn't she, though? Makes most of our soldiers look like shredded wheat in comparison, from what Mike Houston has told me about her."

"You ever meet her?" Ty wondered as he rubbed his jaw. He badly needed a shave and a shower.

With a heavy shake of his head, Morgan said, "No...but I've got a gut feeling that we'll be working a lot more closely with her in the future. Rafe has worked with her for years and swears by her. I understand Inca's got a lot of murder warrants out for her arrest. That isn't good. Perseus does not work with people wanted by the legal system."

"That's what Rafe said." Ty sighed. "Well, if it weren't for Inca breaking in and freeing us, we wouldn't be standing here talking right now. Catt and I would be dead."

Giving him a grim look, Morgan nodded. "No question. The Valentino brothers *own* the Amazon basin around Manaus insofar as drugs and drug trafficking go. I'm itching to take them down, but it will have to be a concerted effort involving the U.S. and Brazilian governments."

"And Inca," Hunter reminded him. "No one knows the Amazon basin like she does."

"First things first," Morgan said. "You're thinking about Catt?"

Ty would never get used to Trayhern's ability to almost mind read at times. Startled, he nodded. "Yes, I am."

"You're going to be a father. Congratulations."

Grinning a little sheepishly, Ty said, "I heard that Laura had twins a week ago. I think congratulations are to be shared all the way around."

Morgan glowed and shook his hand. "Fraternal twins. Neither of us could believe it when the doc did the ultrasound and found two babies, not one. Twins don't run on either side of our family. She had them at home with a terrific midwife by the name of Aledra Scott. It was really something to be a part of...." He smiled fondly in remembrance. "So now we have four in our brood. Laura always wanted a big family and she got her wish."

"Four," Ty murmured with a shake of his head. "I can't imagine four kids around. Maybe one or two..."

Chuckling, Morgan clapped him on the back in a fatherly way. "Believe me, once you see them moments after they're born, once you hold them in your hands, you know that nothing was ever so right." His eyes twinkled with merriment. "You're going to get your chance soon, Ty."

Epilogue

"Home has never felt so good," Catt said in a low tone as she entered her small condominium. Ty's hand on her elbow felt good, too, as he guided her across the shining cedar-wood floor of the entry hall. Her head was aching and she knew it was from the flight and the altitude. Ty brought in their luggage and found her bedroom down the hall to the left.

It was late afternoon and sunlight was filtering in through the lace curtains. Going over to the windows, Catt unlocked them and slid them open. The soft scent of the sweet gardenias blooming on large, shiny-leafed bushes in her small backyard wafted into the room.

She heard Ty return, the heavy step of his boots announcing his arrival. Turning, she smiled a little. "This is it. Home," she said.

Looking around, he nodded. "Feels good." His

gaze settled on Catt. She was still pale and there were shadows beneath her glorious blue eyes, but they sparkled with life when she looked at him. It made him feel strong and good once more. "What I'm looking at reminds me of home," he told her gravely.

Flushing, Catt allowed joy to thrum through her. She moved over to him as he opened his arms. Stepping close, she slid her own arms around his thick neck and savored the feel of him holding her, as if she were some kind of fragile, beautiful flower. All this she had missed because she'd been immature, stung and hurting so long ago.

"Do you want to stay here with me?" Catt asked as she looked up at him.

"If you want me to."

Catt nodded. "I'm not letting you go this time. I'm not running ever again, Ty."

Ty realized how much softer Catt had become since she became pregnant. No longer was that hard, defensive wall keeping people away. She was accessible and vulnerable to him now and he tried to tread gently because of the gift she'd given him. Sliding his fingers through the hair on the side of her head that hadn't been injured, Ty rasped, "Why don't you go get a hot bath and just soak? You're looking tired. Remember what the doctor said? That you should take it easy for a while?"

"Casey already knows I'm on pregnancy leave for the duration. How much more time do I need?"

Hunter smiled a little and held her golden gaze. "After I get the details of what happened to us written up in a report, you and I have a lot of things to work out," he warned her.

"Such as?"

He brushed a few wisps of hair from her brow. "Such as...marriage. We need to talk about the possibility. What you want and expect from me...from us, darlin'. Little things like that."

Sliding her hands across his proud shoulders, Catt whispered, "I'm looking forward to that, Ty. I really am."

"I thought so," he replied, leaning down to kiss her.

Just then, the doorbell rang.

Lifting his head, his mouth inches from Catt's, he scowled. "You expecting anyone?"

Catt twisted her head in the direction of the door. "No. Are you?" She stepped out of his embrace, pulling at her blouse so that it didn't looked wrinkled.

"Let me answer it," he said heavily.

Hearing the warning in his voice, Catt stood expectedly in the middle of the living room.

Ty looked through the small peephole in the door. "It's my brother Dev," he told her, surprise in his voice as he reached for the doorknob.

Catt quickly ran her fingers through her hair. She'd never met the daredevil of the family. According to Ty, this brother was the second born, and a year older than Ty. She knew from conversations with Ty at the hospital in Manaus that Dev and Shep both worked for Perseus. Worry cut through her as Ty opened the door.

The man standing in front of them looked deceptively at ease in navy-blue chinos and tennis shoes. He was as tall as Ty, leaner looking but in obviously good shape, his light-blue, short-sleeved shirt revealing his powerful biceps. His face was square, his intelligent-looking eyes a dark green, with thick, straight brows across them. As Catt stood there appraising him, she thought Dev might pass for anything but a mercenary. Maybe a beach bum, she mused, except for his short, red-brown hair. That was the name of the mercenary game, however—to blend in, not stand out. There was a sense of danger around Dev, and Catt vividly recalled the power she'd felt around Inca. Dev had that same kind of energy, though it was far less palpable than that of the green warrior.

"Sorry to bust in like this, Brother," Dev said, his gaze sliding past Ty to Catt. "I just got handed an unexpected mission by Morgan. I wanted to see you before I left."

Ty nodded and moved aside. "Come on in." Once Dev had stepped into the room, filling it with his considerable presence, Ty made introductions. His older brother was worried; Ty could see that in the set of his mouth, the way shadows hung like a veil in his green gaze.

Catt asked them to sit down on the Victorian couch near the open windows and asked Dev if he wanted coffee.

Dev held up his square hand. "I'm sorry, Dr. Alborak, but I don't have that kind of time. This is a touch-and-go."

"I see," Catt murmured. She looked at Ty for direction. She wasn't sure that Dev wanted her presence. The feeling around him now was one of edginess.

"Go get your bath, Catt. You need to rest," Ty suggested gently. "I'll fill you in later?"

Relieved, Catt nodded. "Sure. That's a good

idea." She looked at Ty's brother. "It was nice meeting you, Dev. Good luck on your mission and stay safe."

Nodding toward her, Dev placed his large hands on his narrow hips. "Thanks. I'm planning on it," he assured her seriously.

Ty waited until he heard the door to the bathroom down the hall close. "What the hell's going down? This isn't like you to suddenly drop in like this."

Rubbing his jaw, Dev growled, "Morgan just tag teamed me with one of his hotshot women mercs. I'm not happy about it. He wants us to do a little bird-doggin' for him."

"Oh? What kind of decoy work?" Ty demanded, feeling his brother's tension. Dev worked alone. That was the way he liked it. Morgan knew that. So why had he teamed him up with a woman merc? Dev liked women; there was no questioning that. He had more women hanging around him than any other man Ty had ever known. Ty wasn't jealous of his older brother; it was just a fact that Dev's devil-may-care attitude seemed to draw women's attention.

"Black Dawn," Dev rasped.

Instantly, Ty's gaze narrowed. "I was in the Perseus jet giving Morgan a final update on what we'd found out in Manaus. Authorities located the blue-and-white plane that delivered the genetically altered anthrax over the Juma village. They traced the numbers on the plane back to the owner, a man who lives in Kauai, Hawaii. An Albanian refugee who was given political asylum here in the U.S. ten years ago."

"That's right. A very rich, mysterious retired chemist, as a matter of fact. There's suspicion that he's one of the leaders of Black Dawn. Morgan is going to send me with this woman merc to see what we can find out."

"How?"

"I'm not at liberty to say. I just wanted to let you know what was going down."

"He's sending you to the island of Kauai?"

"That's right." Dev's mouth twitched. "The Garden Isle of the Hawaiian Islands. And in the midst of all that legendary beauty is, potentially, a bioterrorist. Sort of shoots the hell out of the paradise angle, doesn't it?"

"No joke. Damn. Black Dawn must be gearing up to release that genetically altered anthrax on a city. They were successful with the Juma. Now they're going to stop testing and attack."

Grimly, Dev said, "Not if I can help it. If Morgan's scheme works, we'll choke hold them before it gets to that point." Reaching out, he gripped Ty by the shoulder. "I've got to get going. I have a last meeting with Morgan up in Washington, D.C., where I meet the infamous Kulani Dawson. Though if I have my way about it, I'm flying solo on this mission." Releasing him, Dev said, "I heard about you and Catt Alborak. She was the woman you loved ten years ago, right? How's it going?"

Ty shrugged. "One step at a time, Dev. Catt and I have a lot of history to work through."

"I remember," he said seriously. "And she's pregnant? I'm going to be an uncle?"

"Yes to both questions."

Dev smiled, then concern creased his features once more. Looking at the watch on his dark-haired wrist, he muttered, "I got a flight to catch...so when's the wedding?"

Caught off guard, Ty grinned and walked him out into the hall. "That's something else we have to talk about. Look," he warned Dev, "be damned careful out there. Black Dawn people aren't stupid, blind terrorists. They've got think-tank intelligence. They're ruthless, cold-blooded thinking machines dead set on accomplishing their goals. There's no emotion misguiding them."

Dev held out his hand and shook Ty's. "I'll be careful. If I get my way, this female merc will be history *before* I go on this mission. I don't need anyone tripping me up on this one. See you later."

Catt wrapped herself in her dark blue silk robe after finishing her bath. The steam escaped as she opened the door and padded down the gleaming cedar hall to the living room. Ty was standing at the window, looking out. His hands were on his hips, and she could see the tension in his shoulders.

"Is everything all right?" she asked as she walked toward him.

Ty turned. He'd been so caught up in worry for Dev that he hadn't heard Catt approaching. "Yeah... I'm okay...." His hands slid off his hips and he gazed hungrily down at Catt. Her face was flushed from the heat of the bath. A subtle fragrance of lilac reached his flaring nostrils. He studied the way the silk robe grazed the tops of her well-formed thighs, his eyes moving up to the border of colorful flowers along the collar, before coming to rest on her face. She looked better. Some of the shadows had disappeared from beneath her eyes.

"Let's go sit down on the couch," Catt suggested as she slid her fingers into his hand. It didn't take much to get Ty to follow her to the wonderful old antique couch. This was one of the few pieces of family furniture saved from Catt's life at the ranch. It had belonged to her grandmother and had been lovingly passed down through the generations. The fabric was faded but showed pink-and-maroon roses with dark green leaves on a cream-colored background. Easing down on the couch, Ty drew Catt down next to him. His arm went around her and she leaned willingly against his tall, strong frame.

"Dev dropped over," he told her worriedly, "to tell me he was going after Black Dawn." He shared most of what he knew, leaving out the quandary about the woman mercenary teaming up with his rebellious older brother.

"Whew," Catt murmured, "I don't envy him, Ty. We know how dangerous Black Dawn is...."

Moving his fingers gently along the curve of her silk-covered shoulder, he nodded. "We both think Black Dawn is preparing to drop the genetically altered anthrax on a city."

Shuddering, Catt said, "That seems like their next step."

His arm tightened around her. "Let's talk of happier things," he urged, and slid his fingers along the clean line of her jaw. Her skin was still flushed and moist from her recent bath. The sparkle of sunlight coming back to her eyes made Ty smile.

"I sat in that tub soaking out nearly a month's worth of jungle sweat," she laughed softly. "And I wished you were in there with me. It's a big clawfoot tub, you know. Plenty of room for two."

The deviltry in Catt's eyes took away some of Ty's fear for Dev. Moving his thumb across her cheek, he asked, "And what thoughts and feelings were swimming around in there with you, Dr. Alborak?"

Absorbing his tender touch, Catt sighed and held his dark gaze. "How happy I am. How incredibly wonderful I feel." She moved her hand lovingly across the swell of her abdomen. "And you're here, with me. It's like a dream come true, sweetheart. I wanted to pinch myself a couple of times to see if I'd wake up from this wonderful dream."

Studying her in the afternoon silence, Ty relished the endearment. He'd always been her sweetheart; that was what she'd called him in the past. "I think our past has met and melded with the present, don't you?"

Catt nodded. "The good things from the past are surfacing again."

"I don't think either of us forgot about any of them."

"No, we didn't...and I'm amazed. I really am."

"Because we never stopped loving one another, that's why."

Catt couldn't disagree. She turned and faced Ty, her hands on his upper arms. "Why don't you get cleaned up? I'd like to lie down and just sleep in your arms. That's all I want."

The quaver in her tone touched him deeply. "I'd like that, too."

"It's a start," Catt whispered as she held his narrowing gaze. "I just want time alone with you. Uninterrupted. Ours."

Framing her flushed face with his hands, Ty met

and held her luminous gaze. "I'm yours, darlin', forever, if you want me. I want to be father to that child of ours you're carrying. I want to be husband to you. Somehow, I want to make up for all the lost time between us. I want to make you happy...."

Tears burned in her eyes as she heard the tremble in his deep voice, which moved like a lover's caress through her. "We want the same things, Ty."

Happiness flooded him as he leaned over and gently took her mouth. She moaned softly and surrendered as his arms went around her. Drawing Catt against him, Ty could feel her softness and her womanly strength simultaneously. As her lips parted beneath his heated exploration, he silently promised her that the years of pain, hardship and suffering while she'd struggled alone would be rectified. He would spend the rest of his life making her life happy.

He felt her smile beneath his ministrations, and hot, wild sunlight sizzled through him. Catt tasted sweet as he moved his tongue across her lower, full lip. She was a hellion of the first order, but one with a mission and purpose in life. Ty was proud of her, respectful of her courage and backbone. And within her lived a baby. Their baby. Their future together. Forever...

* * * * *

Look for
handsome charmer
Devlin Hunter's
story when

MORGAN'S MERCENARIES:
THE HUNTERS

continues in October
with

HUNTER'S PRIDE

Special Edition #1274

Here's a sneak preview...

minion nigged at her. He was out of place here.

"**G**ood afternoon everyone. I'm Kulani Dawson, your pilot."

Dev's skin prickled pleasantly. Kulani had a low, alto voice, like honey trickling across his flesh, making him want to reach out and slide his fingers along the slope of her cheekbone. Suddenly his mission on Kauai wasn't looking so bad after all. Kulani Dawson was worth the flight, and then some. His mouth curved recklessly.

"Mr. Jack Carson?" she said, calling out the alias he'd given her from her roster of passengers.

"Roger that," he said with a grin. Now that he'd met her, he felt bad lying about his identity. But that was just part of the job.

Kulani felt her heart gallop unexpectantly at the reckless little-boy smile the tall man gave her. Her intuition niggled at her. He was out of place here.

Assessing him keenly, Kulani moved past his devastating smile. He looked like a tourist, but the way he stood, tall and erect, said differently. His hair was cut military short and he stood poised like a boxer ready to make a lightning-like move. At whom, she wasn't sure. Even though he wore the loud, red Hawaiian tourist shirt, he was no vacationer to her island, an inner voice told her.

Looking down at her manifest, she asked, "How much do you weigh, Mr. Carson?"

He chuckled and placed his hands on his hips. "How much do I have to weigh in order to sit next to you?" Dev knew that the people who weighed the least sat up front with the pilot. He also knew he'd never get such an opportunity, but he wanted to let her know he liked her.

"You could be the weight of a sparrow and you still wouldn't get a front seat, Mr. Carson." Kulani's heart was beating a little harder now. This man, whoever he was, drew her for no discernible reason. Kulani admitted he was drop-dead handsome. He did not have the face of a pretty boy, but one that was tanned, weathered by life. There were crow's-feet at the corners of his eyes. Deep dimples when he gave her that heated, teasing smile of his.

"How about a canary?" he replied, flashing that smile once more.

"How about no?" Kulani said sweetly. She smiled, despite what she was feeling. Who could resist this man? Her heart certainly couldn't.

"I'm crushed, Ms. Dawson. Here I was told you were the closest thing to Amelia Earhart in the islands." He held up his camera. "I was hoping for a photo of you standing next to your bird."

She regarded him seriously. *Bird* was a military term. Was this guy in the military? A spook? CIA? He was something, that was for sure. So why did she feel bothered by it? She had nothing to hide. And then, Morgan's phone call regarding the mission he wanted her on came back to her and she stiffened. But why would Morgan have sent someone here? She had refused Morgan's mission. None of this made sense.

"Sorry, Mr. Carson. I'll be happy to take a photo of you and my bird after the flight, but that's it."

Dev felt a little guilty when he saw her eyes darken with censure over his pushiness. Looking more closely at her, he saw the beginnings of shadows beneath her eyes. And there was a strain around her tender and soft-looking mouth. The urge to reach forward, slide his hand across her shoulders, undid him. Normally he wouldn't run to help a woman he didn't really know. Something about her made him more bold than usual.

He nodded deferentially to her. "I'm in your capable hands, Ms. Dawson."

Kulani shrugged off the handsome stranger's grin. He certainly thought a lot of himself. Still, that engaging smile of his touched her deeply and she couldn't shake the warmth in his voice that blanketed her and made her feel just a tad bit better than she had all day. "You will be the last to get in, Mr. Carson. I'm giving you the right seat window."

Dev realized that was the most prized position of the three seats in the rear of the plane. He gave her another smile. "I think I'm in heaven. No, I take that back. Heaven is standing right in front of me."

"You are incorrigible, Mr. Carson."

"Why, thank you, Ms. Dawson."

As he slid into his seat a few moments later, Dev felt happier than he could ever recall. Since his devastating divorce years ago, a pall had hung over him. Now, life took on new joy for him simply by being in the vicinity of Kulani Dawson. As the aircraft lifted off the tarmac a short while later, Dev laughed softly and sat back. Morgan Trayhern sure as hell knew how to pair him up with the right woman. But he would never have her as a merc team partner. Devlin Hunter worked alone. Now a relationship— that was another matter. In fact, it was a very likely possibility, one oozing with promise.

Silhouette ®SPECIAL EDITION®

LINDSAY McKENNA

delivers two more exciting books in her heart-stopping new series:

MORGAN'S MERCENARIES
THE HUNTERS

Coming in July 1999:
HUNTER'S WOMAN
Special Edition #1255

Ty Hunter wanted his woman back from the moment he set his piercing gaze on her. For despite the protest on Dr. Catt Alborak's soft lips, Ty was on a mission to give the stubborn beauty everything he'd foolishly denied her once—his heart, his soul—and most of all, his child....

And coming in October 1999:
HUNTER'S PRIDE
Special Edition #1274

Devlin Hunter had a way with the ladies, but when it came to his job as a mercenary, the brooding bachelor worked alone. Until his latest assignment paired him up with Kulani Dawson, a feisty beauty whose tender vulnerabilities brought out his every protective instinct—and chipped away at his proud vow to never fall in love....

Look for the exciting series finale in early 2000—when MORGAN'S MERCENARIES: THE HUNTERS comes to Silhouette Desire®!

Available at your favorite retail outlet.

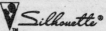

TM *Silhouette* ®

If you enjoyed what you just read,
then we've got an offer you can't resist!

Take 2 bestselling love stories FREE!

Plus get a FREE surprise gift!

HARLEQUIN *Duets*™

2 new full-length novels by
2 great authors in
1 book for 1 low price!

**Buy any Harlequin Duets™ book
and SAVE $1.00!**

SAVE $1.00

when you purchase any

HARLEQUIN

Duets™ book!

Offer valid May 1, 1999, to October 31, 1999.

Retailer: Harlequin Enterprises Ltd. will pay the face value of this coupon plus 10.25¢ if submitted by the customer for this specified product only. Any other use constitutes fraud. Coupon is nonassignable, void if taxed, prohibited or restricted by law. Consumer must pay any government taxes. Valid in Canada only. Mail to: Harlequin Enterprises Ltd., P.O. Box 3000, Saint John, New Brunswick, Canada E2L 4L3.

Non NCH customers—for reimbursement submit coupons and proofs of sale directly to: Harlequin Enterprises Ltd., Retail Sales Dept., 225 Duncan Mill Rd., Don Mills (Toronto), Ontario, Canada M3B 3K9.

Printed in Canada 9/98

HARLEQUIN®
Makes any time special.™

**Coupon expires
October 31, 1999.**

HDUETC-C

```
32602258
```

HARLEQUIN *Duets*™

2 new full-length novels by
2 great authors in
1 book for 1 low price!

**Buy any Harlequin Duets™ book
and SAVE $1.00!**

SAVE $1.00

when you purchase any

HARLEQUIN

Duets™ book!

Offer valid May 1, 1999, to October 31, 1999.

HARLEQUIN®
Makes any time special.™

**Coupon expires
October 31, 1999.**

5 65373 00051 9   (8100) 1 06254

Silhouette ® SPECIAL EDITION ®

Myrna Temte

continues her riveting series.

HEARTS OF WYOMING:

Rugged and wild, the McBride family has love to share...and Wyoming weddings are on their minds!

April 1999   WRANGLER SE#1238
Horse wrangler Lori Jones knows she'd better steer clear of Sunshine Gap's appealing deputy sheriff, Zack McBride, who is oh-so-close to discovering her shocking secret. But then the sexy lawman moves in on Lori's heart!

July 1999   THE GAL WHO TOOK THE WEST SE#1257
Cal McBride relishes locking horns with Miss Emma Barnes when she storms into town. Before long, the sassy spitfire turns his perfectly predictable life upside down. Can Sunshine Gap's sweet-talkin' mayor charm the gal least likely to say "I do"?

And in late 1999 look for WYOMING WILDCAT:

Single mom Grace McBride has been spending all her nights alone, but all that's about to change....

Available at your favorite retail outlet.

Silhouette ®

Silhouette®

SPECIAL EDITION®

COMING NEXT MONTH

#1261 I NOW PRONOUNCE YOU MOM & DAD—Diana Whitney
That's My Baby!/For the Children
Lydia Farnsworth conveniently wed her former flame, Powell Greer, so
they could adopt their cherished godchildren. Although the once-smitten
newlyweds didn't know the slightest thing about being parents—or
reconciling the past—they embarked on a mission of love....

#1262 THE MOST ELIGIBLE M.D.—Joan Elliott Pickart
The Bachelor Bet
Her past had been erased, while her life seemed to begin the moment
Dr. Ben Rizzoli rescued her. Though there was an irresistible attraction
between them, the dashing M.D. tried hard to hold his emotions in check.
As though he was keeping some secret. As though he was desperately
afraid of falling in love....

#1263 BETH AND THE BACHELOR—Susan Mallery
Beth Davis was aghast when Texas bachelor Todd Graham set his
sights on *her*. Didn't the suave, sophisticated tycoon have more sense
than to woo a widowed suburban mom? And could she trust that her
Prince Charming was ready to be a husband and father of two?

#1264 SECRET AGENT GROOM—Andrea Edwards
The Bridal Circle
Life was about to change for shy Heather Mahoney when she found
herself powerfully drawn to her elusive new neighbor. Ultrasecretive
Alex Waterstone was a man to be avoided—that much she knew. Why
then did he inspire dreams of wedding bells and shimmering white satin?

#1265 FOREVER MINE—Jennifer Mikels
When Jack McShane gazed into Abby Dennison's beautiful brown eyes
again, he realized she still had a hold on his heart. *Then* he realized this
woman he'd foolishly left behind had secretly borne him a son. So the
wanderin' rodeo champ vowed to hang up his hat and become a bona
fide family man....

#1266 A FAMILY SECRET—Jean Brashear
Maddie Collins knew Boone Gallagher wasn't any more pleased than she
was when his father's will stipulated they must cohabit before she could
sell him his old ranch house. But the city sophisticate hadn't counted on
unearthing a shocking secret—or the allure of this gruff, gorgeous
cowboy!